A Condo Conspiracy

AUTHOR'S NOTE

Set in a Californian condominium, this novel tells of the trashing of unit owner's rights, and the deceitful diversion of their funds, and their difficulties in finding remedies.

Dwelling units in the form of community title schemes are well established right around the developed world now, and there are many similarities to be found among them, not so much in their legal and administrative structures, or their operating nomenclatures, as in the rights and duties of unit owners, and management arrangements. There is a strong trend toward uniformity in the federated jurisdictions of USA and Canada, so that the present story could be set in pretty well any of their States and Provinces, but not so readily elsewhere, where too often different words are used for the same thing. Unfortunately, reconciliation of those differences is beyond the scope of this work, though the wrongs against unit owners alluded to in the story could happen in any number of like dwelling schemes in any number of countries.

The present story is fiction, yet rooted in actual events. The characters are all invented.

Technical and legal language belongs naturally to unlawful and deceitful events, and condominiums, and I have kept it down as far as I could, and would have gone further but for the risk of disturbing the story. In that spirit I have left out references to homeowners associations. Although they are an integral part of a condominium scheme, they are, of course, only the unit owners associated in a legal entity, and it seemed to me the reader might feel the plight of the deceived owners more directly without the constant mention of a homeowners association. I hope so.

BY IAN SALMON

Copyright Ian Salmon 2013
Design by Jodie Grant
ISBN 978-0-9585852-4-8
Printed by CreateSpace

BY THE SAME AUTHOR

Practical Forms & Precedents
Water (NSW) A to Z
Some Andalucians
French Honour Lost
Amazons and Angels
Fun Tennis for Seniors

CONTENTS

CH	INTRODUCTION TO CHAPTERS	PAGE
1	Barney and Zina Jones become interested in a new off-the-plan condominium development in their district - they pool their knowledge of condo living - they will visit the sales center	7
2	The Jones continue discussion as they prepare to visit the sales center for Gran Capitan	23
3	The Jones meet the sales staff at Gran Capitan - impressed, they read the contract papers, and are unimpressed - but the heart trumps the mind	27
4	Ed and Binny McGinty are introduced - their Queensland connection - its white shoe brigade - Ed learns about condo management contracts there - he leaves his job and looks into condo management in California	37
5	Ed learns about condo management from his broker buddy - tells him about the Queensland system - studies the Californian scene - suggests to Binny they try to make a career from it - they will buy locally if possible	49
6	Barney's brushes with management commence - he studies the legal structure of Gran Capitan - the first managers extend their contract term and then sell to Ed and Binny who become the Onsite Managers (OSMs) there	61
7	Barney continues learning to be a critic - sees options as white for managers, black for owners - appraises fellow condo owners	65
8	Ed gets a little involved in owner politics - the McGintys plan to enlarge their OSM tenure on the Queensland model - they start by sounding out the board	67
9	Attorney Angel Tejero is introduced - his interesting life and times prior to Santa Marta - he and Ed meet	71
10	A clash between McGinty ambitions and Jones pro bono notions looms - Barney sends a circular suggesting management review - Ed takes fright and gets Angel's innovative advice	83
11	The McGintys make a board of directors for themselves - it quickly shows support for the McGintys by a circular - a plan to extend their management tenure takes shape	91

12   The Jones interpret the curious events - they feel extension in   99
      the wind - protection of the condo owners is needed - Barney
      creates a motion to put before the owners - discussion of
      shady activity - owners' losses estimated

13   The McGintys obtain an extra option to extend management   109
      tenure - deception and abuses noticeable - a conspiracy is
      suspected - comparative management modeling emerges as
      an issue - Barney's cause hit by an adverse arbitration award
      - owner's eyes slowly opening - a new board takes charge -
      relations between it and the OSMs bad

14   The new board hammers the excessive compensation of   119
      the management contract - resents the third option - makes
      selling the contract difficult - the McGintys interpret contract
      conditions narrowly for their own advantage

15   The new directors get lucky in the basement - the struggle takes   123
      a new course - suspicions turn into evidence of a conspiracy -
      what to do about it? - President Manuel disappoints Barney

16   The friends review the issues and legal remedies - they   137
      conclude it was and remained conspiracy - in spite of being
      at odds with the directors on the point, they will try to revive
      board interest in a conspiracy prosecution

17   The Jones and Charles Olly continue their probing of the 1988   143
      events - they continue to see conspiracy as the main issue

18   Discussion about remedies continues among the friends - an   147
      insight into Manuel's position - Barney prepares a concise
      conspiracy argument - rescission emerges as a talking point

19   The directors deny Barney's plea for resurrection of conspiracy   153
      - the reasons for denial are unconvincing to the dissidents,
      who turn to other means of justice for the owners - they look
      to rescission of the third option

CH	INTRODUCTION TO CHAPTERS	PAGE

20 A rescission motion is filed - the board will neither support nor oppose it - Manuel and the secretary, as private owners, openly commend it - Barney is more certain the board is split - a director-driven push for compromise of disputation with Ed appears - an owner files a compromise motion which Ed sees as a threat to rescission - he finds a counter - on receipt of the meeting agenda Ed reads the rescission motion and hot-foots it to Angel for advice   159

21 The Jones and Charles Olly are curious about the absence of response from the McGintys to the rescission motion - a telephone call on the eve of the general meeting brings dramatic news   169

22 In which the motions go well for the rebels - Manuel under fire from owners - Charles speculates on Ed's plays post-rescission - celebration of the rescission   173

23 Charles is moving on and some of his past is revealed - analysis of the failed lawsuit - the hoodwinking of owners at Gran Capitan reviewed - ingredients for improvement discussed - Zina makes a shock announcement concerning the Jones future   177

24 Zina's plan for moving to the Towers is discussed - Barney agrees - keeping both condos debated   183

25 Other friends see more fighters for the cause are needed and step up very effectively   191

TIMELINE   196

A CONDO CONSPIRACY

1

Barney and Zina Jones become interested in a new off-the-plan condominium development in their district - they pool their knowledge of condo living - they will visit the sales center

"Let's look at this new place," said Barney, handing Zina a colorful sales brochure. "If you want a change, yet stay in a condo here in Santa Marta, it could be for us." She glanced at it, saying, "Oh, this has been on the television. It sounds quite upmarket. As long as it doesn't have vacation renting and a nasty manager, I'd like to see it." She started reading intently, and Barney left her to it. Later she said, handing it back, "I'm ready for a look. But it's only just started, so what's there to see?"

"They have a display center and plans which tell you a lot. Still, buying off-the-plan means taking a lot on trust. You have to allow for sales talk, and check everything as best you can."

"Knowing you'll only cover half of it, for nothing beats seeing a completed place."

"True. Yet if we want to get into a new building in a decent locality on the north side of LA, this is on our short list."

"Then let's look. No harm in that."

They read all they could find on the luxury, residential only, lake-side condominium development, called Gran Capitan, said to have stunning mountain and distant ocean views. The sales pitch from the big development company, Best & Better Constructions Inc. (BBC), in advertisements and brochures, read well, and for prospective buyers, implied urgency for investigating and decision making. To the two retirees, he from General Electric, she from the LA Philharmonic, both well into their sixties, and no children or parents at home, it was interesting, for they were not entirely happy in Marquise, the condo complex they had bought into a few years earlier. They found themselves readily returning to the topic.

"I know you don't like this off-the-plan business, and you're right, but what do we do?" asked Zina. "Some people buy this way and sell later at better prices, without ever taking possession themselves. When you hear that, you get the feeling of not wanting to miss out."

"But let's distinguish speculators from owner-residents, like us," Barney replied. 'For them it's just the money, like buying and selling any commodity, and for us it's home. If they buy in a boom market they'd better sell in one too, because the falls from boom prices can be very sharp. It's hard to believe in a bust when you're riding high, because the ride gives the feeling that the proper value-price regime has come at last."

"And maybe it shows how naturally hopeful people are."

"Of course. If not, we'd always be saying, why bother buying this thing, its value is sure to fall. But for us, isn't it like this? We accept we're in a boom, so we'd be buying high. We have two buffers though. First, we sell this unit in the same market phase, because it could go south in the year or so before we have to close on the new one."

Zina interrupted to ask: "You think a year? You've heard that?"

"Yep, but we'll check. Certainly long enough for the market to change."

"You seem set on change as in drop, but couldn't it be a rise instead?"

"Yes", answered Barney, "anything's possible. But because we're in a boom right now there's that much more chance of a fall. Remember how we hung on to those Apple shares to make sure we got top dollar?"

The normal serenity of Zina's pale face changed to a frown. "Yes. I was the bright spark, the clever market dealer, wasn't I?" She held up her hand: "No, don't say anything. Don't help me! I said to hang on because my infallible feminine intuition said more goodies lay ahead, and when the price collapsed and I panicked and we sold, you were kind enough to shrug it off, and treat it as a joint decision, when we knew whose it was really. Thanks for that. Pity though, because the price soon climbed up again, and we were on the outer. Now it's my turn to listen. So if we buy at today's prices we should sell at them too?"

"Right. The experience wasn't wasted. We're going to use the left side of our brains and not the part that's controlled by the heart." Zina smiled. Barney continued: "Don't laugh. It must be true. It's in the paper. I just read it. I'll show you. But let's look at the other buffer. Even if we pay top dollar for Gran Capitan we can wear it, because we'd be in our retirement home, and though we mustn't go overboard, it's not the same as an ordinary investment. So in that sense we're different from the speculators."

Zina said: "I see. Won't it be so nice if we like it?" Then, thoughtfully, "Suppose our buyer wants to take over right away. Where would we go? Do I smell a double move in the wind?"

"Most likely. It would be a fluke if our buyer would rent this place to us while we waited. We must offer immediate vacant possession, letting nothing block a sale."

"You mean we must use only the left brain? And so, if I don't like a double move, I must stay here?"

Barney answered: "Something like that. Remember that if either of us doesn't want to do it in a business-like way, we stay put. But just say we were to be homeless for a bit, maybe we could take some of those trips we've talked about, and visit the children, so if we rented a condo it mightn't be for long, and a little inconvenience wouldn't hurt. See, I don't mention a house."

"That's a relief. I'm so used to an apartment lifestyle I couldn't go back."

"Hear, hear! If we buy, and sell this place before the bottom falls out of the market, we will have done very well, and can share the credit."

"I wonder if Gran Capitan values will hold up in a bust."

Barney shrugged: "Who can tell? Certainly not me. Maybe its being in the top end of the market would be some protection. Let's ask the broker when we inspect."

"That'll be interesting. The truth, the whole truth, and nothing but the truth! I must listen in. But y'know, you're convincing me, and so I accept that if we buy there, I agree to selling here, and renting."

"So we're serious when we look?"

"Yes. I think it's time. This place is depressing, and I find it hard to feel it's our real home. Apart from the problems with the manager and the vacationers, it's not well designed, is it?"

Barney nodded agreement, and said: "Y'know, the developer was from out-of-town, one of the desert states I think. He'd heard there were fortunes being made through condo developments over here, and had enough devil in him, and money from his theatres and movie-houses, to try this big place on his own. He got a fright half way along, so it sat half finished, until another boom came. He seems to have kept the same design right through, with all its awkward spots, and cut costs with materials. I guess that after the delay he was ready to do anything to make sales, and clean his slate. It must have been a nightmare for him."

Zina cried, "He may have been a great act in theatres, but surely condos were a different scene. I mean, those different levels on the same floor, the sloping tennis court, and the tiny public car space, right where folks in their apartments can hear the cars going and coming, along with the chatter, plus the exhaust fumes, and the terraces that jut out to receive trash and cigarette butts from above. And more besides, but we needn't list them, need we? We've seen enough. Pity he didn't use the wait time to redesign."

"Or think of security. A place this size - is it 200 units? - needs an on-site patrol. Our manager doesn't see that as his job, and by the time something bad happens and the cops come, it's all too late. If there were a guard here nights, some of those robberies wouldn't happen. You know Gran Capitan will have a 24-hour security team?"

"So that's what fulltime security means in the brochure. I'm mighty glad to hear it. What have we got here? Access to floors other than your own is barred, which is good. The cameras are supposed to capture everything all the time, but we know they don't, and the warning sign in the basement car-park about 24-hour surveillance is actually a fraud, in that it's not activated because it costs too much to run, so we only have the sign."

Barney said: "I didn't know that. Let's hope the thieves don't either!"

"Well, someone told me the other day. I guess the directors don't like to make it public. And as the entrance to the basement is straight off the street, and the door is slow in closing, a thief can follow a car straight in at night, and hide."

"Easily done! Sure. How else do we account for the auto break-ins, and even thefts, like the new Caddie the other night? The evolution is interesting though. Much of our electronic security was add-on to the original design of the place. Compare our Marquise with Royale Canadienne, which was finished a little earlier. Odd they have neither secured floors nor cameras there. They lock up carefully though. I've heard their old lifts can be a toy. Kids can press all the buttons then hop out, and the lift takes ages to get to the top, so the person waiting blames it for being slow."

"It wouldn't be funny if you were waiting," Zina added, suppressing a smile. Maybe it's a safer place because of the type of people who live there. And of course it's also smaller than here."

"I believe they frown on any sort of renting. There's something in their bylaws. Maybe also luck has made up for no electronics; or so far, anyway, as there's a first time for everything. Our set-up is better than nothing. The electronics are sound, and a night patrol firm makes random visits, but I feel a night watchman on-site would be even better. I suppose the extra expense stops the idea."

"And if you start with no guards it could be hard to get the unit owners to agree on employing them later. It's all money isn't it? If the developer of Marquise - I always forget his name - had included watchman security, and better quality finishes, the higher prices of the condos could have slowed his sales. I'm sure some finish items, like power switches and lamp shades and carpets and appliances and door knobs, were run-outs, which you said are especially cheap in bulk buys, and that's why you can't get exactly matching replacements for anything you break, or wear out."

Barney nodded. "Anything to sell the condos, leaving it to the buyers to fix things at their own expense. I think it's like that all over. He's dealing with novices, so puffing up the attractions and smothering the bad bits is a cinch, then like as not they'll fix problems at their own expense, rather than sue him. There's a lot of hassle in making a claim on a builder for faulty work or poor quality. It helps if you're on a surefire winner, and in a group, then the attorney expense can't hurt much. Alone, a lawsuit is daunting."

"Not only that, but I've heard that Mr. What's his name - no, it's Cassini, of course - started this place in the market as owner-occupied, with none of the short term renting they have in the resorts in the tourist precincts. Leases were to be minimum six months. Then he got cold feet, or an empty purse, and switched. The recreational facilities were already ample, actually very good, with the big pools inside and outside, and the gym and tennis court, and those other things, so he decided Marquise should be a vacation resort. He offered refunds of deposits to buyers who had signed and didn't like the change, but most were content, and didn't understand about renters, and stayed on. You never get to know people's stories, but you'd think some would be sorry, now they know everything."

"You bet," said Barney. "And when we bought in later we didn't know much, so we saw and heard only the good bits. We weren't really looking for anything else. So we add that to our data bank for when we get to consider the new place."

Another difficulty for Guido Cassini had been his assurance to a buyer, a French man, that television reception from overseas through a satellite dish and other gear would be on tap, as requested. He was buying an expensive penthouse. Such sales were rare at the time, and when the celebrity status of the buyer became known, Guido dropped his guard, and misinterpreted the advice of his people, that while reception was possible, consistently good reception was improbable. He went on with the installation, and used it as a selling point, which for most people was only a gimmick, of no real significance. It was real for the buyer though, and while the reception was otherwise poor, by coincidence on the first few occasions he was in residence, it worked well enough. When it fell away he hounded the board to bring it back to the level promised him, claiming that if they didn't do so they would not be maintaining the common property of the condo, as was its legal obligation. By then Guido had quit the development, having sold all the condo units, and showed very little interest in expending effort or money in dealing with complaints. The directors tried to make good, through a succession of experts, and even went to the trouble and expense of a new installation.

Marquise stood at the edge of a small tributary for the lake, looking toward a large public recreational park on the other side. Colin Somers owned a condo overlooking the stream, and from which he could see his motor launch moored at the Marquise marina below. Being a self-made business man, he had plenty of ideas about how things should work, and on one late afternoon when he was entertaining the Jones and a couple of other friends with drinks and chat and sunset views, and Barney mentioned his recent experience with the television, Colin's ears pricked up. The board had asked Barney to read the pile of papers the issue had accumulated, with a view to a fresh mind contributing to their deliberations. The president told him of a concern about the mounting expense, and a wish to see that a new technician was doing what he had been engaged to do. Barney took it that he too was regarded as some sort of expert, which he was not, but he was interested in the project, and so accepted the challenge of helping out. The two men entered a small room which was full of wires and switches and electronic and electrical gear. He questioned the technician as he worked. He noted he was constantly puzzled, so intensified his questioning, the answers to which convinced Barney he did not know how to make the connection, or even if the gear in hand was suitable. He said: "Look, if you don't know, just say so and I'll tell the board they've got a mistake, which maybe can't be fixed, and I'll recommend they give up. Y'know, they've tried hard and spent money on this, and it's only for one owner, and the time to end it may have come."

The technician looked at him, eyes shining with gratitude, and said: "Oh, thanks, pal, that's really the best thing. Frankly, I've been thinking this is such a problem it could be a reputation buster for me, so I'm really keen on quitting. I can't say it's impossible, but it seems so for me. I'm very happy to hear what you said."

When Barney reported to the board, it decided it was no longer the responsibility of the owners, as the directors had never promised anything to the condo owner, and if the developer had, the complaint should go there. They believed an obligation to maintain something in working condition could only apply if it had worked in the first place, or could be made to work, and that was not so here. They would do nothing more, and in fact intended to dismantle the useless gear. They wrote to the owner informing him, and he replied it didn't matter, as he had lost interest in overseas television long ago, anyway.

After that story Colin laughed, saying, "When I heard there was a satellite installation for French TV that didn't work, and the board had been pressured into attempting to fix it, and they had budgeted $20,000.00 for the job, I said to Janet - didn't I dear? - that for all the good it would be they might as well stand here on our balcony and throw the money into the water."

But that was in the past when Barney and Zina continued chatting about condo living, with Gran Capitan in mind. "It's so hard to be smart until you've lived in one for a while. All of us who come from our own stand-alone houses risk being tricked, or tricking ourselves, and we're lucky if it doesn't hurt too much," said he. "Particularly if you first come on vacation, and while having a great time, you hear of the good ol' boys and how they made killings, and joining them sounds neat. Some folks are simply out of their tree then, and if they're not real careful they'll buy a condo they don't need, and pay more than they should, and with the brokers so glib and pressing, they believe them more than is right."

"They sure know how to make hot sales pitches," cried Zina. "Hopefully, our experience will help us next time around. Blessed is the one who doesn't get caught sometime during life. But didn't your friend Bob, surely a smart guy, lose almost half when he sold his investment condo at La Jolla."

"Doesn't that show how big market swings can be? He didn't have to sell, of course. His was a lock-up for the family on their occasional visits to the coast, a week or two now and then. He just wanted to consolidate back in Utah. Hardly typical, huh?"

"Let's hope so!" Zina exclaimed. "Now, these papers mention an on-site manager. In case I'm asked, what does that mean? Is it what we have here? Is it the same as managing agent?"

"In a way. It's confusing. I think there's a range of names for basically the same job, being the supervision of an occupied residential building. And there are actual differences in management arrangements among similar developments."

"Okay, we have to find out what gives at Gran Capitan. How do we do that?"

"By being nosy," replied Barney. "I think the starting point is the management that is set up by the developer when it's all his, before units are sold off.

All condo buyers accept that set-up, as they do everything else about the development. As like as not, they'll be given the option, after enough units are sold, of accepting or changing the deal, and most times the majority will just go along with it, as they haven't come to stir the pot, but to start a quiet life in their new home. As a group they know zilch about the finer points of contracts and condo building management. And those who do know, mightn't have either the time or the interest to be worried. Most buyers know much, much more about the desirable concept of residing in a condo, than about the nuts and bolts of the schemes, so they can't ask the right questions, and are easily swayed by the broker. They can hire an attorney, but few of us feel like going into a hopefully pleasant experience like a unit at Gran Capitan hand-in-hand with our lawyer, so like it or not, even against our better judgment, we accept much of what the broker says."

Zina continued, while looking at the brochure, "And it mentions governing documents, almost as though you needn't bother asking any questions about them. You're going to tell me what they are, I hope."

Barney said: "Sure. Let's go back to the developer setting up his condo. It's created through documents that follow a fairly standard style, and which interact. They contain the rules for governance of the development, rules that will apply to all the inhabitants. The documents have specific purposes. For instance, there's a Declaration, or Master Deed, which in effect is the constitution. There's a document - usually named articles of association - that binds the condo owners together, as members of the same development, in a homeowners (or condominium) association. It's only the owners in a collective form, like stockholders in a corporation, but without it an outsider would have to deal with each owner separately. Then there are the bylaws, which are an important code for the day-to-day running of the place." Seeing Zina's puzzled expression, he exclaimed, "Patience please, the end is nigh! And finally we have house rules for living arrangements." He clapped his hands. "There! All done!" He looked at her, asking: "Still here? Too much?"

Zina smiled wryly as she answered: "Just hanging on, but it's alright. I'll be better after looking at them. I don't mean read them right through, of course. So those are the governing documents? Do we get copies?"

"Surely so. We have them for Marquise. They're hard reading though, and of course it's easy to put that off when you're busy with buying and settling in."

"And maybe if a buyer doesn't read up before closing, they may go unread, then he or she lives in ignorance," Zina added. "Are lots of buyers like that?"

"Oh!" cried Barney, "Certainly. Everywhere. But even if folks want to learn, it's heavy going without a legal background, though the house rules and maybe the bylaws are manageable. It's just the way it is. Like all laws, you can scratch the surface readily enough, but going deeper is a hard slog." He paused to think, then continued: "Maybe we can get the hang of things better through the big picture. Condos have common property, or areas or elements

- owned in common by the unit owners - and a set of governing documents, that belong only to the one development. Each has its own set, and its own government, just like a state, or a county, or a city. Governance comes through a board of directors, or a council of management; same thing. We'd better stick to the community title housing schemes called condos, or we'll get lost, for there are others. But condos are increasingly important, not only for us, but for loads of people all across America and Canada, to say nothing of other countries. A condo scheme provides dwellings, not in the traditional styles of houses in suburban streets and farms, but as units in the development. The units and their owners are formally associated through the governing documents, which are unknown in streets and farms, so first-time condo buyers are on a learning curve from the start. That initial disadvantage can't be helped. But, if condo buyers aren't careful, they'll continue in ignorance, and so disadvantaged, for a long time, and maybe forever."

Zina thought that over, and said: "And as we're older, we learn slower. It sounds a little like moving to a foreign country. So to be with it, a buyer should take time out to learn."

"Exactly so. That's the ideal. Look at it through a developer's eyes. He creates the whole thing. Starts with a parcel of land, gets project approvals from zoning and development and building authorities, finds the great sums of money needed, designs dwellings some of which are elevated airspace, like the units here and in Gran Capitan, and others detached like those in suburban streets, and includes amenities suitable for the intended community. He sets aside elements of the property for common use, registers the subdivision plan to create a separate title for each unit, and prepares the governing documents for the functioning of the condo, and gives it an attractive name. He sells the dwelling units, and into them come residents, so the human side is then added to the physical structures, and a mini-city is complete. It's a closed community. Its main rules are hard to change, deliberately so, in order that the residents may live in a stable environment, and the condo owners may expect steady values for their units. The elected board of directors assesses the money needed for operations, and gets it in from the condo owners, and supervises expenditure. The board must act for the benefit of the condo owners, and always according to the governing documents. As condo sales increase, the developer's authority runs down, and ends once all are sold. A condominium is a distinct place and community within a city or a county, just as those in turn are within a state, which is within a nation."

Zina said: "That's a help. I think I get a lot of it. Is it like this with condos? The developer aims from the start to create a community of dwellings and people, like a small city, with rules to keep inhabitants under control in the interests of the majority."

"Yes, and an owner who wants to be a player needs to know that stuff. For the developer nothing happens by chance. He creates the plan and its rules, keeping an eye on the general law which is always concerned with fair dealing for all citizens. He must consider everything, and from all angles. His attorney and other advisers push the boundaries as far as possible. And he will often - not by any means always - want to make money out of the ongoing management, even though once he's done selling the condos, management isn't his business, and to do that he would create a management contract, and sell it. If that's his game, he will also know the easier he makes the contract conditions for the manager, and the longer the tenure, and the higher the compensation, the more valuable the sale. It's equal to selling several more condos."

"So the management contract could be worth a heap to the developer?"

"Most certainly."

"But a developer doesn't always sell a management contract, does he? Haven't I heard of places under self-management, or run by managing agents?"

Barney thought for a moment, then said: "You're showing more knowledge of these matters than I had expected. But you're quite right. It seems sadly true that once a management contract is sold by a developer, the asset has a life of its own, and having the money to buy it can be more important than the type of guy behind the check book. Once management by that sort of contract starts, it may be hard to shake off. It usually comes with a rental brokerage for those owners who want to rent out. That's a set-up in which bad things sometimes happen, even if they aren't found out. There's money held in trust, and the great majority of owner-investors live far away, with trust in the broker."

"So for everything bad we hear about, there's a chance there's more we don't."

"That's it. Why, just the other day I heard about the trick of churning tenants when their time was up, even though the unit wasn't booked onward. The broker moved the tenant to a different condo. Rent stays the same. The unit is let again, and the owner gets billed at the commission rate for a first letting, which is higher than for a renewal. Then there are the charges for cleaning on a change in tenant. The broker adds something most times. So there's more expense than if the tenant had stayed put."

"Uh! Where was this?"

"Somewhere on the south side. I don't know its name. It became news when resident owners noticed the lifts were being used a lot for moving renters' furniture, and that made them wait, as they're very short of lifts there. And suspicions grew, until the directors looked into it, and of course it then stopped, and no doubt was explained away as all being quite innocent."

Zina thought a moment, and asked: "If an investor owns a unit and lives far away, it must be hard to see things clearly. I mean, who can make a special trip just to check out his rental accounts, with no proof of bad things anyway? It's the old story of trust money and temptation. The way it was with that churning, it was the resident owners who found out. Renting out sounds a risky business, but maybe okay if you live close enough to feel the pulse of a place. But tell me please, about contract managers, is it hard to nail one for doing the wrong thing?"

"I think so. There's been some trouble that way here, not that we've taken much notice. The last thing a manager or a developer wants is a contract that can be ended easily by the owners, so I suppose lenient provisions are typical. As the developer wants top dollar in selling the contract, if that's his game, nothing can be included that might disturb the buyer, and maybe foul the sale. The rights of the owners aren't on the table, not for the developer, and not for the buyer of the management contract ....."

Zina interrupted, saying: "Sorry, this is so interesting, but I can't take it all in, so we'd better leave it for a bit. I can see though how all those years in contract management for GE gives you a flying start in this area; and good for you. But before we drop it, tell me how come that fine place in San Francisco your mother lived in was so different. Is it self-management there?"

"Sure you want to go on with this? I don't want to tire you."

Zina replied, "It's okay. I've just got second wind thinking of The Lotus Flower."

"As far as I know the developer was Japanese, and his daughter was the architect. Maybe they weren't in the local development scene enough to learn about selling management contracts, although that doesn't sound right, does it? They were switched on enough to produce a great place, so why wouldn't they know what less clever people do? Anyway, they left the style of management up to the buyers, who chose to employ an on-site manager on a two-year engagement, renewable only by mutual agreement. He's known as the resident supervisor, and doesn't have the long tenure and high compensation of some other places. They've had this style from the start, and you and I know it's worked as well as you could hope for. It's not the only one, of course."

"I wish it were in Santa Marta! The manager is, or was, Guy Robert. I remember your mother speaking so well of him. Does that style require more input from the directors? I mean, if the manager is an employee, and needs to ask the boss for instructions regularly, even if not from day to day, and the development is complicated with many people and much property, the manager may have to bounce plans off a director before acting. That could require the right director being at hand."

"That's so, but if they plan ahead sensibly, and have mutual confidence, it should be fine. That's how companies everywhere get along. Communication and trust are the keys. With both present, it works; with one missing, they'll have to sit down together and find how to do better."

"Isn't competence in it too?" asked Zina. "I mean, a smart manager and smart directors will surely get a better result than plodders."

"Yes, as always. But if they're conscientious, and use common sense, they can get by pretty well. There's a lot that's static in a condo, and even the people are mostly quiet and peaceful. There's never a guarantee about the quality of directors, who don't always get picked on merit, but even so, they can appoint a competent manager, and with him make a good team."

"So, if the manager is well chosen, and the directors allow him to do his job without too much interference, the self-management system can work well enough. It certainly has at The Lotus Flower."

Barney nodded agreement. "It shouldn't be too hard to find the right man. These big places are able to pay well, they need an on-site manager, and so he or she is pretty safe in the job, and there's no outlay of his or her capital to get in. And the owners very probably get a cheaper deal than under contract management."

"I'm happy with nice thoughts about The Lotus Flower and its creators, and I'll defer judgment on others until I know for sure.   I'll ask you later why a manager needs to be on-site, but I really must go now."

Alone with his thoughts, Barney mused: 'I guess an on-site manager, or OSM, could sometimes be shielded against owner complaints through a warm working relationship with the directors, and of them, the president in particular. It's always desirable for those two to work in harmony. If it goes further, into close friendship, the OSM's influence, always strong, could be boosted; it would simply follow on from the close ties. It's something all owners should know about. If they relied on the directors for protection and advancement of their interests - as they ordinarily do - their trust could be undermined by directors and manager being buddies.'

Later that day, as they continued discussing their interest in the new place. Zina asked: "Back to the manager being on-site. Can you tell me why that should be?"

"Well, if he's not there he could hardly know what's happening, so wouldn't be managing," Barney replied. "But maybe you mean in contrast to him or her going home every night?" He paused as Zina showed she agreed. "I think that basically it's size, and personal opinion. I know there are places where the manager goes home nights, especially places controlled by managing agents. But, y'know, even a commercial building that's empty overnight and at week-ends has a caretaker, and condos aren't ever empty. So it's not just to keep intruders out that I would like to see an OSM living in, but also to be at hand in case something that is his work comes up, which is more likely in a large place. I reckon there are plenty of places where money is saved through employing an off-site manager, and residents act as voluntary carers, which would work better in a smaller condo than a large one. The effectiveness of the security system is another factor to consider."

"I see. That sounds sensible. Now this," Zina said. "I sense problems can come up with management, and then everybody has to look hard at the wording of the contract. With so many condos this must be going on all the time, which would bring up questions about changing the contract. Is that a tough gig?"

"Not if both parties agree, but if the OSM is on a good thing he'll not change, not willingly, so the owners cop it on the chin, or take legal action, and those aren't simple choices. Remember these are self-governing places, and so out of the government spotlight. It's natural. State government gives self-government to a small territory and its inhabitants, and within its boundaries it's meant to be self-regulating. The citizens provide their own side-walks and pools and gardens and other common elements, and keep the place clean and tidy, all at their own expense. It's hard for any government not to like that. As the structure and functioning of condos come much more from contract than legislation, the owners can arrange the management of the complex, and their management agreement, as they wish, so long as they observe the laws of the land, which have little to say about those matters. No record is kept of the types of management in operation, and as there are many thousands of developments, it's hard to generalize about how they are run, and problems along the way. A contract can turn out bad, and yet be impossible for the owners to change, at least until the term is up, maybe years away. Of course, it's not only condos that turn out dodgy contracts."

"I bet. But I'm getting the feeling that one side of the condominium deal isn't fully informed. That's the owners' side. Buyers seem to be sitting ducks for a developer."

Barney continued: "I guess we're among the ducks, no matter how hard we might try not to be. We can't get away from the need for professional management in a place of any size at all. Enter OSM. He comes through a written agreement, which states the job specification, which is too complex to be left to a verbal agreement, and faulty memories. There's nothing wrong with that, until we find the contract is long-term, so that changing conditions isn't at all easy. I'm guessing that at Gran Capitan they'll have a contract OSM, like here at Marquise. And though the management of The Lotus Flower is set up differently, it too will have a written contract. If a condo complex appoints a managing agent, as some do, with functions that may pretty well cover all those of an OSM, again a written contract will be used.

"The key is its duration. Say that's three years. So it's not long before changes can be made, and earlier, of course, by consent. If the OSM wants to be re-appointed he'll readily agree to sensible alterations along the way. On the other hand, if a contract is for, say, ten years, there's less pressure on an OSM to negotiate change to meet new circumstances, or accept amendments that most people would see as being fair. Whatever, the unit buyers can't change the contract unilaterally, as rights under contracts are well respected by the law."

Zina said, "I feel maybe I'm being too curious, but here goes. Are employed manager and self-management the same thing?"

"For many people they are, but I'm not comfortable that way, because self-management also means exactly what it says. For example, and particularly, small places of only a few units, where the owners do everything themselves, and don't employ a manager at all. They really do manage themselves. But that can't work in big places. Remember too that an employed manager is there under a contract of one sort or another, as is a managing agent, so contract management is also an imprecise term, for it can mean any of several management arrangements. So we have to watch our words.

"But most owners aren't concerned with contract details. It's hard going for them. Easier to be unconcerned, as long as the elevators and the amenities and common elements function, and are kept clean. The hard way is to personally learn the legalities and rights and wrongs, then you can sort things better, and maybe find loopholes in the contract. I can learn, though I haven't so far. I don't mean to go to a new place carrying a sword and a shield, or as a pretend attorney, but if something comes up that looks like the owners being short-changed, I want to be able to point it out, and criticize, not to destroy, as much as to elevate; but oh dear! I feel that does sound like a knight in shining armor. Do tell me I'm not being too pretentious."

"No. You aren't." The smile that often hovered on her lips grew, as she added: "Still, if I give you a horse you'll know I've become doubtful. But can you take in all that legal stuff?"

"I'm only aiming for what I need to know. This is how we financial guys in GE got to understand contracts. And it's how the lawyers learned about finance. Study the bits you need, and leave the rest of it to the experts. So, if we move, I'll look into it closer. I'll get on top of the governing documents, of which there are only a few, and after that the working documents, such as the major contracts, and minutes of meetings. It would be a hard road for some people, but it seems do-able for me. The starting point is that these are artificial places, with only a few documents through which the whole place is controlled. They're like nothing else. Understand them and you can talk up, and make sense too."

"Zina asked, "Don't city and county and state and federal laws get a look in? Gran Capitan's in America, isn't it? And, by the way, did you know he was a famous Spanish soldier a long time back? Developers must have fun selecting interesting names."

"It would help ignorant slobs like me if they put up plaques to explain those things. And yes, it is in America. I cut corners there. If I said that a condominium, and its inhabitants, are always subject to the general law of the country, would it sound better?"

"Sure, that sounds right."

"I think we need more plain English," Barney continued: "The rules of a condo aren't really above the heads of many owners, but if too much legalese is used, or if information is sparse, they may close their minds; then they're vulnerable, and risk being screwed."

"I fear Gran Capitan won't be much different. If you do get into administrative issues, it will surely earn you some enemies as well as friends, and you may become a contentious figure. But you know that."

"Well, it may not happen. I wouldn't be looking for trouble, but believing as I do that the system can give owners poor treatment at times, I'd be weak if I didn't talk up at the right time. It could bring conflict with those, particularly directors, who may not take kindly to an assertive owner. 'Not your business', they might say to me, and I must be careful to see if that's true, and back out; or even better, not go in."

"Fine, fine. But what if people ask why don't you become a director? That's the usual role for people like you. If you criticize the developer, as many folks will be doing, but stand aside from the board, it may seem you are anti-director too, and then yours might be a lonely voice."

"Fair enough. The fact is I'm a mental elitist. I don't like being on even terms in decision making with muddle heads, and I worry that sitting with them could be too big a strain. As you know, I've had a working life of boards and committees, and some of them were pretty high-powered, and I don't want to be on an equal footing with inexperienced folk with no background that way, or in condo administration either. Trouble is, it's hard to know in advance. So you go for a board seat, and then, too late, find yourself in bed with the wrong people. Anyway, until I know more about the governing documents of a condo I wouldn't consider trying for board, so it's a ways off, and even then I may feel I'd be more useful by raising my voice as an owner. If I were on the board I could feel muzzled. If they do a good job they don't need me, and if they do a bad job I'd like to be free to criticize and suggest improvement, which can sometimes be done better from outside. I know very well how an opinion or a proposal can be distorted by going through the filter of a directors' spokesperson.

"I'm not all that odd, am I? Take any other elected government, local, state or federal. We know that as soon as it takes office many voters, to say nothing of the media and the formal opposition, start questioning its decisions and policies. We accept that. Condos, and their boards of directors, are little private governments. Owners, being citizens, must of course obey their laws, but also should be free to suggest change, or criticize. It's a funny thing that opposition to and criticism of government and public laws, is taken for granted, and is natural outside, but in a condo tends to mark the dissident unfavorably. But I see opposition as rounding out democratic government, public or private."

Zina said: "You're right there, of course. I'd like you to think a little more about that elitist stance though, because we would never have a government anywhere if superior people required their colleagues to be brainstorms, like themselves, before joining in. And if you learn the way you said, and the fire keeps burning, you might naturally want to be part of our little government one day."

"So I should keep an open mind?"

"I think so. No hurry though."

He said: "However that goes, I still have definite views, at least right now. I

20

like living in a condo, but I don't like owners being trampled on by developers, contract managers, and networks of administrators and the power brokers among the directors, even if they smile while they do it. To me, they tend to lean on the ignorance of the owners, especially in the early days of a project. The most serious part of it is when the cost structure makes owner's assessments too high, and may become embedded unless it's contested."

"You mean the management contract sometimes set up by the developer?"

"Yes. If he sells that, he's really selling owners' rights to manage their own affairs. It's a fraud, so obvious, so blatant, it's a wonder the law allows it. Sure, the owners have to approve the contract soon after they come in, but at that stage everything is sweetness and light, so opposition would be a dirty word. Moreover, by probing deep enough you might find some dominant directors at the start were also stooges for the developer."

"Maybe the legislators don't know. Or don't understand. Or are so content for developments to be self-managing they don't see the unfair parts."

"Of course that's true. And developers' lobbyists help keep legislators' hands off. Still, I mustn't blame others unless I've had a go myself."

"That's my boy; up guards and at 'em! Why is it all so hard though? It strikes me you'd have to be pretty dumb not to see how the owners get a raw deal in some of these places, especially where the contract manager has lucrative compensation and long tenure."

"Surely. If government fixed that I could be more relaxed about the rest. But let's look at ourselves. You know now what I want to do if we go to Gran Capitan. I could become a stirrer. If that would bother you maybe we shouldn't go there. I wouldn't want to embarrass you, or have you telling me to slow down. Let's face it before we visit."

"Right. Let's. My view is that you must do whatever switches you on, and that I'm to do some work for you, and leave the front-running to you. On that basis, count me in."

Relieved, Barney grinned, and got up and walked to her, and patted her head, always pretty with its cropped mass of silvery hair, surrounding her pale face with its handsome forehead and normally serene expression. She smiled too, and said: "Thank you. The ride will be interesting. Now there's another slant to condos I've just caught up with. The big D. I've seen a list of the classes of people who have been excluded from condos. It's scary stuff; not only skin color, but also those whose sexual orientation is not mainstream - you see I try not to offend - and includes marital status, physical disability, age, nationality, race, religion, and ancestry. The article said governments are applying anti-discrimination laws to places like condos, if maybe a little later than in public places."

Barney added: "It'll be interesting to see how far they push it, and how much they leave to the schemes to work through it alone."

"How would they do it?"

"You mean extending the rules for Main Street into a condo? It doesn't sound too hard. The government can pass a law that we can't discriminate within its jurisdiction, which includes condos, of course."

Zina stood up. Barney knew the talk was closing own. He was tickled pink the way it had gone. He said, "So we're off to the sales center. Y'know, believing what we've said, buying off-the-plan means taking some things on trust. We can't go there with a condo revolution in mind, else they'll tell us to go jump, and then we miss out. Someone else will buy our condo and be happy, while we stay here in misery? Well, not really happy anyway."

Zina cried, "I don't want us to miss out through being too fussy. I can believe you, and agree with you, and still be keen on Gran Capitan, can't I?"

"Sure. I guess they'll trick us somewhere along the line, but I won't say 'I told you so'."

"Promise?'

"Promise."

2

The Jones continue discussion as they prepare to visit the sales center for Gran Capitan

Next morning, after breakfast, Barney again raised his concerns, introducing them with the question, "Can you handle a bit more about condos?" While Zina was thinking of a reply he went on: "The buyers have no idea about costs for a large unit complex, so have to take the manager contract and its compensation on trust. We buyers feel it's not something to be changed, that it's set in stone, as much part of the place as the roof. And the same with the tenure. In theory there's no upper limit, though something extremely long could be a turnoff for some buyers. The first wave of buyers is vulnerable, and that's when lasting decisions are often made."

"Y'know honey, there's a lot to take in, but I'm doing my best. You really get wound up about all this, don't you? I'm not carping; not at all. It's important. I think I see the cheating way some management contracts are set up. The contract manager sees our homes as a springboard for his profit. It seems to me the looser the conditions of that contract, including the manager's work list, the more the temptation for the manager to cut corners on the one hand, and serve himself some freebies on the other."

Barney exclaimed: "Indeed! Besides, and in some situations where there's a contentious manager with a long tenure, or worse, a succession of guys like that, the loss by owners of their quality of life is real, if intangible."

"When you think of it," said Zina, "Marquise is a bit like that. Anyway, we're ready to trot along to Gran Capitan to find some facts. We can walk?"

"Sure," Barney replied. "As we go, let's remember that the business of both the developer and his selling broker is selling the condos, so they highlight everything that sounds nice, and if they don't talk about legal or management complexities very much, it's because they know that's a sure way of dazing inexperienced buyers. And that would never do. Whoever heard of that stuff in suburbia? Why wouldn't brokers shy away from explaining it?"

"Of course. Simple and sweet are what they like, and I don't blame them. I, at least, had the same experience here at Marquise. The structure is more artificial than I had expected."

Barney said: "But even knowing, it still suits us, and though we pick holes in everything, we want to live in a condo. I bet we find a manager installed at Gran Capitan, and hear that he or they are top of the tree, pick of the crop, et cetera, as though the world had been combed to find him. Yet the truth could be he had two essential qualifications: not currently in prison, and had the cash."

"Oh come, that's cynical."

"Sure it is. And maybe I'm boring you, and had better simmer down. So let's wait and see how Best and Better Constructions Inc. is handling these issues."

"Let's," said Zina.

"We'll overlook that the compensation that lures the manager is to come from us buyers, as long as the manager has a good track record. The less worry we have the better."

Pensively, Zina asked: "Does this sound right? As you said, management expense is unavoidable, and you can't truly tell if it's unreasonably high without a lot of analysis. And I guess the spread of expense over so many owners helps hide some above-market expenses. Take our case. Our share of every dollar spent at Marquise is what - almost too small to think about?" Barney nodded agreement. "So what's a bit more matter? - especially as we can't change anything. And all owners are in the same boat. Our perspective is different from that at a single, stand-alone, owner-occupied dwelling, where we think about every cent. Here an owner's concern is that the unit assessments don't run away, and if they do it can hardly be from the contract compensation, as that's pretty much the same each year, with adjustments for inflation, I suppose."

"You mean, if I didn't complain about management compensation earlier, why now?"

"That's it," said Zina. "I think so. Y'know, the deceit is right at the beginning. The developer presents management as a done deal, telling the buyers they are on a good thing with what he's set up, and we, the buyers, think of it, if we think at all, as a deal between the developer and the OSM, with us as onlookers, more or less. We don't latch onto the fact that every dime of the manager's compensation, at least after the developer leaves, comes from us. It's like we were watching a movie."

Barney nodded agreement.

Said Zina, "Well, well." So we're on our way to have a look. We expect to hear that the set-up is bliss for buyers, and few of us will be skeptical."

Barney cried, "Wow! You sound like an oracle with all that vision. Truly now, would you rather forget it?"

"No, not at all. Its attractions outweigh the rest. We may be wrong in our criticisms, and it may be that the management structure is sound, and that we've been jumping at shadows. If only it were The Lotus Flower number two though!"

"I agree, but it's not, and we want to live here, so this is our best," Barney added."

Zina continued, "We'll have a lot to look for, without expecting to change anything."

"Seems so. But, y'know, even if new laws require a management contract, if set up by the developer, to be approved by the new owners, its different from them being fully informed, which takes time, as they have a whole new learning experience ahead before they know enough to approve or not, and compare the expense under alternative management styles. If contract management is in place, and the OSM is attentive to the condo owners, who know the assessments to expect, which includes management expense, they may be content with the status quo. I think though, as we've said, if a development operated under self-management, like The Lotus Flower, for the first year or so, the owners could get wised up, and know better what they should be looking for."

"I see," said Zina: "You'd like the developer to leave management arrangements for the owners to work out when they've learned what it's all about, and with luck they'll hit upon something that works, and is cost-effective. After all, owning and managing a home is an ordinary part of very many lives, so the management of a group of dwellings in a condo community isn't all that different. Sure, there's new stuff to learn, but ordinary people can get on top of the basics, if they want."

"But what if those ordinary people don't stir themselves?" asked Barney. "Look at our figures at Marquise. Half the owners never vote. I think 80% plus will never even think of becoming a director, or even going on a sub-committee, not ever. Some people aren't fit for that work, but the others are the problem. If enough from that talent bank don't help at some time, they deny the condo access to a great resource."

"So you need healthy competition for board positions, and a pool of good quality candidates."

"Exactly. And those who don't take their turn are mean. They took an interest in management when in their house, but on coming into an apartment they leave it to others. It's not as though they're asked to sweep the footpaths or weed the garden or mow the lawns or put out the trash bin or whatever, but just to use their brains and experience in household management. You'd think every responsible condo owner who had that past experience, and was not prevented from committee work by age or disability, would see it as right that they volunteer. If not, the place tends to be kept in too few hands, which may be fine if, and only if, those hands are clean, and expert."

"You don't feel you are one of the mean ones?"

"Actually, I do, and I must work through that problem."

"Zina inquired: "What about this? Set up a standing committee of owners, a steering committee if you like, to encourage nominations for directors' seats, and present them in a consistent manner, fair to the candidates and to the owners, so that the better qualified folk would stand out."

"I like it," Barney replied. "It would be better than here, where candidates write their own stories, and can put in a lot of nonsense, even his or her prep school, and how many children they have, and naturally only say what's nice about themselves. And if you look closely some of them have never been on a board in their lives, so starting with a complicated thing like a condo would be plain stupid. The other side of the coin is that some folks who write their own CVs are too busy or too modest or whatever to be fair to themselves, so may be overlooked by the voters, which is a pity for everybody."

The weather next morning was pleasant and right for the half-mile stroll to the sales center. The Jones were very happy as they walked, ready to face their important venture. Suddenly, Zina unclasped her hand from his, and halted, saying: "After all that talk and analysis we're thinking of buying off-the-plan. Are we sane?"

"Who knows? It's a worry."

"That's right. Still, I have to say I do like the idea of a brand new apartment with modern finishes of good quality in this district, especially one with great views, and smart security, and no vacation renting."

Moving on, now along a minor street close to their destination, they met a rare sight; a late model Bentley auto, gleaming pale blue, parked by the kerb. They stopped to admire it, and were joined by a passer-by, who said it belonged to 'the broker selling the off-the-plan condos over there,' pointing. The visitors were pleased for its owner, and his apparent success. It seemed a little out-of-place parked where it was, but they soon realized it was less conspicuous there than outside its owner's work-place. They would meet him soon.

3

The Jones meet the sales staff at Gran Capitan - impressed by a condo, they read the buyer's contract papers, and are unimpressed - but the heart trumps the mind

The center was on the construction site. In its several rooms virtual views and supporting graphics made an extensive and representative presentation of the future Gran Capitan. The sales staff of a man and two females, answered every question about the project with a praising of its merits and a dispelling of doubts. Their eagerness led to a willingness to bend apparent rules, and more readily when sales had just commenced and ultimate success was unknown. So when a woman who had been showing some interest said, "It states here no pets allowed. Now we have a little dog that has been our friend for a long time, and we'd be interested in coming here if we could keep him with us until he dies. Pity if we can't, as this seems such a nice place." At that time bias against pets of any sort in condos was general. The bylaws here stated no pets without board consent, and in due course popular demand would lead to change, to permit pets that met the acceptable features of a new code. At this time, BBC's control entitled it to act as the board, and approve the prospective buyer's request, as a special favor. So Henrietta was into sympathy mode right away, her look implying: 'Here we have an obstacle which may block these people from something they have set their hearts on, and I must help them over it.' She said: "That's too bad. Let's see if anything can be done. I'll have a word with Robert." He came to them shortly, took their, and the dog's particulars, and learned the style of unit that interested them. Addressing each of them in turn, with changes in expression to suit the drift, he said: "Congratulations on your preference," and he spoke for a few minutes about its advantages. Continuing, "As to Happy, I'm so aware of the strong bonds between dogs and owners, especially as they all age, and yes indeed, it would be a great pity if he couldn't see out his days in the bosom of his family. I'll have to talk to head office, and no, that won't be a burden, as that's what we're all here for. It's a timely request, because others have also asked about pets, and in fact the company is looking at the rules right now. I think they might allow house-trained dogs of ten pounds or less, and require they be carried when using lifts and paths." He paused, as the man interrupted, saying, "But Happy weighs 14, and is too heavy for us to carry far, and then there's his health." Robert had been paying respectful attention, and showed not the slightest perturbation as the details of the dog came out. He smiled sympathetically, and knowingly, and nodded his head in tune with the story. At the end he exclaimed, "So, so! What can we do for you? Well, you badly want the condo, is that right? Okay. Now, this is what I can try. This will be a one off for a much loved pet with a short life expectancy.

You could find it hard to carry it to the street, so could we say you would use a small trolley instead. You think so? Good! Permission for this dog is what you want, right?"

"Yes, that would be real nice for us, Robert, and it's very kind of you to go to all this trouble."

"Well, there's no trouble in helping people get something reasonable, and skirting the rules if no harm's done. Think nothing of it. I'll get you an answer in a day or so. Right?" said Robert, his eyes glowing with compassion: "When I'm putting up your case would I say you have taken a liking to a particular unit?" They were not ready to answer that, and the woman said, "Just give us a few minutes if you please Robert, and we'll see." The few minutes were no trouble for Robert, and soon the clients were joined by Henrietta, attentive with answers and sensible suggestions. It was not long before they could confirm their preference, and Robert offered to hold it while he checked out the matter of Happy, which offer was gratefully received. He suggested they come back the next day, to have another look, and hear how he got on. In the meantime he would be doing his best for them.

His best was good enough, and next day he was delighted to say that the company would make an exception for that condo for those buyers for that pet, so how did that sound to them? It sounded very well indeed. That being so, what next? He said: "Why don't you come up in the builders' elevator in a day or so, to take in the views from your floor? And what about finance? Some buyers need a mortgage, of course, and for them BBC's bank has made up a fact sheet, describing the arrangements the company has made with the federal authorities for funding for condo buyers at this superior development. Unless you are self-financing, it will pay you to read that paper, and we can give you a copy, which your bank and your attorney should also read to make sure you get the deal that suits you. Even though closing is maybe 13 months on, it's good to have finance lined up before signing up. I happen to know a source of funds that other buyers have found satisfactory, and if I can be of any assistance there, then you good folk need only say the word." Those folk, again, found the advice very helpful, and said they would think it over, but finance would not be a problem, one way or another. Robert continued, "You'll understand that with a strong demand for the units, BBC can't allow contracts subject to finance, although, if it were left to me, it might be different. But you know what a head office is. They make the rules, and I have to carry them out. Subject to that, the team here is glad to oblige folks so taken with the development as to want a condo, which to us seems one of the best decisions they could ever make." Both buyers nodded appreciatively. The woman. whose clothes and gentle manner suggested she was practicing to be a hippy, went further, saying, "Thank you, Robert. We're finding your care and attention so nice we would be happy to put in a good word for you to head office, if it might help you. Would you like that?" That floored Robert, who already knew his value to head office, which was why he had been commissioned to sell the big project. He thought he had better stop the idea at once, as head office would expect him to do, but not so as to disturb his clients. He decided to play for time. He looked warmly and gratefully at the woman, while saying: "I can't tell you how kind that is, nor how very much I appreciate it. The only thing is I must work out is who it should be addressed to, so as not to be lost in all the paper work up there, or fall into the wrong hands. Could you leave it with me please? It may take a few days to get set up, but I'll do my best. In any case, thanks a million." And he finished the affair with another warm smile. With that the woman was content, and his vagueness didn't disturb her at all, as she herself was vague by natural disposition anyway. He returned to the question of finance more decisively. "If you need a little more time, remember my contact. It would be an agreement of preliminary intention to buy, with finance assured should you want it, along with dispensation for keeping Happy in the apartment for the rest of his days, and you could either retain that deal, or replace it with another." The man replied, "We really don't know much about finance, but it doesn't matter, as your man and our own resources will see us through. And yes, we'd like to meet him, as we can see we need to act firmly to secure that unit." They would never know that they were among many 'special clients' whose like introductions would enable them to sign unconditional contracts promptly, so securing to them their preferred unit, and to Robert a sale.

The finance broker was a small law firm, not at all handy to Santa Marta, with links to lines of finance, and Robert. Its guarantees were produced promptly, and could be dropped for a break fee. It was a pleasing deal for all concerned. BBC and the selling brokers delighted in firm sales, and the buyers were getting exactly what they wanted.

Soon after settling the concerns of Happy and its owners, Robert turned his attention to another buyer whose request was that, contrary to the advertised information, he and his wife needed to install a timber floor, because of her allergies, which were stable on wood, but less so on carpet. They, too, liked a certain unit very much, but the floor was the problem. Robert, his look exuding concern for them, assured them the policy of the vendor was to meet reasonable requests, and it was in a position, before the rules were set in stone - not wood, he had added, with a little laugh, but not too heartily, in case the buyers didn't get it, which they didn't, and humor may be better if shared - to consider special circumstances. Unfortunately, he had no power to grant the request, but he certainly could put up a strong case to head office for it because of the special circumstances, and his friends could rely on him doing so promptly. The last thing he wanted was to deny people the chance of living in this fine development. His arm would be strengthened if he had a medical certificate concerning the lady's need, because this would make the case clearly special. The certificate was produced promptly, and said the patient had an allergic condition, and might be more comfortable with a wooden floor, so BBC agreed, on condition that any floor installed met standards to be attached to the purchase contract, and the board be given notice of completion, whereupon it should issue a certificate to protect the owner from any later complaint. The buyers thought that plan perfect, and committed themselves to purchase.

Before proceeding, let's return to Happy for a moment. The dog lived for years beyond expectations, which BBC took to be due its benign environment, and adopted the idea for its promotions, with the slogan "Live here, live longer." The dog was a pathetic eyesore, slightly incontinent, constantly whining, and frequently farting, so that its presence was well and unfavorably known to those who used the same lifts and enclosed spaces as the big trolley on which it lay inertly, with an occasional flicker of its cloudy old eyes the only indicator of life. Its weight increased with the years, but was never known, because the directors had no warrant to measure it, as they had for other dogs, as set out in the code. When its eye-lids finally ceased to flicker the residents had had little to complain about, other than odors, and could not include sheer ugliness, as that was not against any rules. Noise was not a problem, because Happy was never heard to bark, and his other noises occurred more at home than in public. But, by the time of its passing, the dispensation granted his owners was recognized as a mistake, as one Happy might lead to another, and the experience helped the directors in redefining pet policy. Another factor for a time was the near certainty that some residents kept pets outside the rules, and so may not be adequately checked for health. Happy's owners had told Henrietta of a local condominium that banned pets, and in which a fire broke out in the trash room in the middle of the night, causing lots of smoke, but little fire. Residents realized the alarm was not a practice drill, and duly turned out to wait by the pool, and they brought along many pets, which their owners did not want to be singed, or scared half to death, if left at home. They preferred to disclose their violations.

The wooden floor turned out less than perfectly. It was installed by the buyers, faithfully to BBC specifications which, unknown to that firm, were based on flawed research. All was revealed when the original owners had moved on, and the new owner-occupier, who lived quietly with her female partner, held a party, at which women were almost solely the guests, and who mainly had worn high heel shoes, according to fashion, and the occasion. The hostess had taken the precaution of informing her next-door neighbors that a party was planned, and asked to be excused should it produce unusual noise; and invited them to attend. So she was astounded to be called by the duty security officer, toward midnight, with a complaint from the occupant of the apartment immediately below, about noise, being clatter, which the complainant, herself a woman, knew to be high heel shoes on a wooden floor. The hostess immediately recognized that here was a neighbor she had overlooked, and abated the noise, through everybody taking off their shoes. Later she and her partner considered apologizing to the neighbor, though they felt that a direct phone call would have been more fitting, and indeed had it been made they would have invited her to come up to the genteel fun. But the idea was dumped when the hostess found a formal complaint had been made to the directors, and she soon received a letter from the board, noting that consent to the timber floor had not been sought, so consideration would be given to ordering its removal, unless the owner could show reasons otherwise. The formalism throughout made the owner wonder if this was usual treatment of condo owners, or if it had some special overtones related to sexual orientation, which she knew well enough prompted occasional prejudice. But she was concerned mainly because she had had no idea there was anything special about the floor, and also because if she had an illegal construction in her apartment, she may have to remove it, with expense and inconvenience she could not even guess at. She went to the contract of purchase, and found no clues in it. The partners knew precious little about the governing documents of the condo, and neither had the time to read them, so they consulted a neighbor, who was experienced in business. He knew little about them either, but knew where to look, and also knew the original owners, who were living not far away. He called them to discuss the problem, and stressed his interest was only to find the facts whatever they were, and to be neighborly. Their response was quite open. They had acted on the specifications supplied by BBC, and attached to their own purchase contract, and in fact, they had gone further and added more underlay than prescribed. These facts were recorded in papers and plans they had preserved, and which were available to him to read, or borrow. He quickly concluded that the first owners had done all required of them in installing the floor, and that as their doing so rested in contract, and pre-dated the condominium rule, that should be the end of it. They had met the condition of notice of completion to the board, but not received a certificate of compliance in return, and had forgotten about it. The original owners thought their habit of going barefoot, or wearing sox or slippers, could have kept them out of trouble. The current owner still had to pacify the directors, which she set out to do by a letter framed with the help of her partner and the neighbor, which was detailed and factual enough to show the floor was there legitimately, that as hostess she had been considerate of the neighbors as she knew them at the time, and that any noise nuisance that had come from her apartment was innocent, and could hardly be expected to be repeated now its cause was known. The directors accepted it entirely, and the matter was ended for the time being. It would be revived years on, with a new owner of the unit, and a new occupant of the unit below, who would also complain about noise from the floor. By then the board had taken further advice on noise transmission and found the flaw in the earlier specifications, so a general review of installations was made, and new bylaws adopted, all of which became another story, for which there is no room at this point.

Barney's interest in the new place was general, and Zina's mainly on the insides of the apartments. Those most suitable for them were two bedroom and two bath, a study, plus a basement storeroom, and two basement car bays, with a panoramic view of sky, hills, lake, urban areas, and a smidgen of ocean. Zina would want some minor interior changes at add-on cost if they bought in. Robert, in his caring way, broached the subject of signing an unconditional contract, and offered to locate finance, but it would not be needed, and Barney was ready to look over the purchase papers.

He knew courses of study for OSMs and also for administration managers (who organized general meetings, and kept minutes and were active in budgeting and insurance and income tax filings and compliance work generally), were available, and he had seen framed diplomas in some of their offices. Interested to know more, he had followed up to view the content of some courses, enough to see that, in the field of tertiary education for such managers, all was elementary. He considered that lowly diplomas of that sort were worth little, and learned that their possession was not a rigid condition for employment. As to the OSM role, he had also learned that few who took it on had either a former vocation, or a high-level degree, of special significance for its varied challenges. So If an OSM had no practical experience to compensate, he could only learn at the expense of the owners, which was not good, and so the board had a big responsibility in considering the suitability of a new man, or couple. He saw that lucrative compensation, and a chance of capital gain, could make contract management a tempting business opportunity for some people. A broker would have no trouble in puffing it up, while playing down the risks were the candidate to prove unsuitable, whether through lack of appropriate experience, or training, or temperament, or shortage of capital, to name a few significant risk factors for a newcomer.

He had also seen that OSMs made it their business to have good relations with the staff of the administration manager who, apart from the attorney for the association, knew most about the interpretation of the governing documents. Good relations between OSMs and administrators were desirable, if the result was to be fair to the owners of the condos, but sometimes their closeness produced a mutual support deal that left owners out in the cold, and some owners did not understand this. The owner could go to the directors, and in doing so might, or might not, get a fair hearing, because they, if ignorant themselves, would be reliant on advice from the administration manager. It was natural that the contractors should stick together. The interests of the owners could be overlooked along the way. The mutual backing was little known of by outsiders. It was readily implemented through their respective staffs being in frequent contact with each other. But such was only an important instance of the networks of power and influence that operated in some condos.

Barney had been interested in the management set-up at Gran Capitan from the start, and had said to Robert: "I've come across places where the building management is not the best. I wonder how BBC is handling it here." Robert was on top of the issue in a flash. "I know, I know, you're so right, some arrangements are less than perfect," he cried. "I'm glad to tell you, for not many owners even mention it, that BBC has gone to no end of trouble to prepare a modern OSM contract, and you can read it yourself in your purchaser paperwork. And also they looked around for a top team, an experienced team, the best on offer, and have enticed Michael and Gloria Holliday here, who are resting after a long spell at Yerba Buena, which you might know as the biggest condo complex in Ventura county. So with their experience, and both being exceptionally fine folk, Gran Capitan is away to a great start, management-wise. Later the owners will have to approve the contract, and those managers, but both should be okay. You might remember the name: Mike was the top pitcher for the Cardinals until a few years ago. How does that sound for management?" Robert concluded, with a smile that invited Barney's approval, and he answered: "Sounds great. Yes, I think I remember that name. It's a good advertisement for the development, and it'll be nice to meet a star." To himself he wondered what the connection was, but there was no point in being negative with Robert. He said instead: "That's very reassuring, and thank you. I'll look at the contract, but it sounds just right. I'll do that tonight and let you know if we have any queries." He felt that Robert would have been just as pleased had he and Zina signed up without bothering, but nothing was said, and the conversation turned to their meeting the next day, and the procedure to be followed then.

Barney read the contract. Although he had many years of contract experience with GE, he was now in new territory, not having studied the Marquise documentation. There was a lot to take in, and he would have benefited from a checklist of things to look for, one prepared by a skeptical expert, but there was none. He could well imagine how easily the average buyer could take it all as read, and after initial perusal he mused: 'Some of the duties of the manager are not stated at all forcefully, no doubt because BBC couldn't make them too onerous, for then getting a good manager would be tough. But they've gone to the opposite extreme, allowing the OSM to get away with too much. The compensation seems high, but I don't know for sure without a detailed breakdown by an expert, which can't happen, so I'll be consoled by the expense being the same for every owner. The contract is for five years, I suppose from occupancy of units, say 1980. Irrespective of my views, this contract will proceed and there's no way we can become owners of a condo here without it. I fear the manager is treated too leniently in respect of violations, in that he would have to be very bad, many times, before he could be fired. But you have to read the contract carefully to come to that conclusion, and most folks won't do that. I see it has to be ratified by a 85% majority of owner votes at a special meeting after enough units have been sold, and going by the rate of sales that won't be long. The owners are unlikely to hear criticism of, or opposition to the contract, and no doubt there will be a supply of proxies to the chair to help carry the day. The dangers for the owners are the absence of market testing of the compensation, the gentle treatment of violations, absence of a stipulation for finishes to be kept up to a new standard as near as may be, the low level of specification of standards in relation to duties, and no insistence on an OSM personally residing at Gran Capitan. That is such a long list, and I don't know anyone to bounce it off. Robert and his staff could only support what they are selling. The other buyers aren't likely to be interested in grouches like mine, even if they could understand them, and I have no way of making contact with them anyway. So we should give up on this development, and look for another in these parts, one that works under self-management. I'll tell Zina what I think in the morning.'

Zina had known Barney would stay up to read the purchase papers. She took it to be only a formal step, needing little interest from her, and it was not until they were at breakfast next morning that she asked, almost idly, how it went. Barney would have preferred to defer discussion, but instead he replied at once, in between bites of toast and sips of tea, saying, "If you want it straight, then frankly I wasn't impressed."

She raised her eyebrows, and asked, "Seriously, really so?" She felt it was before she spoke. "Is it a little, or a lot?"

"A lot."

"If it's a lot it will take a lot of time to explain, and I'm not sure I'll get it even then. If you say it's a lot, then I believe you. Does it mean so bad we shouldn't go ahead?"

"Before I answer, how would you feel about buying a condo in a self-managed development, the kind we've talked about?"

Zina sat, silently stirring her tea, thinking before saying: "I think I get it. If we use the left side of our brain we leave it. Trouble is, my right side works better and stronger. That's the musician in me. I'd really set my heart on Gran Capitan and its modern everything, and all brand new. I couldn't have imagined being so lucky as to get to live in such a place in southern California, and now I'll just have to kid myself it doesn't matter if it falls over. To answer the question, I can't tell without looking, and if Gran Capitan is off limits, we'll have plenty of time for that."

It hit Barney there was no substitute. Nothing in the locality rang the same bells. Zina wouldn't get over this for a long time, and they would be facing constant reminders of what they had decided against, and all his contentment at not being trapped would be more than offset by her disappointment, spoken or silent. This was their locality, and Gran Capitan was the place for their retirement. He put out his hand and clasped hers. "I won't prolong this. I see that giving up on it is a real blow for you. For me, it starts off the same as for another 400 owners, and if I make it worse for myself by being inquisitive, it's only because it suits me. I don't have to. With your help, whatever I do will be reasonable, and based on principle, so where's the harm to come from that? So the fright's over now, and I'm quite happy for us to go ahead. No tears. No blame, never."

But there were some tears. Zina wept a little as she reached over and clasped his hand, and whispered: "Thanks."

There was no doubt about it now: they were ready for the move, and signed and paid a deposit for their future home, sold the Marquise condo quite quickly, put their belongings in storage, went wandering for a few months, visited their three children successively, where there was neither invitation nor room for them to camp for long, and then they took a three-month lease of a local furnished unit, which ran them to the day when they closed for their new condo. Once in occupation, Barney freely admitted it was all they could wish for, and he assured Zina she had been right.

4

Ed and Binny McGinty are introduced - their Queensland connection - its white shoe brigade - Ed learns about condo management contracts there - he leaves his job and looks into condo management in California

Family vacations in resort condos on the Gold Coast, on the south east coast of Queensland, during Ed McGinty's several years of managing cattle ranches in Australia's north for Georgia Land and Cattle Company, brought him into contact with local resort condos, and incidentally, their management contracts. The staffs of those accommodation towers were always headed up by a main man on-site. As a manager himself, Ed often easily got to know him, and one in particular. Having the time, and the curiosity, he had learned something of the way men came to, worked at, and left the role of on-site manager (OSM) at a resort condominium. He was not personally interested, not even after comparing the seaside life in that booming city, teaming with people and recreations, with the dry and dusty and uninhabited outback which was his workplace, teaming only with cattle and kangaroos. His level of interest would change years later, when he and Binny were looking into condo management in California, and he would then recall the Gold Coast style.

Ed knew that before, and for a decade and more following the second world war, Queensland had compared unfavorably with the more populous and affluent southern states, being poor, large, thinly populated except in the main coastal areas, notable for bad roads and high air fares, and with little at the end to justify getting there. Its inhabitants were unfairly scoffed at as being relatively backward, and characterized in speech by a slow drawl, and teasingly said to be mainly engaged in the occupation of bending bananas, which fruit was a major coastal product. Yet for those who had vision there were abundant resources for the development of the state, and to start it several factors had to emerge. Those varied from time to time, but were always led by a go! go! state government, and go! go! private developers, some local, some not, all with vision, and an urge to advance both the state's and their own interests. Few had real experience in construction, but could plan well, and bring together the necessary elements, lured by hope of healthy profit. Many went heavily into land subdivision and building in the urban areas. Others were agriculturists, and accelerated the rural development of the state, through clearing vast areas of the semi-arid hinterland, and damming streams for irrigation, so that primary production grew, and vast cotton fields and irrigated tracts appeared. Nor were coal or oil or natural gas overlooked, so that when their long day dawned the miners and exporters were also ready to play significant roles in the development saga.

The east coast of the state was, of course, different from the inland. Offshore, the Great Barrier Reef was so iconic among earth's resources that, for the most part, it was preserved from development. Not so onshore. In particular, the general area of the south coast held plentiful beaches of the highest order of quality, and ample coastal lands well suited to urban developments, and a benign climate, rarely troubled by big storms. That area included, to the north of the capital, Brisbane, the Sunshine Coast, and to its south, the Gold Coast, both handy to the capital. To the gifts of nature came the schemes of government and men, and from the combination came a startling change in the appearance of those prime coastal districts.

The state needed capital and people and an entrepreneurial ethos for its development, to be orchestrated by state and local governments. To attract capital concessions were given. To attract people the state tried hard to provide jobs and farms. Southern immigrants came in large numbers, and they needed homes. Postwar tourism grew, and required a steady supply of modern accommodations. Many residential buildings were built. As desirable land right by the favored coasts was naturally limited, the developers and planners soon added towers, which became a unique feature in a state of historically low residential profiles.

Queensland competed with other states for growth factors, and did well through its tolerant attitude to developers and their output. In 1978 it also took the bold step of abolishing state death taxes, so scoring against the southern states, which were temporarily wrong-footed. The move promptly led, as intended, to well-heeled southerners flocking to Queensland to become domiciled there to avoid death taxes back home, and with them came much capital, and a lift to the local entrepreneurial ethos. The Gold Coast was often the preferred place for their residence, and for much of their investing.

There, in particular, in the sphere of constructions, and particularly of residential developments, a phenomenon emerged under the name of white shoe brigade. As used in the media, it meant that major private-sector developers of property had become identifiable as a class that sought, and were liberally given, consents and privileges, by state and local governments, to advance their plans. The ways of achieving success were not publicized, far from it, so it was only occasionally that the general public got a glimpse of what went on behind the scenes, but it was enough to firm up rumors that official consents to proposals came readily, and with minimal awkward conditions, for members of the white shoe brigade, who had ample money and influence. The term did not mean that a formal club or society or the like existed, but only that certain persons engaged in sizable constructions were curiously alike in their successes in obtaining development approvals, which generally far exceeded their failures. They were supported by a network of skilled service providers, in particular, but not only, brokers, attorneys, accountants, architects, and financiers, who became known as serving the top end of town, well and profitably. As all were in the business of development, their good connections with and influence in government and public administration had to be established and maintained, and naturally suggestions of undue influence and more were often made, and just as often hard to prove. Not all successful builders were so branded. And construction standards were kept very high, as stipulated by government edicts. Definite evidence of corruption was unearthed following a change in government, and was followed by prosecutions, and even though many had got away with their party tricks, the lawsuits had a salutary effect on the industry.

The same development climate that served the coastal areas for a few decades from the late 1950s, also facilitated the ranch developments of Ed's employer, Georgia Land and Cattle Company, but he was not aware of anything special coming from the government, even though some of the company's rural neighbors weren't so sure. Certainly though, he had not heard of an inland counterpart to the white shoe brigade, whose coastal activity seemed to him to have done a lot of good for the state.

He learned of a Queensland term, and concept, called management rights, which was a way of arranging the management of a condo, by delegation of many of the management functions of the board of directors to an independent contractor, often called on-site manager (OSM), for a period of years, through a written contract. It was prevalent in the seaside resorts which catered for vacationers, who rented units typically owned by absentee investors. Finding and keeping competent directors were continual problems there, for which an OSM supplying services under contract was a partial solution. Long tenure became a custom. The management contracts were private matters, for the government had a hands-off approach to condos, once established, largely leaving them to manage themselves, and this suited, and was encouraged by, both developers and managers. The tenure was normally quite long, as much as 25 years. Typically it commenced with a base term, say five or ten years, followed by successive 5-year options to extend it on the same terms and conditions, subject only to prior due performance during the preceding phase. Ed learned that as time ran down it was customary for the OSM to obtain extra time, calling it a top-up, to get back to the original period, and that doing so was simple enough, especially with the help of an experienced administration manager, and the existence of a passive body of condo owners. He attributed management rights to the influence of the white shoe brigade, because it seemed to him such a management style was not always in the interests of the owners of the condos, who were outside the network of players controlling the industry.

He found that under the theory of the legislation the initial grant of management rights to a condominium by a developer was supposed not to be sold, that is to say, no fee for it, and that in fact it was a provision designed for circumvention, through thin subterfuge, and for practical purposes could be disregarded. Hence a market in such contracts always existed, and was a quite buoyant one from what Ed had seen. Buyers came with a mind to on-selling later, and in the meantime to enliven the asset if possible, typically by increasing the tenure, so as to realize a capital gain on the way through, and success was frequent, if not invariably so. Ed saw the system in operation in large resorts, but learned nothing about management styles in other places. Had he done so he would have found the same system sometimes applying in large condos that were mainly residential, in the sense of the units being predominantly owner-occupied, and whether or not the building had a small commercial side, such as shops or offices below. The purpose and operation of those unit schemes was quite different from vacation resorts, yet the white shoe brigade developers often arranged for the application to them of resort management concepts, or management rights, scoring well from the laid-back style of successive Queensland governments, and the ignorance of condo buyers. Once any condominium became managed by an independent contractor under a written contract for years, and was vendible, it would be locked into the same management rights regime, resort and residential condos alike, and thus management rights became widespread, underpinned by legislation, and industry custom.

Ed's favorite vacation resort was a high-rise of 22 floors containing 90 apartments of varying sizes, the views from which changed with height, and were often spectacular. Most units were owned by absentee owners who rented them out through the OSM, in his companion role of rental broker, and a much smaller number were not so used, but were occupied by the owners, either permanently, or as second or vacation homes. Each of the OSMs had bought the rights from his or their immediate predecessor, and when the time was ripe would sell, so that every few years change came. As the contracted compensation might not cover the sum of the obligatory outlays of the OSM, plus the capital amount paid to buy the contract, it was essential, and indeed was the custom, that the contract be sold for a suitable sum when the time to move on came. That sum would be far more suitable by first extending the tenure. Sale day always came, because on-site resort management was tiring and constant work for diligent OSMs, and the longer he or she or they stayed on the less the unexpired tenure available to a buyer. It may be taken that once in the job, every OSM applied much mental effort toward increasing the tenure of, and finding the best time and circumstances for selling the contract.

Where possible, an OSM would avoid expiration of the contract by time, as that would put him too limply into the hands of the directors, with unforeseeable results. Better by far to keep directors and owners in full acceptance of the scale of compensation they were used to, and squeeze from them an extension of contract term.

Ed noted that in the management rights system an OSM had a business, more than a job, and the frequency of sales of them, though sometimes attributed to vocational burn-out, was due in part taking a capital profit while it was available. None was a career manager, as he was at Georgia Land. Seen from the stand-point of an OSM who, in buying a contract, needed not only generous compensation, but also a resale to make a profit on the deal, he or she had a moral right to an extension, for that was the whole basis of the sector in which OSMs invested. If it were otherwise, and compensation alone the only reward, the incumbent would have to stay longer than was usual, until the capital outlay was recovered, and if the one no more than equaled the other at the end, he or she would have only been trading dollars, getting in as income the money he had spent as capital, and an income tax bill to boot. Without a sale his or her capital would have vanished.

The expectations of contract OSMs necessarily rested on the backs of the condo owners. For compensation to be profitable it had to be pitched high from the beginning, and be adjusted annually for inflation. If mischance diminished the net return to the OSM, he or she would be at the mercy of the owners, and could be driven into spending less in hiring help, which could translate into reduced quality of service, and even violation of the OSM's service obligations of the contract.

Ed saw that once a condominium accommodated a developer's sale to an OSM of management rights with liberal compensation, with a right of resale, but no right for the board to revise the conditions set out in the contract, entrenched injustice to the owners ensued. But it was part of the Queensland scene, and remediation from a legislature that had stood by and allowed an unfair system to become established was unlikely, and certainly change that reduced reselling opportunities could harm incumbent OSMs. So if it was the law, and the practice, it was legitimate to exploit it. Nonetheless it seemed to him that a contract under which varied services were to be performed over a period of years, should be amendable by negotiation, as nobody had foreknowledge of all future circumstances. Without revision, the parties would have to await the ending of that contract, and start again, which could be unfair, more probably to the owners than to the OSM.

The story of Ed and Georgia Land and Cattle Company (Georgia Land) needs to be told. That company's main interests were in a spread of cattle ranches in various climatic zones of the United States, providing feed in all seasons ample for the turn-off of quality range-fed beef, and as consumer demand became more refined, from company feed-lots besides, including supplies for the fastidious Japanese market. The firm had grown well, yet had remained a private family entity, though the stockholders' loyalties were waning through age and dispersal and competing interests, so that it was frequently and wrongly tipped in financial and agricultural circles that a public offering of its stock was near. Its diversification program had led it into the vast and under-developed tracts of northern Australia, where it had bought up large cattle ranches in the semi-arid monsoon belt of Queensland and the Northern Territory, for operations in the same way as the home division, justifying the activity to the Australian regulatory authorities as having the desirable effects of local jobs and export sales and foreign exchange. As the regulators knew, whether and when such good results might come was conjectural, and they also knew they could not come without consent, with concessions, and this was such a case.

Years later, in order to convert value in assets into money that could be distributed among impatient shareholders, Georgia Land accepted a friendly take-over from Missouri Trust and Insurance Company, which required a current valuation of the cattle operations, home and overseas, and this would prove to be a complex task, much more so than valuing Missouri, whose stock was publicly traded. It was keen to enter into primary production for spread of investment, and cattle production through Georgia Land ticked off well at all check points. The ranching would continue as before, with minimal interference from Missouri. The buyer's investment division decided to employ a San Diegan appraiser with Australian rural experience, and leave the details from that point pretty well in the trusted and experienced hands of Georgia Land. Unknown to Missouri, those hands were not the safest for the task, as Rupert Gilbert, the responsible director, and a major stockholder, was very interested in the cash for his family to come from the take-over, and less in future ranching. He arranged for the appraiser to be shown the Australian assets by Ed McGinty, the local manager, who was briefed by Rupert to do the best he could for Georgia Land. Ed met an almost youthful Gary Hanlon at the Brisbane airport, and described the task ahead. He was a last minute substitute for a more senior man who had taken ill, so he would be more than ordinarily dependent on Ed's guidance. It was his first visit to Australia; indeed outside the United States. As Rupert well knew, Ed had a special talent for endearing self-deprecation, good humor and subtle kidding of his current acquaintance, and could turn on considerable charm, which skills he exercised from the start, to gain Gary's trust and confidence. He was to be both mentor and host to the young man, to learn his pleasures and interests, and meet and satisfy them in all ways possible.

That the McGintys might wish to return to America one day was tacitly understood between them and Georgia Land, and as their four children entered their teens Binny became attracted by the superior tertiary educational institutions near her home town of Santa Marta, where her parents and siblings lived. Ed supposed the reconstructed Georgia Land could not relocate him to California, where it had no ranching business, but that was in the future when Gary came.

Settling him in and briefing him on pastoral land titles and cattle ranching and market information in the areas of their interest took three days, after which they flew north in the company's Cessna Twin to the regional coastal center of Townsville, where Ed and family were based, far away from the ranches, which straddled the Queensland and Northern Territory border, and all of which had their own unpaved landing strips. The weather forecasts were not good, for the monsoon season was coming, and its rainfall was

42

often erratic. The organizers of the appraisal needed to get the job done, and gambled on the rains being light, or late, or both, so that it could be finished during November. If not, it could be delayed for months, which was not part of the plans already made for closing the whole deal. Road travel was not an option, because many surfaces were unformed and often in poor repair, so that even in dry and fine conditions travel would have been unacceptably slow and exhausting. The appraisal team's initial plans had been to fly into each ranch successively, and have the senior hands show Gary around, but intermittent rain became a serious concern. Daily reports from the ranches confirmed the falls were widespread, so that every company landing strip became unusable. It became clear the only way ahead was to view the assets by air, on daily flights out from Townsville, all ranches being at least 300 miles distant.

By refueling at the few paved airstrips in the general locality, the two men were able to make a virtual tour of each property from the air, and estimate the cattle numbers and types depasturing. It took six consecutive days, at the end of which they had got together the basic data needed by Gary, and then he and Ed set to collating it before his return home, where he would complete his report. In nightly calls back home the awkward conditions and their implications had been discussed among the responsible men on both sides, who decided to continue, and review the position after the last inspection. Gary was glad to have finished the very awkward business of inspecting vast areas from the air, and having to take as gospel everything that Ed told him about what they were seeing. To the visitor the whole countryside was largely featureless, and when they flew low, as they often did, to view mobs of cattle and scarce fixed improvements and streams, the denser air and added motion made Gary sick, so that he relied a lot on what Ed told him he had seen, rather than what he had seen in fact. The boss in San Diego knew the difficulties Gary was facing, but had been instructed to continue, as the clients needed the report to close the deal.

Ed had quickly realized Gary's vulnerability. It gave him a desirable opportunity to review the cattle numbers, as the figures he had supplied to base in the past had sometimes been optimistic, so supporting his reputation as a skilled cattle rancher. The medium of an independent survey was a great way to catch up. It was not possible to count properly the cattle running on any ranch without a muster, which was a major event, only rarely undertaken. An alternative was to count the calves on first branding, and then they were part of that ranch, even if they might later stray onto a neighbor's land across unfenced boundaries. Among honest neighbors the system worked well enough, through periodic exchange of strays after branding of calves, and very occasionally through concurrent musters. Yet honesty was not a constant quality among the cattle ranchers of the inland. Rustling from large, sparsely populated and unfenced ranches had developed into an art form, along with rebranding, and corrupt activity from stock police and ranch hands, and the use of very large motor transports to move stolen beasts away from a home area quickly, so as to prepare them for sale in another locality, or to include them in distant herds, if the rustlers were themselves ranchers. Foreign investors were the most vulnerable to cattle theft because it was harder for them, or their staff, such as Ed, to see who to trust among their ranch hands, and they were seen by some locals as intruders who didn't know what they were doing, and so rich that losing a few head of unbranded stock now and then would be of no account. In time they learned how to manage their ranches and livestock and interface with the locals, so in effect they became honorary Queenslanders, and not discriminated against. Georgia Land was still a foreigner. It had to draw its employees from experienced locals, and who were all part of the one backward and enigmatic culture, typically slow in thought and speech, responsive to seasons more than dates, suspicious of outsiders, and often dissemblers. Their culture included protection of their own, at least where it was no more than rustling, and in a remote area where men were well experienced in living off the land, alone, it was good protection. Ed worked hard at establishing and keeping good relations with the people of his region, without ever losing outsider status, or the feeling he was rarely given the full story about anything. He had known from the start that Georgia Land had a long apprenticeship ahead, and in the meantime he would do all he could to earn respect for his employer, who recognized the effort with generous pay and work conditions.

Ed didn't know how many head of cattle had been wasted from company ranches, and the closest questioning of his most skilled hired hands never helped much. He knew the numbers on hand stated in his reports were rather imaginative, but how much could not be exactly known without mustering. He knew that ideally Gary should have required a muster on each ranch, but the time and weather factors made it impossible, about which Ed was content, though careful not to let it show too clearly. So, in the conditions under which they inspected the ranches, Ed was able to point to mobs of cattle here and there as belonging to a company ranch, and by visual count he estimated numbers, which Gary was at a loss to follow, but as he knew no better, and trusted Ed, he adopted them in his own reporting. By these means Ed produced the numbers that would be helpful to Rupert. The appraisal was completed, and reviewed by both sides, whose representatives had had access to both Gary and Ed.

The global headquarters for Georgia Land were in the small city of Newton, Kansas, whose connection with the forefathers of the company dated back to when it was a major terminal of cattle drives along the Chisholm Trail. Ed visited every few months for consultations with senior management, and this custom continued after the change in ownership. On one visit he disclosed his wish to return home, and would stay on and help find a successor and remain while he learned the ropes. They hit upon an experienced Australian, and brought him to Newton for indoctrination, and a year or so later Ed and his family returned to California, where Georgia Land had no activity, so it followed he would retire from its service. In the course of severance discussions he let it be known he was expecting a large termination payment. The company had expected to pay him generously, but there was something in his tone that made Rupert ask why Ed spoke like that. Ed's answer was that he had laid the basis of the favorable appraisal of the Australian operations, as Rupert had instructed him, and if Missouri Trust were to carry out musters the ensuing numbers might show a substantial shortfall from those in Gary's records. Rupert asked what that might be, as a percentage, and of course Ed did not know, but guessed up to a quarter. Both men knew that as the cattle were the most valuable part of a fully stocked ranch, the difference in value could be significant. The numbers of cows on hand directly influenced the projected turnoff of future years, so substantial differences in counts were significant. Rupert became agitated, but Ed calmed him by saying if musters did not take place for years, if at all, then a discrepancy, if one existed, would be absorbed by intervening events, and as like as not, never known. Still, Rupert was greatly disturbed by the discussion, and said so, and suggested to Ed they separate and meet again the next day, when he would have a better grasp of the issues.

Alone, Rupert realized it would be very bad if the appraisal were to become suspect. Missouri might investigate, even sue. The money that had flowed in on closing the take-over had already largely been paid out to the stockholders retiring their investments, and so compensating Missouri, if it came to that, would have to come out of the reduced capital of Georgia Land. That, though, might be the least of the problems, as Rupert had little idea, but much fear, about what a large insurance company might do. On thinking further, he doubted if musters would be held soon, or frequently, if ever. It was one thing to muster a herd on a fenced tract of 10,000 acres in, say, Wyoming, and a quite different one on remote ranches, each of hundreds of thousands of acres, substantially unfenced, in northern Australia. And to be really successful, mustering should take place on all adjoining ranches at the same time, so that swaps could be made, but to get even two neighbors to cooperate was unique, let alone the several neighbors of some ranches. Musters were big events, that took up great slabs of time and effort, and interrupted the ordinary work routines of ranches, and sorely tried key men who were normally as stretched as far as they could stand. The more he thought about it, only two things could stimulate Missouri into requiring Georgia Land, now under its control, to conduct musters: a clear shortfall in their expectations of annual turnoff, or the thought of having been deceived in the course of the sale. As to the first, Rupert knew there were natural factors that produced variations in turnoff from year to year, so he would not become too concerned on that score, at least in the short term. After all, if Ed and Gary had got it wrong, it might not have been all one way, and they could have missed counting some that were there, as well as some that were not.

Missouri had known the difficult conditions of the appraisal before closing the transaction, so the chance of surprise had been present all the time. But if Ed told Missouri enough for it to want immediate musters, serious distrust between the two companies, and review of their deal, might follow, and that was to be avoided. Ed was the key. Rupert knew that his linking the count to the discussion about termination payment was an employee's way of improving his pay-out, and he had to accept it.

When the two men met the following day Rupert was all business. He cried: "I know what you're up to, and it's hard for me to deal with it for reasons which I'll keep private, so don't bother asking. I expect Georgia Land - the old one - will offer you an additional $50,000.00 termination payment if you sign a confidentiality deed binding you not to talk about the Australian cattle count or appraisal with anybody, not a soul, within 20 years, without our written okay. We could sue you for breach of covenant and claw back all our money, if you did. Give me a yes or no answer, and if its yes I'll get a deed made out and have it ready in a few days. As we have no operations in California where you want to be, we have no future together, and could hardly have one in the circumstances. Otherwise, the company appreciates your past service."

Ed said: "I see. I'm not for making trouble, and I'm happy with that pay-out. But I also need a reference, and I suggest that my service justifies a good one. Would it be in order to get it when I sign the deed?"

Rupert replied: "I'll make it out and show you first, as we don't want to hamper your future in any way. Right?"

Ed had nothing more to say. Though hurt to be discarded as he felt Rupert was doing, and to be forsaking the corporate fellowship he had enjoyed, he knew he could not have it both ways, and the size of the additional payment, actually more than he would have asked for, would make up for a lot. He told Rupert he would look at the deed when it was ready, and in the meantime would continue debriefing with Missouri's agricultural managers, and would have no trouble skirting around the details of the count should the subject come up.

Binny McGinty was very pleased indeed to return to Santa Marta, where her ageing parents lived in the same cottage on three acres that had been their home for several decades. They had newspaper stores around, and her brother was in that business and taking over from his parents, and her married sisters lived with their families close by. Binny and her children had been heart-broken to leave Townsville, and it was only education that tipped the balance between staying away and returning to California. The children had lost nothing in schooling in the substantial regional center where they had lived, but Santa Marta looked much better for the next stage. The McGintys leased a house locally, and Ed went to work with his brother-in-law,

Will, and although the two men worked together well enough, and it was a good fill-in while Ed and Binny looked around, it was Will's, and not their future. Ed had no prospects in primary production, as his specialty of cattle raising was not in demand in the district, which was ironic considering that it had been the economic basis of the whole area long ago, when all the land had been open space, except for a few Spanish rancheros, more Indians, and great herds of cattle. He reckoned that current rapid urban growth would throw up something for his future; but what? He learned that an army buddy was a realtor in San Francisco, and was active in condos, specializing in selling condo units, and in brokering management contracts. Ed recalled something of what he had learned during his vacations on the Gold Coast, and decided to talk with Rory.

5

Ed learns about condo management from his broker buddy - tells him about the Queensland system - studies the Californian scene - suggests to Binny they try to make a career from it - they will buy locally if possible

Ed took Rory Salinas to lunch. He had told him ahead he wanted to renew their acquaintance, now he was back, and also wanted some career advice. He was content to travel to Rory's office in San Francisco, expecting that the effort would underline the importance he was placing on the reunion of survivors from an infantry battalion in Korea. The meal mainly over, Ed called for more brandy and coffee to prepare the mood for the important part to come. After sipping, and lighting their cigars, Ed said: "I'm into career change. Out of cattle, into I don't know what. This is where I want your help. I'm thinking about the management side of condos, and I need educating, ol' buddy."

"Of course. Where do you want to operate?"

"Around Santa Marta. It's Binny's home base, and her parents and other family are right by. We all get along fine, and I have no family to pull me somewhere else."

"Hard to beat that LA area, for either living or business. Outside's better than right in, and Santa Marta's both near enough and far enough."

"Thanks. That's a good start."

"I think condos are a coming area. Managing apartments of any kind is good business. I know men who have done - are doing - very well in that line; New York, Florida, California, they're the main states. Here, condo units are the big things these days, and maybe more so than cooperatives. Everywhere else too I guess, being easier to set up, and to run, and to finance. More user-friendly, I reckon. Actually, there's a tendency for co-ops to be converted into condos. If you get a handle on condos it's not much of a management jump to other types of housing schemes, so let's start with them."

"We're talking condo developments. Every building has to be managed. If it's small, say three floors with a total of up to twelve walk-up units, the owners can pretty well handle it alone, and save. If they're clerical types they can even do the paper work. Others have to hire help for everything. Generally anything over 25 units, or if the condos are used for vacationers, is too much for DIY, or self-management, if not today, then soon, because competent and energetic volunteers don't last forever. There comes a point where a management guy should live in. Various ways of that. Names you'll know: janitor, or caretaker, or concierge, on-site manager, or building superintendent, resident condo manager, and more. They overlap. What's in a name? People use different handles right through this business. When I say on-site manager, or OSM, I'm talking of someone to supervise the whole place, keep peace among the residents, keep the common areas tidy and in working condition, get in the assessment money to pay the community bills, supervise the repair men, try to keep the people happy. There's a real lot to it. For a really big place he should take several study courses to be fully prepared, but none does, so everyone knows something useful at the start, which is maybe a fifth of what they should know, and they add to it on the road. If the directors are experienced operators, and take a hands-on interest, and the manager is smart, you can get a well-run establishment. Too often there's something missing up top, and you get black holes. The worst is when the directors are neither clever nor experienced nor industrious, and believe me it happens. What's it matter? Well, considering it's the owners' party, if they're happy, no problem. Y'see, many can go a real long time and not know if their place is well run, or be concerned to find out, and still be happy."

"So they never get to know how much better it could be?"

"That's so. Y'know, much management stuff is an extension of what every homeowner and family man does, in that condos are collections of dwellings, but you need to be smarter because the place is so much larger and it could be many hundreds of dwellings and families, and it will have an overlay of rules and regulations unknown in a cottage. It's serious work, and people management is part of it. Owners want sweetness and certainty around the place, and if you can ring their bells there, life will be easy, and you'll get your way most times.

"The owners of the condos elect a few of their number to a council of management, also called a board of directors, to see that the rules are complied with, and that the staff do their jobs, including the OSM, if there is one. He can be an employee of a firm whose business is condo scheme management, and those are managing agents. Or have a direct relationship with the board, under a contract, and such an OSM can be one or more persons, or a corporation. Naturally, the more a contracted OSM has to do under the contract, the less need for a managing agent besides, but the compliance paper work - insurance, tax filings and that stuff - is usually too specialized for the average OSM, so besides him the board may employ a managing agent, or someone called an administration manager. Or the agent may install its own OSM, who would typically be its employee. There's lots of variation. The important thing is the legal basis. The OSM may be an employee, and work under an employment agreement, or be an independent contractor, also under an agreement, in which the services he is to provide are set out. Typically, the OSM under an employment agreement, or self-management as they say, can't transfer, or assign, meaning sell it; but if he's an independent contractor, he usually can. In that case the term of engagement under the contract normally runs for several years, and is something that can be bought and sold, which is part of my broker business.

"A condominium of any size operates better if the OSM lives there. Take an ordinary household. It's a better one if the man sleeps there. Take a family-size farm. They say the best ones are those where the owner lives on-site, compared with commuting from town. Same with condo management, I believe."

Rory touched Ed's arm, saying: "Jump in if I go too fast, or I'm giving you the wrong stuff."

He slowed as Ed put his arm up, saying: "You're doing fine, ol' buddy, but just let me catch up a bit. Take any big condo. At start-up it needs an OSM. The buyers expect management to be in place when they come in. Who decides the style, between self-management, and contract; between year-to-year and a term of years; between managing agent and contracted OSM? The buyers aren't up with that stuff, nor are they organized. They come from all over."

"You say big condo. Now that's where contract management has a big place. A really big, throbbing condo needs vigorous management, and directors can't always cope. There's something to be said for management through someone at hand at all times, and working according to a set of conditions laid out in a contract. There's continuity to start with. The contract transfers supervision away from the directors to the contracted OSM, and means there's someone on deck even as directors come and go. But if those directors can be relied on to be, in effect, managers themselves, that's not a good argument. Instead, an employed manager might be the way to go. Frankly, I'm not sure. I've seen good arrangements both ways, and things that are good today turn bad tomorrow. You can't get away from the fact that we're dealing with people, or that there are always some unknowns about them. Just be extra careful when choosing somebody.

"As my business is about contract managers and not about employed managers, I've seen more of that side of the business. I guess you know that some developers set up a management contract to run a few years, with good compensation, and sell it, and then they're able to say to the buyers of the units that they're getting a sure-fire management regime that needs minimal effort from any owner, even from owners who may become directors. Of course the compensation is high, to attract good people, and of course the owners must meet that cost through their assessments.

"As a broker in an industry that exists no matter what I think or do, I can't become too judgmental, or carry self-doubts. The people who buy condos are well advised, or should be, and they engage attorneys, and they are, almost without exception, men and women of the world, so let's not talk as if anybody's pillaging an orphanage. This is a business, I'm in it, and if you want to be in it too, I can give you some tips that might help a bit."

"Please do. I'm certainly wanting to be in."

"I match contract OSMs with buyers with enough money, and character, and some education or experience, or better both, wanting a contract as a business. Naturally, in bargaining, the buyer looks hard at the conditions of the contract, and the unexpired tenure, and of course the compensation.

Most buyers are first-timers, so I have a lot of explaining and figuring and negotiating to do, because although I'm paid by the seller, and I'm his man, I keep in mind that the buyer will be a seller one day, always within a few years."

Ed cut in: "Always? You sound definite. Why so?"

"That's how it is. Everybody moves on. For some it's a stressful, 24 hour, obligation they find hard to handle. Some fall out with the wrong people, which is easy to do if your personality isn't right, for there are a powerful lot of people to love in a condo. Others look for the right moment when they can sell, so as to recoup their capital outlay, and then some. The timing is an art form."

"Being able to get along with owners must help."

"Yep. Ain't ever been a condo manager, but my gut feeling is it's like being a politician. You need people skills, and the better they are the better your take. Look after your constituency and they won't mind much if you bathe in life's goodness, or check to see it coming from their own pockets. But you have to have the right contract. No good wasting a lot of love for no dollar return."

"So the job is a mixed dish of looking out for people, and their property?"

"Sure is. Plus a pretty good lifestyle. You'll be better for being energetic. Lazybones are seen by everybody, and attract the wrong sort of attention. Otherwise there's little risk, clean hands most of the time, extra good money. The cream's in the tenure contracts, and not in the employment agreement. Let's not go there. You don't need me for that. You've had years of it with the cattle ranches. Make sure the contract allows the OSM to sell the unexpired tenure, and the conditions to apply. You need attorney advice for that."

"Isn't that the keystone? Why would you buy a contract if you didn't have a strong right to sell it?"

"Yep. Quite so. Now look to see how the manager gets an extension of time. He's the one who wants it most. Remember the directors may be new on the job and never had to consider such a thing before, while a business-like manager will have had it in his mind from the first day. So he says the management services are needed, and extension of tenure won't cost the condo owners a nickel more on their assessments than they've been paying. Maybe a particular OSM can also show he has put in place good systems for the whole development, and did so over and above the call of duty, so the owners might send some goodwill his way on that account. And he may have bought an apartment and an office for the better carrying out of his duties, which shows he has a business, which rests on tenure. He won't need to say too much there, because he can sell them, as will be obvious. His best argument will be that he bought into the management, and expected then to continue it if he did well, and as he has, so he deserves to have continuity, and if that carried with it a right to sell, it would be no more than any business needed. A storekeeper has stock to sell with his business, and for an OSM

52

unexpired tenure is stock. But, of course, the whole question could go on ice if the directors started talking about reviewing the management system. Though nobody knows how such a thing might turn out, talk of it might spook directors enough to cool them on extension. Better not wait for that to happen."

"He can be vulnerable then, even if he has done well."

"Yep. On the other hand, the question of review usually won't come up unless there's a trigger for it, as most owners want to stay comfortable. The OSM might have to blame himself if enough owners become concerned enough to want review."

"Does he always buy in? Is he ever given the management contract?"

"I can't say not for sure. But it seems to me unlikely that any developer, or a majority of owners in a condo, would make a gift of a contract that could be sold by the donee. You'd need to see what the contract said. I fancy a right to sell, and conditions about it, should be written in, and if it's not, maybe the directors need only decline; end of story. But that's attorney stuff.

"An OSM may truly have come into the contract in the belief that an extension of term was assured, ready for when he asked, like a ripe apple waiting on a tree to be picked. Brokers like me, and sellers, and everyone around, must take care not to build up the expectations of a novice buyer too high, and I have to say it's a very fine line for us. As extension at some future date is always a possibility, we can't rule it out, and so kill a deal, and equally we can't promise anything. What the buyer makes of that is up to him. If he decides to take his chances, and falls over, like as not he'll find someone to blame other than himself, so what's new?

"Maybe the biggest hurdle comes with owners wanting to review the whole management system, which we just mentioned. That would slow down selling. While it's in the air the OSM needs to watch his back."

Ed reflected, as he fiddled with his cigar, before saying: "So extending tenure requires both luck and skill. A newcomer needs to do his sums, and at the least be sure of really good income from the annual compensation, in case there's no capital lift through extension of term. Yet if the plan is made well, the risk of failure is small, because management is needed as long as the walls stand up. I suppose contract managers of resort condominiums have a better prospect of long tenure through renewals than those that are mainly owner-occupied?"

Rory smiled at his friend, saying: "What you just said shows me our pow-wowin' has been useful. Keep thinking like that and you can't get lost. As to the resorts, yep, as so many condos in them are owned by absentees, they're only too happy to have the place looked after, with no hassle. But also the job is more demanding: there's a heap of ignorant folks out there and many of them take resort vacations. They arrive stressed, as getting there is always a busy time, and some, especially high-powered business types, can be hard to handle until they rest up, and relax, and start actin' human."

"Would I be right in thinking there's a market in management contracts? That's my real interest."

"Yep. There's a market. Not as neat as the stock market or real estate though, because the buyer has to satisfy the board of directors that he's suitable, stand up to a character check, experience, and that shit. Way I see it y'all buy a fine income for a few years, and when you want out you sell for a big capital gain if, and only if, you got good tenure in place. Ain't no good the guy you buy from getting it, 'cos that's gonna up his selling price, and leave less for you later; not that you can control what he does. It's hard to lose if the compensation is strong, but if you then add long time, wham!, there's a real nice package."

"Sounds neat. Almost easy."

"Whoa now! That's not the message I want you to take. You have to get the tenure extended at the same good annual compensation, maybe even better, though that's not likely; and if it's twice what you spend in doin' your job under the contract, you have a margin; multiply it by the number of unexpired years, and it can look good to buyers."

"From your experience can you pick places where an extension is in sight? I mean you, personally."

"It takes a bit of study. I can tell when there's little hope, which is simpler than the other way. Still, I can guess it sometimes. Start by looking at it this way. The owners want peace and efficiency. The only cost that bothers them is increases in their assessments. When they buy their condo they accept the existing cost structure just like they do the buildings 'n stuff. They know things happen to push up their assessments, so they growl a bit, then pay and carry on as usual. The growl is louder about some things than others, but never will all owners growl exactly the same. They know that real estate has to be maintained, so the query won't go past the timing: do it now or later. The biggest cost, the manager compensation, is unlikely to come under owner scrutiny short of a mini-revolution. Doing the sums would be a big job, and even if one or two owners were qualified to try, they mostly have better things to do. Rely on continuing acceptance of the compensation, until or unless the owners get it into their heads to look at self-management. It can come in so many ways it would be useless guessing, but take comfort that they usually stay with what they know. If it's a peaceful place, with no talk about reviewing management style, and knowing a place needs an OSM, most times an extension is there for the asking.

"I don't know as there's anything a manager can do to head of a push for review, Sure, he can argue that if the thing ain't broke, ain't nothin' to fix, but careful now, as that's owners' business. And he could find other things to say, but if the compensation is actually too high this will come out in the wash, and if it's not, the manager can then jump into the argument. So the smart thing would be to extend the tenure as soon as could be done, and that could push aside thoughts about change. The OSM would have to get the ball rolling, 'cos it's his business.

"If owners are getting a nice environment to live in, one that keeps values up, and attracts buyers, and the manager is a peach, if he asks for extension of tenure there's a good chance of getting it. Y'see, someone has to manage the place, and the guy who's been there on the ground with a broom in his hand and a friendly wave, has a flying start. The people who own the condos want no more than for things to be looked after, and themselves kept safe. A little bit more money in management expense don't matter to people who must have plenty to be there in the first place. When they come in it's a new world and they don't know poo from pennies, but they see the chance to have amenities and services and a location they couldn't otherwise afford; plus greater security than in a private home, and as much privacy. There's little chance of a single owner using all the amenities if there are many, like in a classy joint, but their guests might, and the very existence of the luxuries makes owners proud, especially when they don't have to clean the pool or the tennis court or whatever else their condo owns. And never any gardening. They go away, and when they come back nothing is overgrown, or has died of thirst. The list of advantages is long, and of course longer in an up-market condo.

"People don't buy a condo with a mind to run the place, but to enjoy it. They might take a turn on the board, and maybe find it all so complicated that to do it properly they'd have to take a course in condo management, which few want. So power gets into the hands of a few key players. The natural dominators among them tend to exclude rivals, so folks come and folks go, and power is increasingly held by the survivors, and maybe more and more so because they know everything, so are always a jump ahead of everyone else. Remember too, the owners have only a small interest individually, a spit's worth of the whole kit 'n' caboodle, and for many that's also their level of participation."

"You make it sound like people don't care."

"I don't mean that, though some really don't. Take a rich man in Alaska who owns a seaside condo in California. He comes for a few weeks each year, but only to enjoy himself, and there are plenty ways of doin' that. Expect minimal interest from him about how the place is run. If it's as good as when he bought the unit, and not much more expensive than the rising prices of other things, he never knows the price was too much in the first place. He takes it to be something he can't change, and the last thing he wants is to make waves in his sunny fun home. How can he? He's not there, and knows nothing about condo complexes, only knows what he's told, like civilians in a country at war. He tends to believe because he knows no better, is trusting, and if he starts getting curious he remembers how little he owns, and pays, out of the whole deal.

"But you don't have to be a lock-up owner from cold country to be like that. Many live-in owners are the same. They're like the three wise monkeys, and don't even bother to vote, but if they do, it's maybe in line with some propaganda, which may or may not be true, or even in their real interest. There are as many different reasons for hanging back from any sort of participation that isn't mandated, as there are people, and together they are the indifferents. I ain't seen figures on this, but I'd guess that's a half and more of the total ownership. But it all goes deeper. Of the others, the voters, some are investors whose units are for rent, which is best done by the OSM. So he's the central person, he who looks after their properties and ensures they get tidy tenants. If he tells them how to vote, most likely they will."

Rory sipped his brandy. His cigar had gone out. He tested it and then discarded it. He started to replace it but decided he had better hurry up and get the meeting over. He added: "I believe it's like any other place where people can please themselves whether or not they vote. If the pros play smart they'll get their way."

Ed was watching Rory's hands. They were punching the air now as if he were looking toward the finish. That suited Ed, who smiled at his friend, saying, "Getting near the end, I reckon. So I decide to buy a management contract. Is it worth-while looking for a fire-sale?"

"It could be. Trouble is such things are few, and you might have to wait a long time, then find the only one is in the wrong locality. It can happen, but don't hold your breath, especially in a progressive state like California."

"Thanks. We have to go, don't we? I'm starting to see a gap for a switched-on manager. Y'know, you can't blame a manager for looking after himself, if the owners don't care much. Y'know, my family and I took vacations in resort condos in Queensland at a place on the south coast, and I heard the OSMs there had tenure up to 25 years, maybe more, but that was the tops I knew of. I don't know why, but the habit was to have an initial term of a few years, with a right to extend in 5-year phases, if the OSM wasn't in violation. How would that go here?"

"Interesting. It's longer than most places I've heard of here. When the next five years started, were the compensation and original conditions of the contract changed at all?"

"Don't really know, but I don't think review was a standard requirement. That was the beauty of it for an OSM, you knew what you were getting, and would continue to get as long as you kept your nose clean. With compulsory review your future would be up in the air. Yet it must have happened at times."

"Of course it would. And without it 25 years is a heck of a long time. I don't suppose you know if there were ever lawsuits from owners to upset the arrangement claiming, for instance, the contract was commercially unreasonable or something?"

"Naw, never heard about legal stuff there. I get the feeling there's no law against long tenures for OSMs in California either, otherwise you would know about it."

"True. And all I can add is that my gut feeling is that the longer they are, especially without provisions for revision, the riskier for a guy buying the contract, 'cos in that long time a nosey, switched-on owner, will surely pop up full of questions and ideas."

"OK, I'll keep all that in mind."

That pretty well ended their long lunch.   Rory had to get back to work, and Ed couldn't thank him enough for his time and guidance. He said that if he bought something he would try to cut him into the deal. Alone, he found a coffee shop where he sat and turned things over in his mind. 'We buy management contracts for the supply of services to condos. We buy the contract from its owner, being either the developer, or the current contract owner. The contract is the right and obligation to manage a condominium for a term of years for specified compensation. The OSM supplies nominated commodities out of his compensation, and his job is to produce listed, doing it his way, as long as the result is in order. He's an independent contractor, as distinct from an employee. In self-management the condo pays the manager a salary, and he supplies no commodities. His duties can be arranged to meet changed conditions, so it's a flexible set-up. That's how it was between Georgia Land and me. It can be a very good job, and last a long time, and you don't have to put up any capital. Those are the two extremes. And there may be variations, where the deal is not quite one or the other, and that doesn't matter. Anyways you look at it the owners pay for everything in the end, because their assessments are the only source of funds for manager compensation, and for running the show. As each owner pays only a little bit of the whole, expenses are less important than if he or she picked up the whole tab for everything, as in a suburban house, or a farm. Every condominium has its board of directors which, with the manager, supervises the whole show, and I figure that a smart OSM keeps sweet with them.'

Ed thought of managing condos all the way home, getting fixed in his mind a short list of key points he needed to know more about. And then there was what Binny would want, so a lot of talking and planning and learning lay ahead. Back home, he asked her:

"Do you know what condominiums are?"

"Not really, apart from being places where people live."

"Well, the way I see it, there may be something there for us."

"That's broad enough. Will you make them, sell them, buy one, live in one. Janitor? Maybe …. ?'

Ed interrupted with a wave of his hand: "Honey, you'll knock yourself up thinking like that. I should have said that management is the idea. Someone has to be the caretaker, janitor if you like, but on a grand scale. All those places have to be managed, and that's quite an industry. The managers all work under contracts. That's what we would look at. Maybe become condo managers?"

"Well, I never! Whoever heard of such a thing? That's pretty way out, isn't it?"

"Only because it's new to us. When we look we might find America is becoming covered by condominiums, and each has a manager. Correction: the little ones don't, for the owners do everything themselves. No, it's more than being janitor, or caretaker. It's hands-on management just like any other manager job, with the difference that the manager has a long term hold, and fat annual compensation. Well, that's the sort we want, anyway, for they're not all like that. He employs the janitors and cleaners and makes the contracts to fix the lawns and the leaks, under the supervision of the board of directors. It's like managing a very big house, with a lot of children, called condo owners, and residents. They don't want to, or can't manage the place, as they have their own lives and units to look after, so there's often an opening for a contracted manager."

"And you could do that? Sorry; of course you could."

"Not alone. I'd need you. And it would give you a chance to use that nice personality, and that accountancy training you got back a bit."

"Oh! I remember. It's what I gave up to be a wife and a mother, and now it could be useful! It would be a challenge, and I just might be glad to use it now the children take less time. You sound keen on this condo stuff."

"Honey, it could be something we could do together, and do well, and my instinct is that we can make enough money in a few years to set us up for life, with something good left over for the children. I reckon we could become as cool a management team as any in California. So, if you like, we'll look around."

Binny had a very practical approach to home and people management, and be it in dress, manners, getting along with folks, or personal habits, she was a success, as Ed knew. He said: "Fact is that management deals require man and woman, and the more they are the same family the more profitable the deal. Half the condo owners and residents are women, and dealing with them requires a woman's touch, that is if she's a good woman. It may sound corny, but a manageress is a bit like a mother in a household, and I can't think of anyone better than you. Now we're at this point, let me say that if you declined to be my partner in condo management, the whole idea just went south."

Binny smiled. "I bet we'll make a real good team," she said.

It was time for Ed to read up on condos. The outline of a development was easy for him to follow, but that was a very different thing from being a manager, who operated through a contract, and his financial sense, and information gathered so far, suggested that management contracts would vary in style and in profitability for the manager, and in length of tenure. Unless there were regulations he did not know about, the developer of the condo, the directors, and the OSM or managing agent would all contribute to the terms and conditions of a contract. The developer would drop out once all the units were sold, and the owners would have to decide on keeping that contract and the OSM or managing agent appointed under it, or starting again. It seemed clear to Ed that with many thousands of condo complexes in California, there would be many different decisions.

He mused: 'I wonder if developers sometimes appoint themselves or their subsidiaries as managers? They'd be in the box seat for that. But what an obvious conflict of interest! Still, there's a grey area when the development was nearing completion and the selling and occupation of units had commenced, this being a period in which the development required management, and the better its quality the better for the condo buyers. If the buyers ratify the deal who's to worry? Mistakes in manager appointments must occur, then a place ends up with a son of a bitch who wants all the compensation without any service, or even a happy face. Maybe also some contract buyers pay too much, or borrow too much, then look for ways of making the deal work, like cutting down on services, or even cheating, or selling, anything to end the misery. But as Rory said, fire-sales are rare, especially where you want them. So far I'm thinking cattle ranch management was a breeze, and if condo management is harder, I have to make sure it pays better.'

6

Barney's brushes with management commence - he studies the legal structure of Gran Capitan - the first managers extend their contract term and then sell to Ed and Binny who become the Onsite Managers (OSMs) there

After a few years on the job, first six years at Yerba Buena, then nearly five at Gran Capitan, Michael and Gloria Holliday became a little worn. The cares and stresses of the work had taken their toll, so a long rest, and maybe a career change, beckoned. Their initial 5-year term would expire in a few months, early 1985, and before that they would exercise an option to extend the term, which had been granted them in 1980, concurrently with the commencement of the initial term. That would run the contract to 1990. Consent from the board was not needed, only notification, though the board could deny the notice, for cause, such as violations of contract conditions, but there would be no warrant for that. So, on the verge of their second 5-year period of management, 1985-1990, it seemed business-like for them to seek an additional option, for 1990-1995, to be exercisable in 1990, and so identifiable as the 1990, or second, option. They had quietly raised this prospect with the board, and especially with the president, who had then asked around, noting in doing so it could help to keep the Hollidays at Gran Capitan, and they were a good team, and somebody had to the job anyway. He found no complaints of substance against them, or against the grant of the proposed second option, and in due course the board put the question to the owners in a special meeting. The matter was of such little interest that the meeting failed to attract a quorum, which automatically triggered a further meeting, for which the governing documents allowed a reduced quorum, and at which the proposal was voted in, and shortly afterwards the grant of the second option had been evidenced in a deed. That important matter settled, the Hollidays took a sailing vacation in the Mediterranean with their friends, the board president and his wife, and if any questions were raised by owners about that, they were certainly not answered. But the chance of a useful sum on the sale of their contract grew in their minds, one advantage being an even longer vacation. So they commenced inquiries of brokers, and found in their contract the procedures for selling, which included the stipulations that the intended buyer show good character and experience and financial capacity, and that the owners in special meeting approve the transfer if it passed scrutiny by the directors. Their attorney assured them that the attributes required of an intending buyer would not be especially onerous, and it was unlikely the board would, or even could, frustrate a sale. Moreover, he and the selling broker also both advised that upon the board being satisfied, it was inconceivable that the owners would, or could, disallow the transfer.

Prior to the second option being sought, some observant owners had concluded that the quality of cleaning of the common areas was declining, and was lower than was right, and when they recorded complaints the president had denied them, as effectively as the OSMs themselves could have done for themselves. One complaint was based on a test by an engineer-owner who secretly cleaned parts of foyer tiles to show how ordinary attention would produce cleaner surfaces. Another was that scum marks were showing on the floor of the outdoor pool, and becoming worse. Those owners had decided that the cleaners were inefficient, which in turn was a management deficiency. Moreover, they were unreasonably slow, and perceptive owners were puzzled to understand the special circumstances that allowed their continued employment. They also felt that Michael's own cleaning efforts were perfunctory, and performed in the most prominent places, apparently to create an illusion of constant personal effort. The handicap for those so concerned was they did not know their remedies, if any, and any inquiry they made of the directors, or the staff of Prince Inc. - the administration management firm - were met blandly, usually through the OSMs, who gave excuses and reasons and denials that were almost invariably endorsed by the board, and often also accepted by the complainants, at least by those nervous about conflict with authority. Though dissatisfaction with the cleaning standards was not widespread among owners, a small precedent for inquiring about contract performance was set.

Another issue that annoyed a handful of residents concerned the tennis court. Michael had decided that the court hours should be reduced, and to some owners the purpose was to humor the tenant of a small apartment, owned by him and his wife, that adjoined the court. It was obvious that the court and that unit were not well matched. Oddly, for a court so close to several condos, the bylaws allowed unduly long hours of use, so that it was very likely a reduction could have been easily negotiated. But the first that owners knew of change was the appearance on the wall at the court entrance of a large bronze plate, stating reduced hours. This was complemented by the promulgation of a new house rule by the board, without reference to the owners, which technically wasn't needed, if in fact the board had power to make the rule. The amended rules were printed, and distributed to all owners by Prince, as procedurally required. Barney and Zina were tennis players, and were annoyed by the way the restriction had been imposed, though not averse to a review of the hours. Barney then saw that as the court hours were set out in the bylaws, they could only be changed through bylaw procedure, and a house rule was insufficient. Therefore the change required approval from the owners, and until then it was beyond the power of the board. He also found a dispute resolution procedure in the bylaws, of the type he had used at GE, and so he went ahead with a case. The board obtained legal advice that its position was quite hopeless, and that the association should scramble out of it as best it could. Then, rather than face Barney, the directors engaged Prince to talk with him, and its executive officer, Grace Gambell, readily accepted reality, and saw error by a Prince employee, who had been over-anxious to meet the wishes of the OSMs. Prince advised the board to remove the sign, and treat the house rules as unchanged; that was to say, trash the new printing, and the sign.

But Prince had another current problem with Barney. He had objected to a house rule imposing penalties for late payment of assessments as unconscionable, in that the penalty was usurious, and even if valid could only be imposed by change in the bylaws. Prince tried to make it a condition of remedying the tennis court fiasco that Barney withdraw his penalty objection, and he declined. Prince, for itself and the board, then caved in, and Barney's complete victory assured him of the lasting resentment of Prince, and Michael and Gloria, and some directors. He had expected this to happen sooner or later, and he knew not to rely for support in the future from those sources. But his complaints had the effects he sought, promptly and completely. The plate was taken down. Prince could not allow misleading rules to remain in circulation, so had to print and distribute restored sets. Barney supposed the cost of those matters might be blamed on him, against which he was powerless, because denial would require a circular at his expense, and he didn't care that much. He thought it unlikely that either Prince or the OSMs would bear the cost of their own errors, or even own up to them. As few owners at Gran Capitan cared about tennis anyway, or the changing of the penalty regime, and Barney didn't push the issues into the public domain, they didn't become widely known. One enduring consequence of those events was Barney's closer interest in the affairs of the community. In this he was also driven by the ease with which Michael and Gloria had secured both their options to extend their management tenure without a stipulation from the board that the original terms and conditions of the OSM contract, including compensation, be revised.

He continued reading the legislation and governing documents, for he knew that a condo development, as an artificial entity, rested on a platform of special regulations, which had to be mastered so as to know one's way around. He soon realized he was one of very few among the owners so engaged, and took it he had been uniquely prepared for an understanding of them through his work at GE. As he had no wish to appear as the local know-all, he wished for the appearance of other informed owners, but seeing none, he sensed that whatever their qualifications might be, they were generally there for the quiet life, and content to go with the flow of management.

Barney recalled that when Robert had talked up the merits of Michael and Gloria their permanence had not been mentioned. He lamented to himself he had been slack in not pressing the point, just to see how Robert would handle it, as all managers must leave some day.

Ed and Binny started searching in earnest for a contract to buy, and were very pleased to hear that management of Gran Capitan was for sale. They knew it as a most modern and prestigious complex, and being in Santa Marta, ideal for Binny's family considerations, and well enough for Ed. They told Rory, who then had himself added as a selling broker for the Hollidays, and he negotiated a sale to the McGintys. They had to borrow some funds for closure, but were able to handle the purchase without strain. Though they had no prior condo management experience, both had accountancy diplomas, and Ed had many years cattle-ranch management experience, where the subject matter had been some people and much property, and so had some similarities to a condo. His references included a good one given by Georgia Land on his retirement. The McGintys were seen by the Gran Capitan board as satisfactory purchasers of the management contract.

7

Barney continues learning to be a critic - sees options as white for managers, black for owners - appraises fellow condo owners

The fire that had burned in Barney for a time before and after moving into Gran Capitan, had pretty well gone out before Michael and Gloria secured the second option for contract extension. This event fired the embers, and he decided to become more active. He may as well be poking away in public, he thought, as boring Zina with his concerns at home. He knew he would incur displeasure and worse from those whose interests he came into conflict with, but if he was right, and acting justly, he would expect owners to find that to be so, and some warmth and support would flow his way, to bolster him against attacks from the offended interests. Yet he saw that owners generally were pretty well conditioned to the system, the same one as when they bought in, and their satisfaction level was reflected in their approving the board's recommendation to give the OSMs the second option. Nobody inquired if review of the terms and conditions of the contract in the interests of the owners should first be undertaken.

His interest renewed, Barney turned his thoughts to the owners generally. They were the key to any improvement. He saw them as loners, with very little intermingling, a few private arrangements apart. None that he had heard of took classes about condos, or studied the governing documents and relevant statutes, or even summaries of them, so the acquisition of knowledge was haphazard. Chatting with other owners might amount to nothing more than sharing prejudices, or false data. Potted information such as was published by Prince, went only part way, and left many questions unanswered, especially such as might relate to directors or OSMs who, for Prince and its kind, were part of the management network, where special positions had to be respected. That at times such respect could work against the interests of the condo owners was never admitted. Careful observation, which many owners had no inclination for, showed mutual support often in play within the network. Owner's sources of information pre-purchase were mainly the broker and the attorney, if one was engaged, and denigration of anything about the development by either would be inappropriate. Whatever might be the private opinion of any local attorney engaged for buying in, he or she would shun a reputation among condo brokers of being a deal breaker. Communications from the board, or the OSMs, or Prince, may or may not be helpful on a particular issue, especially as the line between information and propaganda was often blurred. So the lonely condo buyers had to let much go. Separated into their concrete cells of airspace, alone with their thoughts, trusting and ignorant, their views were readily shaped by the community leaders, being both knowledgeable about condos, and in power. It could have been different had the developer appointed an independent attorney to advise the buyers, but it was not in its interests to do so, and in the absence of a law, would not be done. Predictably, BBC advertisements referred only to the nice features of its developments, and never about the value for owners' money in the management contract. Barney supposed that one day calculations would have to be made to see if value had been lost to the owners through excessive manager compensation, but that was ahead. So far, the isolated owners had no ideas on that. But he had become interested, and after preliminary work on the limited range of figures available to him, was convinced enough of being on the right track, and was ready to go further. Seeing no move in that direction from any other quarter, he would have to start the ball rolling on his own.

8

Ed gets a little involved in owner politics - the McGintys plan to enlarge their OSM tenure on the Queensland model - they start by sounding out the board

Ed and Binny McGinty were not of a mind to cut corners in their work, being aware of the generosity of the compensation under their contract, and that their duties read very reasonably. They calculated that their capital outlay for the contract purchase would be substantially clawed back as compensation over the several years ahead, but of itself that was not enough, because it would come as ordinary income, which was bad taxation strategy. They needed more, in the form of lower-taxed capital, for a really good deal, and for which they had the precedent of the Hollidays. They drew on Ed's vacation experience in Queensland, as fleshed out in discussion with his broker friend, Rory. He recalled the length of management contracts there, and looked to its emulation in California. He learned from both Prince and his attorney that there was no legal barrier to the board, with approval from the owners, granting a manager any term of years, but business prudence and practice, underpinned by the actual or potential requirements of banks or other lenders, and insurers of loans for condo purchases, kept terms at not more than five years at a time, and if the contract carried an option for extension, five years was again usual, apparently because extension could be made to depend upon compliance with the conditions of the contract during the preceding phase, and maybe also set up an opportunity for limited revision of the original conditions of the contract. Successive terms might then amount to a total of many years, the making of contracts being a matter for the parties only, that is to say the owners, or even the board only in some developments, and the OSM. That meant to the McGintys the certainty of considerable variation in management provisions from one condo scheme to another, both within the state, and in other places.

During their second year of management at Gran Capitan the McGintys - or, rather, Ed - became embroiled in an owners' row over travelling expenses for non-resident directors. Maybe fired by antagonisms based on other local matters too small to mention, or even to identify, interested owners, not in all a majority, tended to form into opposing groups, one for reimbursement, another against. An observer from afar, having noted the passions in play, could hardly have believed their cause was so insignificant. Ed came out in support of reimbursement, and because of it, when the enabling motion was voted in, he had lost some of his image of OSM neutrality, which of course was noted by owners on the other side, as Binny had warned him.

Months later, in the warm glow of owner cordiality and appreciation of McGinty efficiency and friendliness, both still at a high level notwithstanding Ed's foray into owner politics, they decided it was time to start campaigning for an extension of contract tenure. They had their attorney in San Diego prepare a management contract that, with the inclusion of options for extension of term, could run for 25 years from date of signing, and would replace the existing contract. They proposed no change to the established compensation, or the other conditions, taking the view that those had served owners well, and so needed no amendment, for if that path be taken there was no knowing when or how it might end. They sensed they had the goodwill of the directors, and if they were to rubber-stamp the proposal, as expected, it would be a big step forward, because the owners would probably follow the leaders, and also approve it. The McGintys had observed that many owners took little part in communal activities, few as they were, though they included occasional social nights that Binny and friends tried hard to establish, and lack of interest was taken to be chance, and perhaps not permanent. But they both had frequent personal contact with many owners, which they could readily expand if they tried, and therefore their views on management had a fair chance of acceptance by many owners.

The directors took the request seriously, and cordially suggested change in some contract provisions, which Ed was prepared to consider. He reminded them that on-site management was the McGinty business, for which they had outlaid a large sum, some borrowed. A condo the size of Gran Capitan needed OSMs, a suggestion that implied no disrespect to the excellent qualities and energy of its current directors, but only that it could not be assured that directors with like attributes would always be at hand, and on-site management was therefore an assurance of continuity, to the advantage of owners. That the owners of a smaller development, say 12 units all owner-occupied, with no leasing of condos permitted, might well get by another way, was not relevant for a large and complex development. As to compensation, it had to be profitable for the solvency of the manager, and for the due performance of duties for the benefit of the owners, and as the compensation set at the start of the condominium had been sustained without a word of complaint, it should be taken by all to be appropriate for the development. And for their management business to be successful, security of tenure was essential.

The managers knew that extension through the exercise of any option was subject to prior due performance of the contract, and were content with that. They acknowledged their view of length of tenure was affected by Ed's acquaintance with Queensland, which they understood to be in the forefront of condo developments in Australia, and 25 years appeared to be a commonly used tenure in that state, and for all they knew there were even longer terms there, or indeed, in California for that matter. Long tenure enabled management to plan ahead, and added certainty for the condo owners. When the McGintys came into the business they had understood from discussions with experts that what they were now proposing was not unreasonable. In discussions with the board Ed advanced the foregoing and like arguments, against which the most the directors could suggest was that it seemed very long, which Ed acknowledged, while reminding them it was only long in total, whereas in fact it came in 5-yearly phases, none of which could be availed of if there were pre-existing violations, so it could be thought of as a 5-year contract, as much as a longer one, but he was careful not to make too much of that point, and the directors didn't either. Nor did he say that a few years on, when the 25 years had reduced by the passage of time, an incumbent OSM could be expected to look for new options, or top-ups as they were known in Queensland, to bring the available term back toward its original length. He was not asked to speculate on how managers in possession of such long terms chose to employ them, as between selling, and personally serving out their terms, nor did he see fit to volunteer anything there. Similarly as to the theoretical length of time that a condominium could be subject to contract management under conditions and compensation stipulated, perhaps, decades earlier. As long as the walls of the condo stood up? The same with the possibility that the compensation had been unusually higher than fair market at all times, which could only be known through expert analysis. Was that ever to be looked into? Moreover, what to make of a situation where successive OSMs appeared to make capital profits on selling their management contracts? Where did the money come from? Was not the financial root of the system the owner's assessments? The owners and the directors were either not sharp or not interested enough to press questions on such issues, though they surely would have done so if Gran Capitan had been their private business. On the other hand, the OSMs, and their fellow networkers among the employees of Prince, knew pretty well the likely answers to all questions, but sustaining the system, and not changing it, suited them well enough, and so they were silent.

Discussion about the proposed new contract, which concerned mainly minor changes to cover the inadequate wording about some managerial duties, but not compensation, proceeded slowly, Ed not wanting to seem too anxious, and the directors, not being aware of any urgency, needing time to digest the data. None was experienced in reading and understanding complex contracts, which disadvantaged them in discussions with the McGintys, who in consequence came to expect board support, even if prolonged discussion might precede it.

9

Attorney Angel Tejero is introduced - his interesting life and times prior to Santa Marta - he and Ed meet

Sancho Tejero was a civil engineer exiled from Franco's Spain at the end of the Spanish civil war in 1939. As a major in the defeated Republic's army engineers battalion, he had reason to expect severe punishment from the fascistic victors. He had escaped with his wife Pilar, and young children Angel and Isabel, into an inhospitable France, shortly before the border was sealed against further inflows of refugees. There the family was interned in a concentration camp near Perpignan, and after enduring serious privations, the Tejero family were chosen in March 1940 to emigrate to Mexico, which had been consistently supportive of the Spanish Republic throughout its short life. It was also keen to attract educated migrants, of whom there were many among the exiles.

In Mexico, Señor Tejero was warmly accepted into the national water service, and in due course took up residence, with his family, in Ciudad Juárez, on the other side of the Rio Grande River from El Paso, and worked for a joint authority for equitable river water management between Mexico and the United States. Several years on, he went into private practice, in the course of which he was engaged from time to time by US water authorities in the region, and as that work was more readily available to US citizens than foreign nationals such as himself, and well paid, he changed residence to El Paso, and from there successfully applied for US permanent residency, and in due course, naturalization. His son, Angel, after qualifying as an attorney in Mexico, worked in an El Paso law office, while completing a US law degree part-time, through which forward planning he would become well set up for border practice.

Angel was good for his employer, Simpson and Sitwell, a long-established multi-partner firm, where he specialized in litigation and personal injury cases, especially those where a motor vehicle caused personal injury. Because awards of damages included economic loss, mainly loss of income, arising from the injury, the pay-outs could be high, and the lawyer for the successful plaintiff would be entitled to a percentage of it, as much as one-third. Angel noticed that by using certain techniques it was easier to attract clients in those cases than in others. All that was needed was an injured person, a motor vehicle, and a keen, sympathetic attorney. As victims were as likely to be Mexicans as Americans, the young man was able to establish his name across a wide range of prospective clients. By talking up his successful cases with the assistance of some strategic media contacts, his name became well-known, so few injured persons in the district would not have heard of him in the context of vehicle accident cases. He worked up an early contact system.

As he could not personally meet all victims, or chase every ambulance, he engaged agents to keep their eyes open for accidents, and to put his card in the victim's hand, as a precursor to direct contact. Then the opening play would be that he had understood that the victim wanted to speak with him about his or her unfortunate circumstances. As often as not the victim had not so far formed such a wish, but absent contact already made with a lawyer, and even sometimes after, Angel would receive instructions to act.

His litigation practice grew well in all directions. He sought maximum publicity for his cases, and went out of his way to help court reporters in their work. He issued writs for practically all plaintiff cases, even where there was no real contest about any part of it. He had so many writs in circulation his name occupied in local trial court lists as much space as those of all other practitioners combined; and so an aura surrounded him in the auto-plaintiff field, and to a lower degree, other personal injury cases besides. His reputation impressed the insurance company representatives who acted for the defendants, and he ensured he had good personal relations with them, which made easier the finalizing of his suites, and improved the pay-outs. If they defended, and Angel felt the case was winnable, he prosecuted ably and vigorously, and his success rate helped to limit the cases of his the insurers defended.

The numbers of Mexican-auto injury cases in the El Paso area grew through a marked inability of Mexicans to drive safely, which was due, in part at least, by their taking up driving later in life than Americans, and consequently not acquiring the same reflexive driving skills of those who learned when younger. Besides, Mexicans, being poorer, drove many unreliable and unsafe vehicles. And being poor, and aware that injuries in motor vehicles were sure-fire paths to compensation, and that pain was not something readily diagnosed, a curiously large number of accidents came from their vehicles crashing when carrying several male passengers, with very little damage to the vehicle, but personal injury to the passengers. Invariably they were singularly poor in English, making investigations so much harder, at least until insurers began employing bilingual investigators, after which the tide of those claims started to fall.

The injury litigation side of Simpson and Sitwell became very, very profitable, and Angel was duly rewarded for his efforts ahead of the normal time for a young attorney in a conservative firm, by appointment as a full partner when aged 30. The appointment was not as much a case of the other partners reaching out to him, but the reverse, the alternative being, he said, for him to leave and set up a rival firm. That made for hard choices by the partners, and they took him in. His new status, coupled with his reputation, meant more clients for the firm overall, even though he had neither the time nor the experience to deal with all who wanted to hire him. The only way out was to second them to other attorneys in the firm, handling each client carefully to make the transfer seamless. Not that it always worked, as Angel's reputation was such that some clients would prefer him handling their cases regardless of type. And the hand-me-downs were not always welcomed by the other attorneys, as they were a reminder that the upstart was a rain-maker, apart from which it was hard for some to be concerned with the affairs of clients who had not preferred them in the first place. But such difficulties apart, everybody tried to make the system work, and it did. As recognition of the value of the Mexican connection, a branch office in Ciudad Juárez was opened.

The ethics, or lack of them, in Angel's aggressive approach to his cases was known to other local lawyers, who were muted in criticism, for displaying jealousy would do them no good, and anyway some belatedly tried to copy his tactics. It was difficult for his partners to see the ethical problem clearly, as he had an answer for everything, and also much of his communication with clients was conducted in semi-secrecy in Mexican-Spanish, or even dialect, and there was no getting away from his financial value to the partners, so he was no push-over in any sense of the word. He was pleased to be a partner in the solid old American firm, and his parents and sister were happy that he was doing so well.

After the other partners had accepted, and found excuses for Angel's conduct for a time, they lost moral superiority. The public were unaware of the ethical aspects, but knew success when they saw it, and in a popular sense Angel was the most successful lawyer around. He also projected affability, and a personal style of being all things to men, and was invariably courteous and cordial toward women, many of whom saw him as a good catch, and scheming to arrange a match for him was a pastime of some mothers, especially Hispanics. But the truth, to some stranger than fiction, was that he had not the slightest interest in sexual activity of any kind, except as the basis of dirty stories, to which he was partial, both for telling and for listening.

James Groat, a law partner of Angel's, was unhappy about losing a file belonging to his client's dispute with Pedro Gonzalo. The client, Henry Watson, thereby lost an advantage. He did not let up on James, going through the possibilities time and time again, to make sure the attorney was addressing the matter seriously. The possibility of suing the firm was there. James had to be careful to do everything possible to satisfy his client. He knew a case about a lost file was not the sort of publicity that was good for lawyers, so he was on edge all the time. He had no basis for tackling Angel about the coincidence of Pedro's presence in the office one evening near to the time the file was noted as missing; not, at least, until much later when Pedro, while drunk, had boasted about how he had won his contest with Henry Watson by taking charge of some essential documents, of which there were no copies. Unfortunately for Pedro, and eventually Angel too, the boasting, which would mean nothing to most people, was overheard by an acquaintance of Henry, to whom she repeated what she had heard, without understanding its significance. But he did, as did James, whom he tackled about the matter promptly. Loss of a file through presumed inadvertence was one thing, and theft another. Nothing less than a vigorous investigation of the incident would satisfy the client, who reserved his rights to claim damages.

James was in a quandary. He consulted with the senior partner. Together they discussed the problem with Angel, looking for an innocent explanation for Pedro's remarks, and the loss of the file. Angel said that if Pedro had said something like that, it was maybe only foolish boasting, or drunken nonsense; but he had no other explanation to offer. The senior partner considered calling in the police, which might lead to more information from Pedro, but did not push it, as the lawyers should be able to deal with the matter in-house. Angel undertook to ask Pedro what he knew, if anything, noting he could hardly accuse his client of being a thief unless he had proof. Angel reported back that Pedro knew nothing, and that maybe the woman had got the story wrong. So that line of inquiry was a dead end. Henry Watson sued the firm, its insurer met the claim, up to its legal liability, leaving a gap to be covered by the partners, in addition to which they made a confidential settlement with him, so that he could not talk about it later, and he was content with the outcome. But at the end all partners were convinced that Angel was hiding something from them. He had probably been complicit in the loss of the file, they thought. And, unknown to them, he had not in fact questioned Pedro. The firm had not lost a file in its previous 80 years.

The continuance of the Mexi-auto crash affair suggested to insurers there was organized collusion in some cases. The incidence and similarity of the cases was noticed by insurance companies to be peculiar to the El Paso district. Many injuries suffered were either soft-tissue, or invisible, and always painful, often located in back or neck, and made the victims unfit for work. When the insurers swapped notes, they took it that a mass production line of minor but painful vehicle-related injuries was operating. Angel's involvement at one level or another was apparent throughout, and when the insurers showed more resistance to the claims, he became unusually ready to settle them pre-trial, which increased and confirmed their suspicion. They chose cases to fight to the end, and in the process received verdicts for defendants, whereupon the claims slowed sharply.

The insurers requested the Texas Bar Association to look behind the cases, against the chance that one or more of its members was running the show. Inquiries came to Angel and the firm, and his partners were furious. Their collective attitude started to harden into one of: 'We don't need him, or the extra money, that badly. We've lost trust in him, with this coming after the Watson case. If we don't act he'll do something worse one day. We'll ask him to leave.'

And they did. But in the course of negotiations for the break he made it known that he knew of how, before he became a partner, the then partners had shared a windfall sum of a missing person's money. A man, hitherto unknown, named Carlos Bertoldo, had come to John Simpson and asked him to hold in a safe place, anonymously, a package, which he had opened to show $250.000.00 inside, before wax-sealing it, and handing it over with firm instructions that it not be recorded, but placed in a safe deposit box at the lawyer's bank until Carlos came for it. He spoke of flying his own plane on to Lubbock, Texas, for negotiations with an oil broker about an investment in some oil and gas acreage, which would require much larger sums, although the how and who and when of their source was not explained to the attorney, who took it the money was hot, and that in some undisclosed way it, and probably other funds, would be laundered during the prospective oil deal. Then came news that Bertoldo's plane had crashed en route and killed him, the sole occupant. It was rumored he was a mafia figure. Knowing that the police were making routine inquiries about the death, John Simpson volunteered that the deceased had consulted him a couple of days before the crash, on an entirely personal and confidential matter, unrelated to the fatal flight, the exact nature of which Simpson was unable to disclose, on the grounds of attorney-client privilege, except that it had no criminal aspect. His information did not perturb the police, as deceased had made several contacts in the city about the same time, and none was at all suspicious. The police conclusion, later upheld by the coroner, was that the crash was simply pilot error through being caught in a thunderstorm, whose turbulence had sheared the wings off the plane. Experienced pilots at El Paso airport told of warning the pilot of the danger, and that he had claimed he could fly away from the storm if it came his way, and ignored their advice, even after they had stressed that was far easier to say than to do.

Having custody of such a large sum of money worried John Simpson, especially as both its source, and intended destination, were unknown. He was not unused to dodgy cash transactions, of which the firm ordinarily practiced several types, in the interests of superior clients. Such transactions were simply part of legal business, and their repeated usage, yielding gain for the firm and hence for the partners, had long numbed their ethical qualms. But the current circumstances were unique. 'Is this a case of no owner?' John asked himself. 'That's rare, but surely there are cases where ownership is so vague or fragmented that nobody can assert title. A man of business, an owner of property such as an airplane, would carry so much cash only for special reasons, just as he would be driven by special reasons to ignore the expert advice given by the experts at the airfield. If I disclose this money it might be taken into trust by the state, and who knows who might claim it then, and if I did, mafiosi might take an interest in me, and that would never do. And without a claim it would become public property. Any publicity now could bring to the notice of the Bar Association that I had handled the money outside the trust account system, and they wouldn't like that, or me. If it had been known to be held by Bertoldo, surely news of it would have appeared in reporting his death. Like 'Reliable sources claim dead airman carried millions of dollars cash.' So through those and like reflections, aided by simple greed,

John moved farther and farther away from giving up the pile, and closer to a proprietary interest in it.

The bank had no knowledge of the contents of John's safe custody box, in which he kept valuables, and opened it upon need, and its officers did not know of the coming in or the taking out of the cash. He kept it in a brief-case under his bed for a couple of weeks, until the strain of its presence, including the probability of his wife coming across it, and demanding an explanation of the inexplicable, pushed him toward the most anonymous depositary he could think of. He had no experience with Swiss banks, and rather than acquire it from anyone local he anonymously learned the procedures from a branch in New York, and flew there, to be met at the airport by a security officer, who accompanied him to the bank, where he put the money on interest-bearing deposit in his name alone. He then placed the receipt and account details in an envelope addressed to himself personally at his office, and posted it before boarding the plane for home, as protection against accidents. He would have placed the money in the firm's name but for the bank's rules requiring more signatures and details than he felt it prudent to give. He arrived home content with progress, and nobody any the wiser about his secret. His wife, of course, suspected he was up to something, but knew from experience when to inquire, and when not to.

He delayed telling his partners what he had done, so that if trouble came they would be better out of it. But almost two years later, it was time. The others were greatly amused. Another year on, with their agreement, he had returned to New York, withdrawn the money and accrued interest, in cash, and flown home with it the same day, to be distributed among them, in secret, according to their shares in the firm at the time of Bertoldo's death. Although the distribution was made after Angel had become a partner, he was never told about it. However, that he was on the trail appeared from some remarks he made during the discussions about him leaving the firm.

He had said: "You guys are saying I'm not fit to be in the firm. You say my practice is unworthy of its standards, even though you've taken the money as I brought it in. You want me to leave with minimal rights. You're going to say you kicked me out, and trash my name around town." At the sound of protest about that, he had raised his hand, saying: "Let me go on. No, you haven't actually said that, but I get the message anyway. Now hear this. Much as I like and respect y'all, I know you're not the lily-white lads you make out. I know the way you fiddle cash, and I've been part of it, so I can't complain. But now I've got bad news for you." He stood, and moved back a couple of paces, the better to survey the group of seven men seated around the table. His expressions normally ranged from mildly serious, through calmness, to happy. Never angry, never surprised. Impassivity, his most usual countenance, often seemed about to give way to a smile, but not now. The partners looking at him noted, if they had not done so before, his large, well-spaced dark eyes set below a large forehead topped by receding dark hair, and supported by a

76

round face. The effect was of wisdom, and thoughtfulness. Certainly he was patient, and a good listener, attributes they knew rightly made him popular with his clients. He was also slow, unpunctual, and inefficient in organizing his work, which most attorneys tried hard not to be. They watched and listened with mixed feelings. He spoke gravely. "I know that before I came in y'all shared a windfall. It was a large sum that seemed to have no owner. Now before you reach for your worry beads be informed that the owner has no idea what happened to his cash. I don't know who he is, but the current leader of a branch of the family in Chicago has made noises. That's a man - not a gentle man - called Alvarez. If the mob thinks that Carlos Bertoldo - I'm sure you'll remember the name - had it, they'd also think it was lost when his plane burned, so the chances of tracing it to Simpson and Sitwell, or anybody, are zero …. unless …." He paused, and noticed every partner alert. With his gaze drifting across the anxious faces, he continued: "Unless there's another accident." Then he paused again, for longer, aware of the consternation his words were causing. Continuing, he said: "Now the good news is that I'm going to be very happy to treat all that as a fairy-tale if we can deal reasonably on this partnership split. I want nothing more or less than a fair run. I'll be ready for another discussion when you are, but not today. Good afternoon." And with that he slowly walked out of the meeting room. Closing the door, he paused for a moment to listen: predictably, concerned discussion had commenced. He smiled.

Angel knew less than he had made out. He had made some informed guesses, and a few inconclusive inquiries. He vaguely remembered the plane crash and the rumor that the pilot had been a mafioso. That was before he became a partner in the firm, and it had meant nothing to him. Much later he had noticed a run of unusual personal expenditures by partners and their wives. It seemed as if several of them had thrown over their normally conservative style of expenditures at about the same time, in favor of an easy-come easy-go style, which was a rare thing indeed. As he was genuinely interested in money, and its uses, and counting it, as a pastime, in much the same way as others might enjoy chess, or supporting a community activity, or any of innumerable other activities, he observed these strange new habits of the people close to him, and felt a lot of money had come to them suddenly, but you had to be someone like him to work that out. Still, none of it was his business.

Being on good terms with as many members of the border police departments as possible was, though, important for business. Through the friendships he cultivated with his undoubted charm, and flattering the cops by associating with them, he had more affable contacts in that area than any other attorney around, which led to introductions to criminal clients and victims of vehicle smashes. Not many lawyers could, or wanted to, operate in that manner: Angel could, and enjoyed doing so. It was said of him, by both attorneys and police, there was no better stroker of police feathers in all Texas. One of his particular friends, with whom he had a few drinks occasionally, was a senior detective in El Paso PD, one Billy Fallon, who said, while they idly chatted one day:

"I saw one of your partner's names on file today. It stood out because the illustrious gents at Simpson and Sitwell don't get in our records much. John Simpson's one of yours, isn't he?"

"Yep. I hope the dignified gentleman isn't in any trouble. I insist he's innocent before you start."

"Don't worry, you won't have to defend him. It's just that I was closing the file on a plane fatality and saw his name."

"No, it wasn't John. I saw him in the office this afternoon. Very alive."

"Ha, ha! No, he was only one of several people the deceased pilot had spoken to during a stopover here, not long before the crash."

"What crash would that be?"

"Well, it's all over long ago, but this man flew his plane right into a big thunder storm just a couple of hours after taking off from here. A rumor went around he belonged to the mob somewhere back east, but we never found anything about that, nor figured out why he had to fight a thunder storm."

"Maybe only 'cos he wanted to. What was his name? Was it a big one?"

"No, a no-name. Carlos Bertoldo. Seems he had no known relatives, or address. Surely a mystery man."

"Some of it comes back now. Poor man. I wouldn't ask how John was connected, of course."

"Of course not. And I wouldn't tell you either. It didn't matter anyway. But I guess if John had made a will for Bertoldo he would have said. Anyway it's all history now."

"It sort of puts you off little planes though."

"Don't it just."

Angel believed Bertoldo's visit to Simpson, the talk about the mob, and the subsequent big spending, might be connected, but it was too tenuous to treat seriously. That is, until the partners started to squeeze him out of the firm. Although he was not given to self-pity, and could absorb more insults and rejections without resentment than most men, he felt they were unfair, so he had to find a weapon to use. And in time he found it, and told the partners in their conference. He had no way of knowing if he was right, other than from their attitude, so if they continued negotiating with him, he had guessed correctly. Otherwise, he had just added attempted blackmail to his other shortcomings. He would soon know, as another meeting was certain.

Angel had had another problem with the bar association, years earlier, when he was a sole practitioner. A client, Harry Hills, complained he had short-changed him long ago. Through pressure of work, and complications in the client's figures, Angel had delayed accounting to him for several transactions. The accounting, when at last finalized, showed a small balance due to Angel, and for which he made no claim in view of the delay. He took the statement to Harry with his apologies, and was greeted affably. The statement showed that a small amount had been transferred years earlier before in payment of some legal fees run up with Angel by Harry's son, who had been accepted as a client only because of the father's insistence. Angel had taken Harry to have authorized that transfer, orally, and their friendship at the time made that credible, especially as the son had no money, and was foolish by nature. Angel had gently closed the relationship as he found their heavy drinking sessions less fun and too time-consuming, and was unaware of Harry's resentment at being spurned, so he didn't see the trap being set. He had turned on Angel, and complained to the bar association, and had painted a dark picture, and the case found its way to the desk of a sympathetic investigator, who was at once gullible, and harsh on suspect attorneys, bringing an accusatory style to the work, alike, in Angel's view, to officers of the Spanish Inquisition. The affair had a long history, and was ended when Angel gave in, confessed error, presented character evidence, persuaded the tribunal the case was a lot about very little, and was formally reprimanded, and ordered to pay back the small amount Harry had complained about, together with interest which, compounded over several years, was a large amount. Angel took Harry to have become an alcoholic, and obsessive with petty issues, but such could not excuse him from culpability on the main issues, and attacking the integrity of a former client hardly seemed a good idea, nor even a defense in front of the ethics tribunal. For some reason he never learned, his name and his case and his reprimand were not published in the usual way, and he didn't check the cause, but was content to let the sleeping dog rest.

The law partners were unaware of that case. With another coming up about the accident claims, that could not last. They would say Angel should have told them when he became a partner. Their relations would be worsened on that score. His future relationships with rival local lawyers might also be at risk, as the Simpson and Sitwell partners were influential, and their reputation had served as a shield for him so far. Angel devised a plan for them to consider. He would take the hit about the Mexi-auto collusion cases on behalf of the firm. It was not a really noble gesture as he had been responsible and the partners, although beneficiaries, had not been activists, and rushed for cover when the time came. He would be glad to be away from that brand of loyalty. He would avoid official punishment by volunteering not to renew his practising certificate in Texas, and suggested the firm undertake not to accept plaintiff's instructions in running down cases for a period of time to be agreed upon. That package might be acceptable to the regulators, as being sufficient protection of the public interest, coupled with sustaining in practice a prestigious and long-established firm. As Angel would be acting the fall-guy he could claim generosity in his retirement pay-out, provided of course he kept the earlier reprimand concealed; and he did. And so his practice in and around El Paso wound down.

He chose Santa Marta, a growing coastal urban area with a strong Hispanic population, as his destination. Leaving El Paso was hard, involving as it did closing down so many aspects of his life and work. At times it seemed too hard, so that he had regrets about his decision. People asked questions, and he had agreed with the partners the basis of the answer was to be their irreconcilable differences. If anyone thought that didn't cover his leaving town, he pointed to his being single, and the partners not, and he had planned to see something else besides the border one day, which had now come. Yet he could return, as nothing was forever. Of course, alternatively, he could stay, but the undisclosed condition of his move was that he would not work in the law locally, and to practice somewhere was highly important to him. Because of his make-up, which gave him few close friends and many not so close, he was able to make a friend as readily out of a chance acquaintance as from people he had known and been intimate with over long periods, and along with his placid temperament and optimistic outlook, few men were better equipped to handle change than he. He would stay in the south and rebuild. With ample money for a single man, and considerable ability, he had no major concerns, once over the pain of disengaging from El Paso. He knew his style of practice would have to change, because with a bad name among insurance companies, any work involving them would have to be treated with care. He thought of taking a job with an established firm, but they would want to know more of his background than he could divulge, and if he was not forthcoming they would make their own inquiries and get what was missing, or else they would want him as a trial attorney, which could run into the insurance company problem pretty quickly. So he would go into practice on his own account, take on limited trial work for the time being, and move into real estate, and in particular condos, which were a bigger feature of the housing scene in California than in Texas. He decided to live in one, the better to fast-track his understanding, while researching their legal aspects, and hopefully his efforts would lead to something. When he applied for admission to the California State Bar he produced warm character references, disclosed that he had once received a mild reprimand from the Texas Bar Association for delay in accounting, and showed he held a current practising certificate in Texas. Figuratively turning his back on that state, he invented a phrase to console himself: 'Hell had no fury like a woman scorned …. until that motherfucker Harry Hills came along!', and toyed with putting it up in his waiting-room, until his business sense overrode his sense of humor.

Angel opened his law office alone, and with his engaging personality and Hispanic background and bilinguality, was soon as busy as he could wish for. His office was in the commercial center nearest to Gran Capitan, and his own condo was close by. A county director had his office nearby, and on meeting they got on well, and when asked his line of work, Angel responded that it had been trial work, but as a practitioner on his own he could not afford to be out of the office as much as it demanded, so he was doing more real estate work, knowing that condos were rapidly increasing.

Soon afterwards, the director casually mentioned to Ed what Angel had said about an interest in condo work. As Ed's own attorney was distant and that was at times inconvenient, especially when volatility was growing in the McGinty affairs, he called on Angel to size him up.

Across the desk, Angel saw a large man of vigorous appearance, with sandy hair, and a strong face with watchful, inquisitive green eyes. Ed saw a rather short and solid man, balding, with black hair, a round, pale face, and large brown eyes, exuding calm and attentiveness. Ed told Angel he could possibly be useful to him, for he had condo owners and tenants who needed legal advice from time to time, and if Angel was interested he could maybe send him some work, which Angel was pleased to hear, and he said so. And Ed was as good as his word, and sent business to the attorney, and encouraged his friends among the local managers to do likewise, so that Angel got a useful flow of new clients that way quite soon, more or less attributable to Ed's good offices. So, they being in touch from time to time, Ed commenced discussing the situations that were troubling him personally at Gran Capitan, and Angel took his concerns to heart. For his ambitions as they then stood, Ed could hardly have made a more suitable contact.

10

*A clash between McGinty ambitions and Jones pro bono notions looms -
Barney sends a circular suggesting management review - Ed takes fright and
gets Angel's innovative advice*

An unexpected hurdle for the McGinty hopes of contract extension was
Barney's developing skeptical interest in the value to condo owners of
management contracts of several years duration, like that at Gran Capitan,
and that were also vendible by their owners. After a slow start he had become
familiar with the governing documents of the condo, and the contract, and
had also acquired an outline of the new one the McGintys wanted. He had
identified the nature and sizes of the outgoings for which the OSMs were
responsible, and added a generous allowance for their profit, being suitably
good rewards in a successful business. He had obtained copy accounts from
owners of units in two large condos nearby, both of which employed an OSM
on two-year contracts that were renewable with mutual consent, without any
right of sale or transfer for the manager. The directors and the condo owners
there took their arrangements to be self-management. From those sources
he formed a sensible view of the position at Gran Capitan, and concluded that
the owners could likely save money through a change to self-management
from the current contract management, after existing 5-year phases ran out
by time; thus 1995. Expert comparisons and analysis would be required,
besides board and owners considering the issue, and voting on a plan. So
there was a selling job ahead if he were to continue, and he wasn't sure he
cared enough to bother, especially as a change in management style couldn't
kick in for several years. His interest might have paused there, but for Ed's
proposal for a 25 year term, which was put before the directors in June 1987.
The possibility of something like that being granted without the owners
first considering self-management appalled Barney. The long tenure was at
the forefront of his dislikes about OSM contracts, because no matter how
acceptable an incumbent might be, a sale to the wrong person could turn the
place upside down, as he had heard about, and also had seen at Marquise.

Feeling now he should become an activist owner, Barney had first to
bounce the prospective change off Zina. He had so far talked with her only
about shortcomings of various sorts in the Gran Capitan set-up, and she had
patiently listened, with varying levels of interest, without completely sharing
his passion, which she recognized as desirable for someone, but whether it
should be Barney sometimes crossed her mind. She consoled herself that
by listening she was storing up a fund of goodwill for the times she wanted
an audience for her own concerns, not least of which was comparing hands
she played in bridge competition with those she would have played, if either
her partner, or herself, or both, had been more alert. But challenging the

style of management was a major step, and would expose Barney, with certain resentment from some quarters, and an unknown level of support from others. It was new territory. There would no point in doing it by half measures, or making out it could be resolved by dispassionate discussion: the financial interests of the OSMs were too strong for that.

Barney wasn't too sure about Ed. He certainly presented with charm and cordiality, and his performance of OSM duties was above reasonable complaint. Yet Barney sensed some was façade, intended to woo the owners so that one day they would be content to do as the McGintys wanted as regards the contract, whatever that might be. Barney did not mind, except where OSMs' interests might clash with those of the owners, who were generally of trusting dispositions, shown through the lengthening of contract tenure via the second option shortly before the Hollidays sold, without review of the conditions of OSM service. To him, common sense called for the owners taking a hard look at the figures and costs of running Gran Capitan. The proposal would require promotion, and he was the logical proponent. It would put him under public notice. Inter-personal difficulties would become part of his life. None of that would make life any easier for either Zina or himself, and so he was of half a mind to leave it all to someone else, and to do that properly a clean break was needed, and that meant they should move house, and buy into a place under self-management, an equivalent of The Lotus Flower. He had plenty of other ventures to keep him busy, so would not miss the challenge here, where even with eventual success he would get nothing out of it, in that the few insiders who would know of, and appreciate his efforts, would be balanced by the enmities sure to arise along the way.

Zina heard Barney describe his dilemma, then said:

"You have to do what you think is right. I confess a personal interest, in that I don't want to leave, but it's your call. Do exactly as you feel is the right thing, knowing that I'm right behind you. I don't pretend to understand everything, but if the owners are being ripped off then something should be done about it, and I don't know of anyone better equipped for that than you. Is that okay?"

"Yes, thanks. I don't mind the battle. I've done most of the ground work so it would be a shame to waste that progress, as will happen unless we take the next step, and tell people. I respect your wish to keep on living here, as it's our home, and a good one. If you can put up with me as an agitator then I'm happy."

"Well, honestly, it can't be much more than I'm used to. This business has been on your mind and a worry for you for a long time, and I've listened, and in that way been a part of it, so going a bit further doesn't change things much. Maybe there'll be some nasty words – so what? You can't stop because of that. Nothing would ever be improved that way."

"I don't intend to put up anything as other than coming from me, in case you might feel as if my stuff might come across as a joint effort."

"Oh, I'm not qualified to get deep into these problems, and if anybody thinks otherwise, they'd be pretty dumb. Don't pause a moment on my account. Just tell me when you want a hand."

"Right we are then. The way I see it, with Ed looking for that long tenure, 25 years or so, I should tell owners my view of the management issue, and why we should look into the pros and cons of self-management soon, to see if that would suit us best when the second option phase ends in 1995, and if it seems it could, to put further extension on hold until we get it sorted. I've got to find a way of getting into owners' minds. I can't rely on the directors, or Prince, to put my case."

"You want self-management to be looked at before the owners consider Ed's request for additional tenure, whether it be 25 years, or anything past 1995?"

"Exactly. It would be too late after. If self-management was a good idea it couldn't have legs until the existing tenure expires, about eight years on. It's far away, but the idea needs to be floated before Ed gets an extension. If eight seems distant, imagine the hopelessness of us planning for a change that couldn't take place until later again, say 13 years. If self-management couldn't be implemented until too far into the future, few people, ourselves included, would be interested in talking about it today."

"Why don't you send a circular? That would put everybody in the picture. I think it'll be hard for lots of people to get their minds around self-management, they being so used to contract management. Give them a simple story to start. You write it, and I'll find out how to print and send."

"Fine. Good idea. We'll have to pay, as I don't like asking the board for favors, even though it's a community thing. Besides, they might sabotage us. So let's find out the cost. If it's a fortune we'll consider taking the hat around the owners."

"I'll check it out."

"And I must check the rules in case we're not allowed to do it, though I don't remember anything."

"You want a proof reader? Here she is! I've been an examiner of music students, remember?"

They went to work, and reviewed progress a couple of days later. Zina approved Barney's circular as drafted. She had learned the cost of printing, and enveloping, and bought from Prince's office a copy of the list of owners and their addresses, and as addressing the envelopes would be tiresome, they agreed on merely folding them for the letter boxes of the resident owners, and they made the drop themselves in the quiet hours. That left about 120 envelopes to be mailed to absentee owners, and for them she got help from a few friends at morning coffee, and at the same time introduced them to the cause.

The circular stated:

Dear Fellow Owner

The purpose of this message is to get us thinking about managing Gran Capitan, in which we all have big personal investments, and pay for its management through our assessments.

The condo commenced with management all laid out for us by the developer, BBC, who withheld from us buyers the right to decide how to manage our place. It did this by making a contract for on-site management, and selling the benefit of it for its own gain; not a nickel to the owners. It was to run for several years, with generous compensation for the on-site manager (OSM), and when we buyers came we agreed to go along with the set-up. We, of course, were pretty ignorant of condo management, while BBC was experienced, and also surrounded by expert advisers, but still we must accept what we did. That contract has eight years more to run, assuming the OSMs take up their existing option for a 5-year extension, 1990-1995; and why wouldn't they, it being a valuable gift?.

Maybe we're paying more for management than is fair and reasonable. At the start BBC did not have our interests in mind, while ensuring that manager compensation, and contract conditions, including the standards for the OSM to meet, were attractive for a contract buyer. Only careful examination can reveal the truth.

I suggest we look to the future, even if it's years on, to decide what type of management we will want then, and the most cost-effective way to get it. We need to know if we are paying too much. We need to know if the rights and duties under the OSM contract, fixed years ago, suit changing times. We need to know if on-site management under a long contract is our best style, or if we should be planning for something shorter, or a form of self-management, such as operate at many other condominiums, local and distant.

I suggest the board should compare the costs to owners, and the contractual conditions operating here, with those of similar developments, including in particular those under self-management.

Please think about the above issues, and vote in any proposal for comparative modeling of management that may be put up, for that seems to me the best way of meeting our true interests.

Thank you,

Barney Jones [Unit 257]

Zina noted the cost of the circular was less than she had feared, and said to Barney: "You can afford to send out another sometime. Do you like that idea?"

He laughed, saying: "You're teasing me; but yes, I do. Still, I mustn't become a chatter box. Get such a reputation, and they will be a turn-off."

"Of course. It's not as though the owners are just standing by, calling out for guidance, is it? Y'know, a couple of those friendly girls who helped seemed not to care much about management issues, so I guess we've a long way to go."

"That's sobering, but it's as well to know. It will teach us not to take too much for granted. Surely some got the message, though?"

"Sure they did – all did. Some warmed to the cause at once, but not all, or not then, anyway. Not a word against though."

When the circular came out Ed and Binny had been running a good ship, and were hopeful of extending their contract, without significant amendment, as they felt no need for that, and had heard nobody suggest it either. The clause allowing transfer had been there from the start, and had produced them, and could again produce good people. It was an industry where people buy the contracts with the expectation of selling, hopefully lengthening tenure along the way. Their views seemed to follow past practice. They had heard about Barney's ideas - and he was not alone - that the condo should have self-management, that with it the assessments could be less, and the chance of transfer of management to a party less responsive to the needs of the owners than Ed and Binny, would be reduced. That line of talk disturbed them, who saw in it risks to their business and their financial security. They had bought in hoping an extension of tenure would be available to them, and without which their prospects of capital profit would drop. However, neither the owners nor the directors had influenced them in their purchase, nor held out not any promise for the future. No nods, no winks, nothing. They had got to where they were with their eyes open, and now must make the most of it, which meant helping themselves.

Barney's effort was not aimed at the existing contract and its option, but only at life afterward. He felt owners were entitled to decide how to manage their condo, including the activity currently within the scope of the OSM agreement, as they saw fit, and had been denied that right by BBC, but that need be only a postponement, until current OSM contractual commitments ran their course. It was possible that modeling would not lead to any change in management style, and if so, the review would still have been worth the effort and expense, because the owners would have found the optimum system for Gran Capitan. But his calculations so far, and the fact of other condos being self-managed - meaning any of several systems falling short of the Gran Capitan style - made him think that in the end change would be preferred. And that was apart from the risk of owners being saddled with an uncongenial OSM down the line, and who might prove hard to dislodge, while with self-management remediation would be more readily available. There had to be a time when the matter was set to right.

The McGintys saw the threat in the circular instantly. The message was mild, but clear, and even if many owners might not get it at once, or be inclined to put off thinking about something so far into the future, every time the issue was raised, their prospects of extending contract tenure would be reduced. The message was a warning shot. Any more from Barney, or anybody, concerning self-management, would be hazardous for their plan to lengthen their tenure. They would have to act promptly.

A few months prior to the annual meeting of the owners to be held in November, Ed lobbied the directors for a firm indication of support for the revised contract he had put forward, if not in the terms of that submitted by him, then at least using that as a basis. But as any decision would have to be mutual at board level, and it was known that some directors thought it too early to even discuss the matter, he made no headway. He believed that had the board accepted his submission they could have put it to the owners at their forthcoming annual meeting as being reasonable, and then, more likely than not, the owners would have fallen into line, for they trusted the directors to make wise decisions and recommendations, and in giving that trust they were absolved from the trouble of learning about the legal structure and financial details of the place in which their homes lay.

Ed took his concerns to Angel. Not expecting much, he still thought it worthwhile just talking about the dilemma he faced. Apart from Binny, he had nobody else. The attorney quickly formed a strong idea of the risk facing the McGintys through Barney's proposal. He said:

"Leave nothing to chance, but instead be busy in the director elections coming up. You need a stacked board, which you must make through lobbying, to dissuade outsiders from standing. If possible, the voters will have only one group of candidates to vote for. It's important that others be frightened off, in case somebody like Barney makes the cut, and once on board, he or she could deflect decision-making from the path you need, and also leak confidential plans, and either line of action could endanger your interests."

Ed sat as if spell-bound by this daring proposal, and took it home to discuss with Binny. She felt, and looked doubtful, so Ed asked: "You don't like the sound of it, do you? Is that because it's a new idea, or can you see something wrong? I asked Angel, and he said not."

Binny replied: "I can't find the right words, but it feels wrong for us to interfere with elections."

Ed thought a while before saying, "Angel said its legitimate. We're unit owners ourselves, and entitled to our say. By us putting up a ticket, other owners aren't stopped from doing the same. Doing it seems so very important for us, I think we should look for reasons for, rather than against. Let others do that, if they object."

They continued talking in like vein during the next couple of days, until Binny fell into line, and Ed was able to return to Angel with instructions for him to help advance his proposal, and so the McGintys were soon into electioneering, starting with confidential sounding out of suitable owners to be on their ticket. The boldness and ingenuity of Angel's idea had startled them at first, but they soon got used to it, and the lure of a sympathetic, even compliant board, kept them working, and increasingly able to put aside any qualms they felt about their path being ethically or morally rocky. Angel stressed at all times they should shoot for 100% success with their nominees, with which all things would be possible for them.

11

The McGintys make a board of directors for themselves - it quickly shows support for the McGintys by a circular - a plan to extend their management tenure takes shape

So the McGintys went to work with Angel's plan. They used and abused procedures designed by the governing documents for the owners to elect directors having the sole purpose of serving owners' interests. Although the McGintys did not say outright to their nominees 'the prime purpose of the new board will be to help us get extended tenure', that was the implied basis on which they chatted up their director nominees, and they satisfied themselves of loyalty to that effort before short-listing them. The McGintys made out that existing discord among directors, and between some of them on the one hand and Prince staff and the OSMs on the other, justified a push to get a board that would heal the wounds. They didn't mention that a primary cause of any discord was their own wish for a 25 year contract. Owner interest in the administrative area was low. It was hard to identify the cause exactly. Possibilities were a shortage of communication and explanation from the directors, and the owners viewing activities at their condominium like disinterested and unaffected spectators. Ed and Binny gently made it known they expected their nominees to succeed, and the few others possibly interested in standing became discouraged from doing so by the clear prospect of either defeat at the ballot box, or belonging to a powerless minority. Some regular directors were due to retire anyway. As the McGinty lobbying proceeded as per plan, the numbers of owners who saw through it grew a little, but it was too late, and many didn't care anyway. In short, many owners were so ignorant of local politics and ambitions it did not occur to them that electing a board at the nod of the OSMs could make it unduly responsive to their wishes and be harmful to the interests of owners. They had yet to learn. In the meantime any vague concern an owner might have, such as Binny had on first acquaintance with the Angel plan, about its propriety, stayed dormant. It was beyond any owner's experience, and as the chosen ones apparently saw nothing wrong with it, maybe it was in order. A couple of owners who spoke in condemnation of the ploy were ignored by their colleagues, which left them with a choice between silence, and individual action; but the latter was too hard and too expensive to contemplate for most owners. Barney knew there was something wrong, but had enough on his plate already, so let it pass, and only later realized he had been wrong, and that the ticket from the McGintys, and their canvassing for owner votes, arguably constituted unconscionable conduct by the McGintys, and if so, the governing documents made it unlawful. But it was one thing to believe that, and quite another to commence and sustain legal proceedings to prove it, and find a remedy.

Not very owner approached by Ed or Binny to accept nomination had agreed. Those who declined were not rude in doing so, no matter how they felt, because there was no point in conflict with them. It was easy enough to find excuses, and all that was asked of those who declined was that they keep the invitation to themselves.

The electoral campaign wasn't worked out in very fine detail at the beginning. Once Angel's advice to aim for a clean sweep had been accepted, the identities of the preferred few were still to be learned. When they were, a voting flyer, signed by Ed and Binny, stressed that the candidates shown - six men and one woman - together, and only together, represented a new dawn for the embattled owners of the condos. That they were neither in need of a dawn, nor embattled, didn't matter. Tell them, Angel had said, and they would believe. Unlike the slapdash approach to selling themselves employed by most board candidates acting singly, a smoothly orchestrated effort would be impressive, and voting the ticket would be attractive for many voters, being simpler. It was out and about before nominations closed, to wave off unwelcome candidates. The result was, as Angel had predicted, the candidates on the ticket all succeeded. The board as elected seemed to be a useful mixture of directors of prestige, and ability, and hands-on experience, and was enthusiastically praised by the McGintys for those merits, and also for the prospect of working harmoniously with them for the benefit of the owners. But it would appear in time that was largely pie in the sky.

Each of the new president and vice president and secretary, had plenty of bias in favor of the McGinty interests, and the two first mentioned had no experience in condo administration, and little in other areas that might serve as a basis for rapid learning either. The secretary, a director, and an attorney, didn't lack experience, but his principal home was in Oklahoma, where he was a busy attorney and entrepreneur. Of the other four directors, two had held office before, and the final two made up the numbers, without any known interest or experience in condos. It would not take long, even for an undiscerning owner, to realize that the board was not formed on merit, nor for the benefit of the condo owners, but with another purpose in view, which would appear fairly soon.

The president, Bernard Brooks, was well and favorably known in the district for participation in community affairs with generous energy, and as a leading orchardist, and as a breeder of racehorses. His details looked very well in the electoral papers, where his lack of experience in condo administration was disguised. He was easily promoted as a fine leader, who would add prestige to the board, and hopefully look more inspiring than his predecessor, who lacked little in experience, and a great deal in leadership. What Bernard concealed, and friends helped conceal, was that he was a ferocious gambler, and was in a bad losing streak when Ed first came to him, and when he came the second time he told Ed he was considering the matter, and could see the prospect of Ed doing well out of his plan, and he wondered how Ed would feel about recognizing Bernard's contribution to such an outcome; but he would not embarrass him by dwelling on the topic, at least for the time being. He was content to have sown a seed. Ed, suspicious of the idea, which to him had undertones of his departure from Georgia Land, did not commit himself, but merely said he would think it over.

Still, the prestige of Bernard Brooks was a selling point for Ed in hunting up other prospects. His next prime target, for vice president, had similar prestige, being a retired forensic medicine specialist from the New York PD. He, Josh Spinks, was well known and respected, following his assistance in solving a serial murder case that had scared the community. He had done so by helping an investigative reporter from the local paper, and that work had got his name liberally before the public. Ed had given him vital clues to identification of the killer, after they had come his way by chance. Josh was a large, vigorous and fast-moving man, aggressive by nature, and given to strong views on many subjects. It was not widely known that he was in the habit of writing letters to people who disagreed with him. Though his words were not at all clever, his meaning was always clear, and forceful, and as often than not, openly demeaning of the recipient. Those who received them, after recovering from the shock of the tirade, and the revelation of extremism in opinion which in another man would suggest he was something of an odd-ball, usually concluded that to respond could well be a complete waste of effort, and likely to keep alive a difficult matter. Those of that opinion didn't reply. Their invariable concern was that Josh's local standing was such that should the issue be made public, natural loyalty and respect toward him would result in observers taking his side, or at least failing to see the matter objectively. Others, annoyed, replied in like vein as used by Josh, which made them feel better, and so the exchange would end, as he never responded.

Josh's eagerness to have his views known had appeared publicly during the months prior to the election of directors when, as an ordinary owner, he had sent a circular to owners, denigrating a handful of their colleagues for resisting an owner's proposal to change his condo by the addition of a piece of airspace that was part of the common area, though useless for the amenity of other owners because of its location. It was a strong attack, and its scathing tone, including a suggestion that the protesters needed psychiatric help, surprised owners without knowledge of his style, and besides, many had no interest in, or even knowledge of, the proposal. But still, the recipients of the circular - not the victims - seemed not to think any the less of him, but to take it that a man of his discernment could be right, and the targets wrong.

So Josh was an inviting prospect for the McGinty voting ticket. Although he was not of the pool of more or less regular directors, he was presentable, and few owners could have anything against him, and most would likely be impressed by his condescending to serve them. The style of Ed's approach, including generous flattery, and assurance that his not knowing much about condos or meeting procedures would not matter, as experts such as Ed and Binny, and the staff of Prince, were at hand. Moreover, he would be assured of being vice president under the excellent leadership of Bernard Brooks, and the board would appear to owners as prestigious, and the more so for his own participation, which fitted well with the high opinion Josh held of himself. He agreed to stand, first seeking assurance he would succeed, because his vanity would not allow of his contesting office and being defeated. Angel told him his profile made him a shoe-in; and it was so. For the McGintys it was an inspired choice, as Josh assumed from the start a concern for their interests, and asserted a degree of influence unusual for the holder of his office. In fact, he came out as an in-fighter for them from the start, actually better than their best hopes had allowed. His support was unequivocal and unquestioning and constant. Ed, in turn, responded so that, in a sense, the board became a two-man show, though Ed was not on the board, except that as an OSM, he was an ex-officio member. Nonetheless, proper procedures were followed to the extent of giving the appearance of a normal board, functioning by the rules, a picture made more possible through disinterest by some directors, and their willingness to give proxies, so ensuring that meetings did not fail for want of a quorum. It would be easier to see what had happened, how due process had been ignored and subverted, later, than at the time.

Ed did not know, because the gripping financial scandal had not yet broken, that Richard Rowe, one of the carry-over directors to whom he gave star billing on the McGinty voting ticket, a man of impressive financial qualifications, spent great amounts of his time away from home, in Chicago and in European financial capitals, pursuing value for his clients through complex transactions, but losing more than he made, and in increasingly large amounts, hence the scandal. But he was away from town so much he hardly registered in owner perceptions, notionally existing in meetings of the board through giving his proxy to others attending, and so for the McGintys no harm was done. They encouraged him to stay aboard, for if he went, for any reason, prior to their plans being implemented, and through a fluke he were to be replaced by an unsympathetic outsider, derailment might follow. In the result, the original board from the McGinty ticket stayed together for long enough to achieve its original purpose. Richard turned against Josh and company later, and became a board critic, which was like a pot calling a kettle black, but by then he was a spent and disgraced force because of his business record.

The election ticket had read quite well, being led by three men of relative eminence and excellent education, and whose other members were also presented as well experienced, and all of a mind to be attentive to owner concerns. Owners were impressed. As the voting for the ticket was very strong, even allowing for the lack of competition, the warm regard held by the new directors for the McGintys grew.

The owners too were content. The message they received was to expect less bickering, and a prestigious and competent board that would work well with management. The picture was not clouded by Barney's ideas about self-management, which so far had but little impact.

After having their ambition for tenure extension frustrated by the previous board, the McGintys could hardly believe their luck in securing an openly cordial and potentially compliant board, and were encouraged to turn again to the long contract of their dreams.

Soon after the new board took power, and under the guidance of Josh Spinks, who had already emerged as its de facto leader, it sent a circular to owners. The content was little concerned with their affairs and related board policy, and much greatly with the excellence of the service of the McGintys, and how it would serve owners well to sustain them in their post, for if it should appear that owners intended to let the contract tenure run out, the disappointment of the valuable managers would cause their interest in the job to decline, with a reduction in the high quality of their service. It stated that the McGintys had never asked the current committee for a 25-year management term, without saying why something that had not happened needed to be mentioned, and the reasons were, if a reader thought about it, to cede credit gratuitously to the OSMs, and also introduce the prospect of extension. Because sensible explanations did not appear in the circular, owners assumed things had happened without their knowing, and most supposed it was their own fault for not paying closer attention to condominium news. The circular was so warm for the McGintys it could not have suited them better had they written it themselves.

Here it may be noted that of those owners who were at all interested in the managerial side of the condo, representing no more than half the total number of units, many had little understanding of the complexities of their artificial entity, and tended to believe in the integrity of the directors, as the people's representatives, all of whom were also owners, and who no doubt had given their concerned and expert attention to the issues. Who then, among the other owners, could say they were wrong? The interest held by some owners in the condo, low level so often, was satisfied, in a clumsy way, by their effort in voting on issues presented to general meetings, and as they had no reason to vote no, and the option of entering an abstain mark had little appeal, additional votes in favor of any motion that had board approval came quite readily.

Outsiders could not know if there was something secretive behind the board's circular, but Barney supposed there was. He took it as calculated to mislead owners, though its style made analysis hard. He did not know what owners generally thought of it, illustrating again their fragmentation. Help seemed far away. The directors were effectively under Ed's influence. The staff of Prince were of no use, being concerned to keep in the good books of both the OSMs and the board, with whom they worked constantly, and who would be the main players when it was time to consider renewal of the Prince service contract.

Unknown to Barney, a few owners hadn't accepted the board's circular as either a reasonable exercise of its function, or sensible according to their own understanding of contractual relations in business. In particular, two lock-up owners, men of business in their different cities, were separately prompted to write to the board, in the care of Prince, both claiming the circular contained much that was commercial nonsense. One received a letter from Josh Spinks in the same hectoring style as used in his other letters in which he insisted he knew best. Barney too was angry about the circular, and circularized a critical response among the owners.

A factor of unknown weight in voting in condo business is the level of understanding the average condo owner has of the underlying legal structure. The advantages of those dwelling complexes are well known, and are more readily stated and assimilated than are the regulations through which they function. Owners may know little of technicalities and law and governing documents, and so be heavily independent on advice and information from others, especially those who have gained their confidence. At Gran Capitan, in early 1988, many owners had confidence in the OSMs and Prince, and the new board. Owners generally were not aware of the McGinty tenure ambitions, though they had surfaced briefly a few months earlier, and even if aware, they had no present reason to be upset. They had not known of the McGinty plan to control the board, nor that at the same time as the new board circulated its views to owners in March, it was running secret negotiations with the OSMs for a new, long-term, contract, and which could be fairly described as a contract made in heaven for incumbent OSMs. Its term, with options, was to run for 25 years to 2013, the compensation was to continue at the past buoyant level, and the duties of the OSMs and the circumstances for deeming violation of them, were no more strongly stated than before. This contract could only have been produced through the combined efforts of partisan directors and the OSMs, and it was quickly printed and ready for submission at a special meeting of the owners, as required by the bylaws. It was clearly of great prospective value for the OSMs, quite apart from a curious clause that arguably could make its term, with extensions, indefinite if the OSMs so wished. Ed wanted the board to bring the new contract to a special meeting of the owners promptly, and it was sympathetic to the idea. It may have been a bit much to expect the owners to vote such a supremely advantageous contract for the OSMs, but its proponents saw it as a distinct possibility. The McGintys had produced directors unanimously sympathetic to their ambition, both they themselves and the directors were in good repute with the owners, the board had approved the new contract, so who was to know it would not be rubber-stamped by the owners?

Had they linked the voting ticket to the board's March circular, condo owners may have understood better the faint rumors that the board was chosen more for its willingness to dance to a McGinty tune, rather than function as representatives of the owners. They would one day, and then would also see the board's actions in relation to the management contract in a different light.

12

The Jones interpret the curious events - they feel extension in the wind - protection of the condo owners is needed - Barney creates a motion to put before the owners - discussion of shady activity - owners' losses estimated

By circularizing the owners about review of management style, Barney had placed himself in open opposition to the board and the OSMs. He sensed that, if nothing else, the directors' March circular indicated that activity about the OSM contract was afoot. He said to Zina:

"Though it's crassly worded, and altogether a puzzle, it shows, above all else, real concern for the McGintys' welfare. But the board's duty under the Declaration is to serve, and protect the interests of, the unit owners. And look at that stuff about the length of tenure. The contract must have been on their minds for that, like it's been on McGintys for a long time. So what was the purpose of the voting ticket?"

Cried Zina: "Even I know that. The McGintys wanted a board to suit themselves. That was clear from their circular congratulating and praising the new directors, and suggesting the owners would be better off under them than before. Why would the managers care that much, either to run a ticket, or to sweet talk the new directors afterwards, unless their target was a longer contract?"

"I agree. So they've been doing their best to look good to both the directors and the owners. They're certainly succeeding with the directors. If you subtract from that circular the stuff about the OSM contract, there's practically nothing left, so if the McGintys' hope is for an extended term, it sounds like they've now got the right board for the job."

"They're moving while they see the space. They must fear your review suggestion. It's so clearly a threat that not only the McGintys, but every director with half a brain must see it. You can bet your life there's something being cooked up to beat it."

Barney said: "And the circular is part of the plan. If they lengthen the contract, the chances of reviewing its conditions, and modeling alternative forms of management, are reduced, being pushed away in time."

"What is it now?"

"About eight and a bit years."

Zina thought about that, then said: "Let me get this straight. If the owners looked into the whole contract business and wanted a change, it couldn't happen for eight years. Would some owners, not necessarily your opponents, say it's too early for modeling at present?"

"They could well do that. Then I'd say we need to know soon, as it might turn up flaws in the contract, and also show that self-management should be cheaper, and no less efficient. And owners would need time to digest the findings, which may be contentious. Ed and Binny couldn't argue too loudly that it's too soon, because only a few months ago they put in for 25 years; no question of waiting on their part. That's their target. Ours must be to delay contract extension until after the owners have reviewed their management possibilities. As they didn't pay for extra, and the condo didn't promise any, if the McGintys are reasonable, and if the directors aren't to be traitors to their duty, they'll all see that modeling now, in advance of talk about increased tenure, is no more than is due the owners. We know that Ed and Binny do their job well, for which they are compensated paid generously, but that doesn't entitle them, or anybody on their behalf, to trample on owner's rights. Say they got a long tenure, and then sold the contract, as the Hollidays did, and the new man turned out bad. That could be a terrible burden on the owners."

Zina said: "Another one! Y'know, if there's any concern about your motion for modeling being too early, it should spill over to the McGintys and the extension they want, as they have no need for it right now; not for years actually."

"Except to head off our modeling idea. Remember though, we're dealing with smart guys. They snowed the owners to get their own board voted in."

Zina, looking puzzled, asked: "But what's holding them up? It's quite a time since the election."

"It's hard to know. I had thought our circular would have spurred them on. Surely they must be close to calling a special meeting to consider extension. Whatever, I'm thinking we should go on with a motion for management modeling. If it's filed prior to their motion, then correct procedure would see ours dealt with first. If the owners voted that, surely they wouldn't agree to extension, at least until the modeling was done, and maybe never. Say though, the extension motion was up first on the agenda, and say it was for quite a long time, and was passed, the modeling motion would have less punch, and even if passed, would be neutered until the contract ended, which could be like waiting for the next ice age. Yet I don't know that we could complain, as long as both motions were there before the owners, for the owners could see and compare both in the same breath. So we need to file our motion so as to be on the same agenda, and desirably listed first. Why don't we jump in right away; get front spot, or at least be there for the owners to see and compare? I can start drafting it right now. What do you think?"

"I agree. But I think that if they have an extension motion in hand, they won't give us front spot, no matter how fair that would be. It seems to me that self-management and modeling and Barney Jones must all be dirty words at the McGintys', and with some directors. You're not worried about being offside with all those people?"

"I think I'm already there. Pity, but it can't be helped. They played a lousy trick on the owners with that voting ticket, and that many owners still don't quite get it changes nothing. If the directors were innocents, and believed their role was to serve the condo owners, then as soon as they saw the unorthodox play they were in, like puppets on a McGinty string, they should have protested. Even though that would be too tough for weaklings, or committed McGinty people like Bernard Brooks, you would have expected at least one director to protest. The whole thing is quite bizarre to me, after forty years of seeing people elected to all sorts of representative positions. I'm surprised that more owners haven't tried to shout it down, for I'd bet few, probably none, have ever seen the like, no matter what their vocations have been."

"Maybe owners will get wiser as we go."

"Let's hope so. It's their condo, and we're only looking for the best deal for them."

Barney already had an idea of the motion needed, and it was ready for their joint review over a drink before the evening meal. In essence, it provided for the board to hire a qualified person or firm, to analyze the provisions of the management contract, including compensation. Then compare the results with two or more local, self-managed condominiums of similar size and amenities as Gran Capitan. The purpose was to help the members decide if self-management, or contract management, or some other style, should be preferred. The modeling was not to suppose that the directors would have hands-on, as distinct from supervisory functions, the difference being shown in small condominiums where, to keep costs down, owners personally did much of the day-to-day work and maintenance. The motion was expressed in the formal language necessary to ensure it was not shot down because of technicalities, but those details are not necessary here.

Barney said to Zina, "The words we are using will hopefully prevent trickery either in the setting up of the analysis team, or in the selection of the condos whose data would be the basis of the modeling." She nodded her acceptance of his word, and the motion was settled and signed by Barney and filed. In the covering letter he asked for it to be dealt with by the next general meeting of owners, as stipulated by the Declaration, where it dealt with owner's motions. He explained that the motion brought up a new matter fundamental to the welfare of Gran Capitan owners, both present and future. If the board did not agree with the request about dealing with the motion, he would like to know right away, so as to consider his position. He and Zina knew that language was bold, but believed it was correct, and essential, given the evident pro-OSM bias of the board.

After three weeks, and no reply in any form had come, Barney wrote again, enclosing a copy of his first letter, stating that if the board was planning to extend the OSM tenure, which may have been indicated through its March circular, it might be disposed to ignore the modeling motion. That would be unreasonable, considering it was for the benefit of all owners, and the OSMs would be the only beneficiary of lengthening the contract tenure. He received no reply to this letter either, which he took to be complete disdain, attributable to the purpose of favoring the McGintys. Though the Jones felt isolated, as the owners generally were unaware of those events, they took comfort in believing that due process by the directors would necessarily see it handled correctly.

Prince published records of proceedings of the board, and other matters relevant for the owners, and in May 1988 a minute appeared showing that the board had received the Jones motion. It said the board thought that as no action to implement it fully could be taken while the management contract had several years to run, present expense and diversion of board effort in modeling could not be justified, and the owner would be written to accordingly. But for four aspects, the board's attitude as so expressed might have appeared reasonable. The first was that the board had no discretion in the matter of an owner's motion for a general meeting. It was bound by the governing documents to list it for consideration at the next following meeting. The second was that the Jones were not advised what the board decided, even though the record said a letter would be sent, so they only had the garbled account in the record of meeting to go on, and it was inadequate for their needs, and so they had waited. The third aspect was that the implantation of the motion was unlikely to engage any notable time or effort by directors, as the task was to be executed by Prince and an external consultant. The fourth, because another minute of the same meeting had the board approving the provisions of a new management contract, even though the existing contract, with an option, had several years to run. So to those biased directors modeling was years too early, but extending OSM tenure from a date equally distant was not. The record did not show, and in fact it would not be exposed for several years ahead, that the extension contained in that new contract was very generous.

For an owner who was not familiar with board activities, and could only be so through its communications, or as an insider, the true nature of proceedings could not be understood. At Gran Capitan, when Prince was administration manager, and the Brooks board was in power, reporting was usually inadequate. It was well known to keen observers, but not generally, that the staff of Prince who worked the Gran Capitan file had become extremely supportive of the McGinty interests, and against any owner who was not. It was as though they were there to serve the board and the OSMs, without reference to owner interests. The mixture of inefficiency and bias kept owners in the dark. The board seemingly exercised little or no control over those shortcomings, and the reason was its composition; it was a McGinty board, and Prince staff members were their allies. Ed made the main plans, and Prince staff members followed through. No derision of opponents was too biting for those zealots. The president of the board was totally in the McGinty corner, without ever getting to understand how a condominium was supposed to operate. The vice president was the driving force of the board, and although he knew little about meetings generally and condos and their governing documents, Josh Spinks knew what power could do, and was obsessed with conferring on the

McGintys an extended management tenure. For whatever reason, he took it to be their due, and he would see that Gran Capitan gave it to them, by any means at hand, including cheating. He was forceful, and as de facto chairman most of the time, whatever came up touching upon their interests had to go their way. The reason for this attitude was never explained, but it was a fit with his style by which a stance once taken was not for changing, as shown in his written communications. What a psychologist might make of him is unknown. For other observers, how any person so afflicted could succeed in a superior vocation was unclear. In some circumstances bribery could be the key, but there was no evidence to suggest this was one. The secretary, no less biased toward McGinty interests, and who had the particular duty of administrative oversight of records and meetings, simply failed, continually, in the duties of his office. In his case, as with Spinks, speculation as to causes can only be idle, and is not attempted.

Though some of the lesser lights among the directors showed less interest in board affairs as 1988 proceeded, that was not so for any of the leaders, whose allegiance to the McGintys stayed firm, and they always had enough support from the others to make up the numbers. No issue was more important to the future of the condo in 1988 than management arrangements, and none received more effort from the board, always with the aim of protecting or advancing the McGinty interests. It is not to be supposed that every director had that aim, but each was either an avowed McGinty ally, or a close supporter of one who was. Thus Angel's vision achieved reality, and not least through the drive of Josh Spinks, and his willingness to subvert due process, and lead fellow directors along wrongful paths, littered by deceit and abandonment of duty.

Ed and Binny saw nothing fundamentally wrong with their ambition. Management was needed. That it was profitable for the OSMs was both normal and essential. Ed and Binny were not an inferior management team: far from it. Among condo complexes under contract management it was usual practice to extend tenure and sell the unexpired contract, so there was nothing untoward in their approach. It was not reasonable to interfere with the established system. The owners all knew of the management structure and its expense when they came, and nothing had changed, or was sought to be changed, on that score. By whoever and however the property was managed in the future, it would cost owners.

While the McGinty attitude was not without merit, it was incomplete unless the rights of the condo owners were counted in. Those owners who had voted, years earlier, at start-up, for retention of the management arrangements made by BBC, had not been fully informed, were new chums, and under the influence, directly or indirectly, of BBC, who in effect pushed on to them a contract that was commercially unreasonable, and in doing so the form of democratic process had been followed, without its reality. The owners should be given the chance to work it out for themselves, and that was Barney's idea with his motion. By proceeding with it the existing OSM contract would not be disturbed. They had not been promised anything more than was in their own purchase contract, so the risk of future change had existed as a business hazard from the beginning. Certainly their future prospects might be affected, but the details of that had to await the modeling. The owners were not going to be unfair to the McGintys in terms of what they had purchased, nor was the move in any way personal. If they had got the wrong idea about extension, and the owners had not given it to them, it was unfortunate, but life was like that.

The looming strife at Gran Capitan illustrated the problems of unit complexes generally, and of condos in particular. They were communities run under their own regimes, controlled by the elected representatives of the owners. In the forms of government of both city and county councils and states, there was at all times a risk that governance would not proceed as efficiently, or as honestly, as community ideals, so finding the same features in condos was not to be marveled at. If the scheme developer was shady, of course there were prospects of a bad future for owners, who must help themselves, or succumb.

Unit buyers are often at sea on arrival, particularly if they have no prior condo experience through condo residency or ownership. Being rather clever, or experienced in a superior vocation, doesn't help much. Unless he or she comes knowing about the operation of a condo scheme, and its legal and financial aspects, a buyer will be far behind the developer in knowledge, besides negotiating power. The developer knows from deep experience what is and what is not possible or appropriate, and doesn't lose the role of decision maker until sales are well advanced. It's not enough to say that the buyer does not have to go ahead. If he or she likes a unit, and is looking for a home like it, and is unaware of deception by or on behalf of the developer, that buyer is impelled by the ordinary forces of honest business to proceed. And deception is no less so for being sophisticated. But to sue a developer, hood-winked owners need to be busy, and get expert counsel promptly, lest the time allowed for suing overtakes them.

The Prince contract had been renewed at the same general meeting, in November 1987, at which the McGinty election ticket succeeded, but only through the expertise of Prince's senior staff in manipulating proceedings at special meetings of owners, where they had deep experience, and directors and owners but little. It was thereby secured in its position for another three years, amid widespread wonder and genuine disappointment. As with its predecessor, the new board sustained disapproval of Prince, and requested it to surrender office, but as the contract was lucrative, and the job prestigious, it gritted its corporate teeth and remained. It could do so the more readily because the staff members who worked Gran Capitan enjoyed good relations with the OSMs and their staff, who did not fully share the dislike of Prince by the directors. Ed knew most information for owners came from or through

Prince, and that it had the capacity for reporting in a flattering manner, which Ed found useful, being alert to the importance of a good public image. It could also report maliciously, as Barney knew very well. Prince's shortcomings were tolerated by the Bernard Brooks board so far as they served its purposes, one being non-disclosure and obfuscation of a proposed new and secret and very long tenure OSM contract, and another the manipulation of the agenda and associated papers for the 1988 special meeting that would unlawfully omit the Jones' motion from the agenda.

Owners did not know, but soon after the new directors took office, Ed commenced urging them to extend the contract term. He said that if they did not, the McGintys would have to sell the contract, the value of which was declining as its unexpired term diminished. Without an extension, he foresaw - or, at least, stated he saw - a capital loss, which would become greater through delay. The directors only had his word to go by, and being infatuated with the McGinty welfare, were content with it. He claimed they must sell right away, or be granted a long contract. The board reacted as if there was no need to take into account the owners' interests. In their own words the McGintys' interest in an extension was centered on the market value of the contract for them, and the board adopted those concerns for itself, without any need to do so, and a duty not to. It was a repeat of the McGinty push the previous year for 25 years, with a different outcome, made possible by Angel's advice that the McGintys get their own board. So the board could have required review of the terms and conditions of the existing contract, as a precursor to negotiations. Or could have let the OSMs go ahead and sell. Had they done so, a new manager, absent the special influence of the McGintys, could not have obtained an extension of term before a decision about modeling had been made by the owners who, if they were to favor the modeling process, would likely not want to extend a management contract prior to its completion; and maybe not after.

Modeling was in the wind because of Barney's circular, and later motion, and consequent owner discussion. But such were unimportant to a board so obsessed. They chose the path that would most benefit the manager. So, starting April, as mentioned, a new contract for 25 years at least, (Plan A) was negotiated, and by 31 May had been approved by the board, and agreed with the McGintys, and printed ready for early consideration by the owners in general meeting. It was not created at arm's length between freely negotiating parties, with the board looking out for the interests of the owners, and the McGintys for themselves. The board was no more concerned for the owners than BBC had been in the original contract formed in 1980. Owners didn't know what was going on, and the board was gung ho for the OSM's interests exclusively.

That contract, always ambitious, and never shown to owners, was dumped after cooler heads among the directors saw the danger to it of the modeling motion. The two would sit oddly together before the voters. So convinced,

105

and at Ed's suggestion, acting on Angel's advice, the board adopted Plan B instead, which was to be a grant of a third option for a 5-year renewal, 1996-2000. Thus, the OSMs already held a second option, 1990-1995, exercisable in 1990, and by Plan B would be granted a third, to follow. Hence a total of ten years in options, on top of the unexpired term of over two years. The shortened span understandably disappointed the McGintys, but with self-management modeling in the air, they saw no alternative.

To proceed with Plan B, the board would need a special meeting of the owners. The board did not disclose to the owners that calling it, and its business, were both special favors to the OSMs, and carried no benefit for the owners. Unless there is advice otherwise, owners naturally take a special meeting to be official business, put forward by the directors for the benefit of the unit owners, and so take it on trust.

The board had sidelined Barney's proposal for modeling prior to its decision to call the special meeting, though Barney would not know this until later. He had no information sources when he needed them most. The whole power structure of the directors and Prince was biased toward the McGintys. Very few owners were interested or alert enough to run down the occasional small indicators of irregular behavior. A search among the directors for a cheer leader calling: 'Let's hear it for the owners!' would have rung hollowly. The fiction of that board representing owners had collapsed. They had shown their treacherous colors. The board's task was to get the McGintys 'over the line', as vice president Josh Spinks was to say later, and they did. Allowing for variances in motivation among them, and some belated dissatisfaction, director's loyalty to their leaders and the OSMs had stuck long enough to get Plan B to a general meeting. At the least, all were complicit in the scheme, if only through being passive in the face of illegal conduct, when it was their duty to be active for the owners. It would come to be seen as a condo conspiracy.

Barney calculated that a 5-year contract extension would rob owners of between $2m and $2.4m, being the increase in their assessments compared with self-management, had it applied. Allowing for interest and inflation, and it became more like $3m value transferred from owners to OSM, above a proper and reasonable allowance for management expense.

Another calculation could start at the beginning of Gran Capitan, to the notional end of the Plan B contract, being 20 years from 1980. As the base contract remuneration was to be constant, the primary figures could be multiplied evenly, and when inflation and compounded interest were slotted in, value wrongly wrenched away from owners, and to the OSMs, seemed close to $15m.

The annual impact on the assessments for any condo unit through such a transfer of value could be found by proportioning its interest in the common areas, or elements, or property, on which assessments were calculated, against the total value.

Had they known of it, the money factor alone might have suggested to owners they change the management system at first opportunity. They did not know, because Barney had come up with the figures lately, and the opportunity to press them home to owners was lost when his motion was omitted - as will be seen - from the agenda. But money aside, the contract management system in operation at Gran Capitan also disturbed resident harmony, by conflict with the OSMs, to whom the contract was a business asset, whose value lay in the bottom lines of both annual income and prospective capital gain, concerns about which took precedence above owners' interests. The contract had also been a business asset for BBC when arranging the management of Gran Capitan for its own advantage, and in so proceeding it was arguably in breach of a fiduciary or trust duty to its initial condo buyers to deliver a management regime suited to a residential unit scheme, to use BBC's own marketing language. BBC had got away with it, and it remained to be seen if the McGintys, in a different situation, also would. Happier people, and useful savings too, were seen by Barney as probable results of a change in management style at Gran Capitan.

13

The McGintys obtain an extra option to extend management tenure - deception and abuses noticeable - a conspiracy is suspected - comparative management modeling emerges as an issue - Barney's cause hit by an adverse arbitration award - owner's eyes slowly opening - a new board takes charge - relations between it and the OSMs bad

The agenda for the special meeting of owners held in August 1988 contained only one motion. It was a proposal from the board that the management contract be changed in one particular, namely to grant the OSMs an option to extend the contract term by five years, to take effect from September 1995, the exercise of it to be subject to the same conditions as for the two options previously granted. Those were that notice in writing be given to the board during the three months prior to the end of the preceding management phase, and that the optionee not then be in default under the contract. So the OSMs had only to give notice, after which it was for the board to accept, or else deny it because of default. This procedure would be followed in September 1990, when the OSMs would exercise the second option, for 1990-95, without hitch, as the new board was not disposed to block it, unlike the attitude it would adopt toward the exercise of the third option, when the time came. The difference to them was that unlawfulness had produced the third option.

The third option was Plan B for the OSMs, but it was not generally known until much later, as will be shown, that an earlier plan had been preferred by them and the directors, until its abandonment. That was not information in the public domain, for it was a secret deal of the conspirators, and the aura of secrecy was continued to hide its collapse. The third option would not be exercisable before 1995, for the phase ending 2000. Just as the contract conditions had not been reviewed, as commercial prudence would have suggested, it was not made subject to the McGintys still being the OSMs upon exercising it in 1995, and so, in effect, it was to be a gift of a few million dollars from the condo owners to them. For Barney, this freebie had neither moral nor economic basis and, as importantly, was unlawfully created. He could also see that if the option were granted in accordance with the board motion for the general meeting, owners might see little point in modeling when the results could not be applied for 13 years. Eight years was bad enough. But no matter: the modeling motion was not before them for consideration, for it was not on the agenda. So they could only vote for, or against, or abstain from voting, the option motion.

Barney's fears had been sound. The OSMs had rustled up a board that would do their bidding. They had found leading directors to act as powerful agents for their ambition, using their influence among the other directors to sideline owner interests. The leaders were Bernard Brooks, Josh Spinks, and

Abraham Mayer, being president, vice president, and secretary respectively of the new board. Barney became angry, as he was now convinced of deceit, which he called conspiracy, without being sure it was the correct legal term. He complained by letter to the board through Prince, who replied that the omission of his motion from the agenda was a simple clerical error, and it would be dealt with at the next general meeting, which most likely would be the annual general meeting. Barney replied that was unacceptable, given the terms of his letter to the directors enclosing the motion, which letter was in view at the board meeting, as the record showed. A future general meeting would be of no use if the third option had been granted already, as implementation of the results of modeling could then seem too remote. Omission was de facto invalidation of his motion. The record of the May meeting held said he was to be written to, and he had been waiting for a letter that never came, and if it had he would have been warned earlier, and been able to act to protect his interests, which in reality were owners' interests.

Barney's letters had been such strong stuff, concerning as they did, matters clearly of the highest importance for the condo, that a reader could hardly help being alerted to their significance. And it was a normal function of directors, and managers, to read important material they were to deal with. Barney read the record of the May meeting again, and realized he had not interpreted it accurately at first. He had not read it as being a decision to omit his motion from the agenda, and now saw that was really both its intent and effect. He had asked for an undertaking not to call a general meeting that would frustrate his motion, and without coming out and refusing his request, board treatment of it was the equivalent of plain denial. His slow comprehension had delayed his complaint, just as the board's and Prince's silence had done, and he saw now, through the necessary implication of their own words, the directors had acted inconsistently with the rights of the owners to due process for his motion, despite his specific request they not do so. It was now clear, and it was artful, in that neither the board nor Prince had come out and said outright his motion would be omitted from the agenda. He would soon see it was also unlawful.

Barney wrote the board to make good the omission by calling off the scheduled meeting, and substituting one whose agenda included his motion. This was refused, after which Barney declared a dispute, and called for the application of the dispute resolution section of the Declaration.

The correspondence about the complaint of wrongful omission was handled for the board entirely by Prince. Barney pointed out that the bylaws mandated that a motion for a general meeting must be placed on the agenda for the next meeting convenient for its inclusion, and that there was no apparent justification for his to be excluded. The directors' meeting in May had not stated his motion was to be excluded from the next general meeting agenda. Inadvertence by Prince should not be a weapon to harm the interests of owners, such as himself in relation to his motion, and the general body of owners in dealing with their proper business. Prince adhered to the line the omission was only clerical error, and that his motion could still be dealt with at the annual general meeting. To Barney that was pure nonsense, because if the meeting with the deficient agenda went ahead, and the option motion passed, the lead time would likely be too long for his motion to be practical. It was obvious to Barney that he and the owners were being deceived, and so he circularized them with the facts as he saw them, and received considerable support in his plea for owners to vote against the single motion on the agenda. However, Barney knew that the motion for extension, coming from the board, could only help the OSMs, as many owners typically fell into line with board suggestions, in effect letting the board think for them. The same undiscerning owners might also ignore Barney's additional complaint that the motion from the board did not provide for a review of terms and conditions, so that any flaws in the original agreement were to be perpetuated. The complacency of owners would be aggravated by the failure of the board to include an explanatory statement of points for and against the motion from a condo owner's standpoint. The motion for the extension, and the papers and propaganda surrounding it, did not mention anything but the proposed grant of a new option, and not why, or if, it was in the interests of owners. The McGintys lobbied owners to vote for the motion, with a naïve plea for an innocuous sounding top-up of their term, implying they would not thereby receive more than they had had in the past. But that was wrong, as they had never held an unexpired term of 13 years previously. Though Barney saw the ruse, he did not always have the time or the resources to contend against every misleading statement associated with the option affair, and regretfully had to pass on that point, among others.

He knew that Prince could not act, or refrain from acting, in an important matter such as was at hand, without board approval, for the very good reason that by exceeding its authority at any point Prince would thereby bring itself closer to being fired, which was an event never far away. So it seemed that what Prince did in relation to his motion had the full backing and authority of the board, though all directors were silent on the issue.

Ed put out a flyer with the voting papers for the general meeting, and its content appeared to Barney as deceitful and self-serving. Later analysis of the governing documents in respect of general meeting procedure would show it was also unlawful, in that statements allowed to be sent with the meeting papers had to come from the sponsor of a motion, which was the board, not Ed.

Barely a half of all owners turned out to vote on a matter affecting the long-term finances and management of the condominium. At stake was the success or otherwise of the OSMs diverting to themselves, via a conspiracy, over two million dollars of the owners' money. It would be decided by ordinary resolution through a secret ballot, as stipulated in the Declaration. The vote count showed half plus one had favored the extension, and those

111

included two votes from the McGintys, based on their ownership of two units. Barney believed that had the motion been sponsored by the OSMs personally, and not by the board, the owners would have turned it down, but as it came from the board, the feeling that directors looked after owner interests had produced extra votes. Moreover, the meeting was not told that the cost of the special meeting was to be borne by the McGintys, and maybe disclosure of that alone would have driven into the minds of some owners that it was not ordinary business before them. Also hidden was the fact of the board having secretly settled a new, long-term contract with the McGintys - Plan A - only to suppress it upon Barney's modeling motion appearing, and hidden so well that not even Barney knew of it until a few years later. Of the votes cast, some had surely come from the owners in the OSM letting pool, as it was known the McGintys had dipped into it for support for their directors voting ticket. But even so, the numbers showed blind faith in their board by some owners, proving that at Gran Capitan at that time, directors could get away with things that should not be. It would take time and painful events to educate the average owner of the need to pay more attention.

Barney had warned the board that if the third option motion succeeded, he would take proceedings of some sort to have it set aside, and for his own motion to be justly treated. He selected arbitration under the dispute resolution provisions of the bylaws for path, this being a proceeding that could produce a fairly quick result with less expense than a lawsuit, with which the board agreed. As he had experience in that field, he felt no need to hire an attorney, especially as the fees could be his to bear alone. He could have taken the hat around the owners, but pride and the time it would take made him decide against doing so. He accepted the risk of an order for costs against him if he lost.

Following the August meeting, Barney had been despondent about pushing his motion at the forthcoming annual general meeting, presuming that the Ed-Josh group would talk it down. Then he found that the arbitration hearing would take longer to commence than he had expected, so he became keen for his motion to be approved, in time for the result to be part of the material before the arbitrator. Accordingly, by circular and word of mouth, he encouraged his fellow owners to vote for his motion, and they did, in good numbers, despite intense opposition before and in the meeting by the OSMs, and some directors, and their cohorts.

From his wide experience of boards and committees, Barney suspected that board cohesiveness was fraying. The records of their occasional meetings showed increasingly frequent apologies for non-attendance, with much use of proxies, which were often needed just for a quorum; four directors present in person or by proxy being required under the bylaws for a valid meeting. He felt director's enthusiasm had dropped, but that need not mean rebellion. Then he received a confidential message from a director, Richard the financial expert, offering support, but wishing to remain anonymous, which was of little use to Barney, who felt that a man who could disagree and keep it to himself during meetings, and neither openly dissent nor have his dissent recorded, and not resign, the while leaking confidential board business, was of doubtful value. Yet he desperately needed inside information so far hidden by the network of conspirators, being Prince, the board, and the McGintys, so any information at all from a mole was to be welcomed, without trusting him. But the mole proved to be coy with his information, and the most Barney got was copy communications showing the board and Ed taking attorney advice on the lawfulness, and technical correctness, of his modeling motion. It alerted him to their continuing antagonism, and that they were searching for an excuse for the chairperson of the annual meeting to rule it out of order. Bu the advice they received was contrary to their wishes.

The annual meeting of owners at which his delayed modeling motion was comfortably passed, December 1988, was disappointing for Barney in respect of the composition of the new board elected then. Unlike the previous election, when the OSMs had presented a voting ticket which had succeeded completely, there were now more candidates, and the Bernard Brooks group had set out to retain control. While their board numbers had dwindled, the same three most influential figures remained, for they had been elected unopposed to the three executive positions. The Brooks group put out a voting ticket for the other seats, which coincided exactly with a like ticket from the McGintys. It succeeded well enough to return the Brooks group to power, as one ordinary vacancy had been taken by a Brooks supporter, apparently the only one among those other candidates, and that seemed to come from her name starting with A, and the voting list being alphabetical. So the power bloc had four out of the seven board seats. The intervention of the OSMs in the board elections again was, to Barney and some other owners, an abuse of the power of their position, yet they could not see how to prevent it. They had protested against this ruse for the previous elections, and the board had taken no notice, and another protest would surely also be denied. The wrongfulness of the intervention could therefore only be countered, if at all, through court action, and here, as always, Barney had the problem that there was no fighting fund, not even to obtain preliminary advice. Even sending out circulars was costly, and when he had asked a few supporters to kick in to help defray that expense he was dismayed at the disinterest of some owners, who were on his side, but only in words, and if it wasn't for the generosity of others he might have thrown in the towel. The McGinty group - reduced at the top by Binny's showing her face less and less in the politics of the condominium - had no such restriction, as the resources and services of Prince were always at hand, paid for by the owners through the board. Its employees were wise in procedural matters of condo administration, and for that to be available to the power bloc, but not to Barney, put him at a continuing disadvantage.

It seemed to him the donkey vote had returned a director allied to the nucleus mentioned, so neutering the hostile minority directors. Barney predicted that such a board could not work harmoniously, and would continue the biased governance he had long complained of. This would extend to control of the arbitration, and nothing could be more suitable for Ed, or more damaging for Barney. The board engaged an attorney to represent the condo there, and it nominated secretary Abraham Mayer to instruct him, which was a means of the power bloc getting its way. Substantially the same directors had engineered the August special meeting that gave the third option to the McGintys. They had represented the OSMs then. Now one of them, Mayer, the leading one for the matter under consideration, was to give instructions in the arbitration. They were now representing the board. It was unlikely that those instructions would undermine the board's approval of the third option for the OSMs, and so their damaging influence of the McGinty stooges would continue. The brief to the attorney was mainly oral, and not publicized, so Barney could only guess at its content. Still, he considered his case to be pretty strong, even if the board's case were to be put in terms that the McGintys would be pleased with, and would not reflect any wish at all by the board, representing the owners, for the August meeting to be invalidated, and a new meeting held with Barney's motion on the agenda. Although unethical, that did not surprise him. He was left with trusting to luck, and the good sense of the arbitrator.

But the arbitration went the wrong way for him when the award came. It concentrated on several points: one, the commercial consideration of denying an OSMs an extension; and that even though the owners had later voted for the comparative modeling, that did not mean they would have voted against the extension had the analysis motion been on the same agenda; and the owners had not lost the right to self-management should they want it, which was a decision far from made. The findings were a blow to Barney and his friends, who believed a different award might have come had not the power bloc had control of the owners' case. He suspected too a judicial trend of sympathy toward OSMs, maybe because the contracts were their livelihood, but he had no proof of the notion, which he admitted to himself was bizarre. The power bloc was content with the award, and said so at the next board meeting, where the president said there was a need to finalize the matter, longstanding and disruptive as it had been, so if there were to be any move to upset the award the board should hear and deal with it promptly. Josh Spinks added that he had asked around about such a step, and had been advised that it could turn out to be a very involved lawsuit, which would cost the association a very large amount of money, with very little prospect of success. Still, it was open to directors to pursue the matter, or at least test the feeling of the board with a suitable motion. After this the minority group met, in dismay, to discuss the matter. They did not invite Barney into their discussion, which he did not mind, as his policy was to be free from obligation to directors, and by declining all opportunities to stand for committee, he had no claim to the status of de facto director. He was sure though they had been spooked by the Spinks' commentary, including as it had, reference to a risk of personal liability of the directors for the costs of an appeal, which he took to be so much humbug, as they would have been indemnified, on his understanding of the governing documents, where directors acting in good faith and without negligence were protected. He was not surprised when, in July, the board resolved, unanimously, to accept the award, so that for the board and the owners the matter was closed, and the third option stood. The unanimity incidentally protected the power bloc directors from any risk of being sued for bad faith in their handling of the arbitration. Not recorded was a stipulation, required by the minority directors, for the board's legal expenses of the arbitration not to be charged to Barney, as might otherwise have been the case.

The board implemented Barney's modeling motion through a committee, required by the motion to be the treasurer and two co-opted members, being former directors. By a tricky move the co-opted members were not strictly eligible, and definitely not within the range Barney had in mind, and he was not consulted on this clearly contrived appointment. Management of the analysis was entrusted to a firm to be selected by Prince, who also were to be active in its administration. The professional qualification - independent accountant - required was stated in the motion, but the firm selected was not of that sort. Barney objected to those non-compliant features, to which Prince did not reply, and the only response was from the then treasurer who, without addressing the objection, insisted the procedures were in order, and Barney let it be, as he believed the treasurer to be commercially naïve, and unfamiliar with business language, and in the McGinty camp anyway. Moreover, the analysis had no immediate significance, and any results it produced could be reviewed later, if a change in management style continued to be of interest to owners. And Barney put around that he would seek review when the time was ripe.

A condo with several points of similarity to Gran Capitan, if a little older, stood nearby, and had been under self-management from its beginning. Barney had been concerned that this other, The Towers of Gold, be included in the analysis. In one of his circulars to owners, a habit essential for getting his arguments known, he had commended it as an ideal reference point in measuring expenditures under different management regimes. It had seemed so obvious that it never occurred to him that the study would not take it in, because even without his prompting, the people doing the analysis could not have failed to see the construction, large and handsome, and close by, so he knew the owners had been taken for another ride, this time at the hands of the committee handling the modeling, and he wondered how so many the disturbing events could have occurred in the one condo, and figuratively shook himself in case he was dreaming.

The analysis had been worthwhile, even though flawed. It was almost as if the research firm had been instructed, maybe secretly, to ignore self-managed condos of like size to Gran Capitan, but even so, the result showed self-management to be less costly than the McGinty contract, and this finding compensated a little for the expensive damage of the third option. It showed a flash of hope that the conspirators weren't sure to win every round.

By now Barney and supporters were accustomed to Ed's team always working for their star regardless of the interests of the owners, and the McGintys had little need to personally promote their cause any more. With the arbitration concluded in favor of the power bloc and the OSMs and the third option, Gran Capitan faced long years of the same type of management. Moderately encouraging signs for the future were that many more condo owners had come to see the truth of the management issues, including that the contract was lop-sided, and that its terms and conditions, including compensation and standards required for works, should have been revised before any question of extension was entertained. And that the election of the 1988 board had been rigged, and the owners duped. And that the board under the power bloc, aided by the devious Prince style of reporting board business, kept owners in an information fog, and by diverse means bullied dissident owners. And that the modeling motion had been kept off the meeting agenda as part of a conspiracy to help the OSMs and harm the owners. Those matters, and others less important, became talking points among owners; or rather, those owners who were interested, only rarely a little more than half the total. Although owners were never united on an issue, enough were sickened by the apparent conspiracy and maladministration of their condo and the activities of the OSMs to withdraw respect from the McGintys, and replace it with hostility, which discomforted the OSMs, who tended to react aggressively, in ways too petty and numerous to mention, none of which endeared them to owners. The records of board meetings showed Prince in tune with the OSMs, following an established style. Ed took to sending out circulars denigrating his main opponents, including the minority directors, and often including two owners, former directors who had openly opposed the McGinty push for a 25-year term a couple of years earlier. Barney was not usually on the hit list, and he could only guess at the reason, without concern.

It was to be expected that the strained and divisive atmosphere of the Gran Capitan community would drive the McGintys into selling their contract, especially as its value would have risen with the addition of the third option. The power bloc of the 1989 board, with Josh Spinks in the vanguard, showed great prejudice, and open bullying, against the minority directors, and against non-supportive owners, but the atmosphere still continued oppressive for the McGintys and, separately, they took up residences elsewhere, which they claimed was justified by the wording of the contract. The owners were nonplussed by neither OSM living in, and it did not please them. However, it was legal, as it appeared the OSMs could meet the residence condition through a nominated employee spending his nights at the condo, and standing in for the OSM on other occasions. In addition, and as an illustration of the emerging gulf between the owners and the OSMs, Ed advised that although the office had been open for certain hours from the commencement of the project, those hours did not need to be kept, as the contract only stipulated something less, and so they were reduced. And other contract issues, of little real significance, became debating points in the embittered atmosphere.

Although it was a great pity that owners of condos at Gran Capitan did not see more clearly, and earlier, where their true interests lay, and how they were being misled, and their trust abused, it is necessary to understand their average position. Essentially, they were vulnerable as they entered into ownership of their condo units. Who among them had previous experience in the specialized area of complex contracts, such as those for the management of a condo scheme? Sure, upon purchase, they had the governing documents and the management contract to read, though for many the documents might as well have been written in Aramaic; that is, if they took the trouble to read them at all. Or they could have them explained by their attorney, and thereafter could not reasonably plead ignorance, but often were so in fact. Most came ill-prepared to face clauses in complex contracts for the supply of services by independent contractors, being OSMs. The area of options for extension to such contracts was also perplexing. In a sense, mini-agreements in their own rights, they were also add-ons to the main contract, so problems of interpretation were magnified. If that was how it was for an owner, little wonder that he or she became reliant on others for guidance, and here they generally looked to the people in power, and this attitude was quite acceptable to the likes of the McGintys and the 1988-1989 power blocs. Absent a sea-change in control, passing from those unable or unwilling to observe the law of the condo, as stipulated in the governing documents, to others who would, many owners were set to long remain mental captives of their strange environment. It had been created by a rapacious developer, and nurtured by crooks known as directors and the administration manager, and by OSMs determined to advance their personal ambitions above those of the owners at all times. The longer change was delayed, the more extensive the damage to the development and its inhabitants. Legislatures would have served their constituents well by closer supervision of the initial phases of condo developments, when new owners were ignorant, and often leaderless, without impinging on a general hands-off attitude. Callous developers and managerial crooks see the dividing line well enough. Decisions made early in the life of a condo often affect later waves of condo owners, as well as the early birds. And probing might show some of the key figures in the early life of some condos to be little more than stooges for the developer.

By the time of the annual owners meeting in December 1989, when the election of a new board was part of the business, not only were many owners disillusioned with the past control of their joint property and affairs, but felt divisions and suspicion everywhere, so that the traditional openness of neighbors in casual encounters among themselves was diminished.

But new blood was available for the new board. A voting ticket for them was promoted by rebel owners, led by the Jones. The former power bloc had lost much allure and unity, and no longer were they or Ed influential in owner's voting patterns, yet he presented a ticket headed by its remnants. The new-broom ticket was completely successful, to the great and obvious disappointment of the former power bloc members. It was not all clear sailing though. The OSM contract had several years to run, even without counting the contentious third option, and Prince remained the administration manager, with a year of its contract to run.

The McGintys apparently did not see that by not selling the contract while the conspirators held the reins, they were missing their best opportunity of capitalizing on the swindle. Maybe success had dulled the sharp edge of apprehension. Maybe they were preoccupied with domestic concerns. A window of opportunity for selling the contract with the third option intact had been opened by the board's decision not to contest the arbitrator's award, and was closed when the power bloc lost office. It had been open from July to December, when the election results closed it with a bang. It would have been barely possible to sell such a complex asset within that period had the OSMs acted swiftly, and had they done so the third option would have been a legitimate part of the offering. But upon the new directors taking charge, among them some smarting from past denigration by the conspirators, and Prince staff members, and Ed, the OSMs previous unduly cozy relationship with the board and with Prince instantly dissolved. Ed knew he would have to deal now with a hostile board, without the staff of Prince at his beck and call. In addition, the new board showed immediately that it would contest, by any legal means available, the validity of the third option.

A small pointer to the future, and to the personalities of the dominant men in the deposed and new regimes respectively, was an encounter in the meeting room right after the election meeting, while people were milling around before leaving. Josh Spinks was talking with another man, when the new president, uninvited, butted in to ask: "What do you think of a vice president who is in the manager's pocket?" Before the other man, taken aback, could reply Spinks, a sometime linebacker of the New York Jets, responded savagely: "Come outside and say that and I'll knock your block off!"

14

The new board hammers the excessive compensation of the management contract - resents the third option - makes selling the contract difficult - the McGintys interpret contract conditions narrowly for their own advantage

Manuel Martin was the president of the new board. Darkly handsome, taller and fairer than most folk of Hispanic ancestry, articulate, he carried an alert though cordial expression which served him well in meeting and negotiating with people. He had long experience in costing contracts in the course of his oil industry maintenance service business, and nothing could be of greater value for the fleshing out, in table form, of the basic work already carried out by Barney. And by obtaining, and adding in, the figures from Towers of Gold, which had been wrongfully omitted from the modeling implemented by the former board, Manuel shortly came up with a worksheet to confirm the excessive compensation the owners would be paying the OSMs under the third option, as compared with hypothetical self-management for the same period. He showed firmly what the figures meant to each condo owner per year through enlarged assessments. The owners could now see more clearly what Barney had been telling them: how their pockets were hit for millions by the management regime imposed on the condo at its inception, and prospectively, by the grant of the third option. It was one thing for a single owner, such as Barney Jones, to make and report on his calculations, and another for the president to use that work and add to it, and make a further report which carried the stamp of authority. Ed contested the figures, and his own were pretty well done, and like as not, if left alone, would have convinced most readers. But Manuel was not to be bettered, and returned to the fray by dissecting Ed's minutely, compelling doubt on them, and causing Ed to withdraw from the battle of the numbers, leaving many condo owners convinced they had been suckers of the first order from day one. And to add to Ed's discomfort, Manuel made clear his board would contest the validity of the third option, if at all possible.

The McGintys soon became very keen to sell their contract, while no doubt kicking themselves for having missed the boat after the arbitration had been finalized. But here they struck a snag. When a prospective buyer came to be interviewed by the directors, because they had responsibilities to the owners to ensure that an incoming OSM was suitable in character and in experience and financially, Manuel explained the board's attitude, which included an intention to deny the third option if lawful grounds were to be found. The inquirer asked how that could be, as he had understood the grant had been through the arbitration mill, and had come out clean. Manuel replied that while that was so, his board saw the matter as so grave, and so colored by strange activity of the former board, and of such enduringly adverse financial impact, the board was duty bound to put it through any mill available. He was not wanting to put the buyer off, and indeed it could well be that the owners would be very glad to have him serving them as OSM, but he felt obliged to state the exact position. The buyer pressed for more details, and Manuel replied that the board would not say anything that might limit its position. So many disturbing events had occurred, and their analysis was an ongoing affair, but underlying all was the belief that the third option was suspect because of apparent deception in its creation, and his board did not believe it was morally right that the McGintys should keep it, yet of course they may do so, if that were the law.

The buyer took this story back to Ed, and dropped out. Ed hit the roof, and through Angel Tejero sued Manuel, alleging that Manuel had defamed him by telling the buyer he should not go ahead because Ed was a bad man to deal with, and so had lost him a sale. There was a little truth in the allegation, if not as much as Ed said. Manuel called the buyer and told him of the suit, and wanted to clear up any doubts about what he, as board spokesman, had said. He went over his recollection of the discussion. The buyer replied that was pretty well as he recalled the meeting, and that was what he would say if called as a witness in the case. Still, Ed must have seen more in the matter than that summary, as the McGintys sustained their suit, and were not put off it by Angel, even though he advised it would be long in getting to a hearing in court, and expensive to lose.

Ed tried again to sell the contract, but the word was about that the third option was not assured, so he had to factor that into the asking price. However, little happened, which may suggest to the reader that even after the price was lowered, few prospects thought much of the asset, and that among the factors to be weighed was fear of a carry-over of the widely-known board antagonism toward the McGintys.

Barney's retired and elderly attorney friend, and neighbor, Charles Olly, occasionally helped him with legal aspects of his Gran Capitan concerns, without claiming any expertise in condos. Of course, that changed as he took an increasing interest in the local troubles, and Barney and Zina got deeper into them. When he heard of the board's attitude probably having the effect of deterring prospective buyers, he had said to Barney:

"I wonder if attitudes aggressively aimed at frustrating a sale might have the result of harming the owners. Say Ed were to sue on the basis of the directors having a general duty to support the contract, which duty was violated by blocking a sale without substantial cause, based on suspicion, and the hope of something turning up. He just might have something. Besides, you said you think the board is hopeful of pinning contract violations on the OSMs, as a path toward termination of the contract, including the third option of course. Now, I'm a little at sea in this area, but I'd guess that violations should be disclosed to the OSMs and complained about promptly, as delay could deny them the chance of making good, and so they might not turn out to be as powerful against the OSMs as we would like. But I'm not familiar with the procedures, which I suppose are set out in the governing documents, and also in the management contract for dealing with violations of all types, and I hope Manuel and the directors are following them carefully."

But the board had not asked for advice from the Jones/Olly corner, being seemingly self-contained in the area of legal analysis, so the friends kept quiet, and waited to be invited, with this exception. Barney successfully proposed to the 1989 annual meeting, as a follow-up to his modeling work, that each year the budget report should include comparisons between the actual expense of management for the past year, and the hypothetical expense had Gran Capitan been operating under self-management. As he said to Charles and Zina:

"For one year it doesn't matter, but add the figures over the years before self-management can kick in, and the total could be telling in a tight vote on that issue."

Zina asked: "What if the figures aren't your way?"

He shrugged a reply, "Too bad. The owners deserve to know the facts."

The McGintys were not badly placed though, despite not selling. They had a couple of years to run in the present phase of their contract, and an expectation of extending the term by the exercise of the second option in 1990, and the prospect of further extension, in 1995, under the third option. The latter aside, they could still do well under the current detached management arrangements, where they resided away, and supervised performance of the contract through employees, in much the same way as managing agent firms operated. By living away they also reduced embarrassing contacts with owners who had been their friends, and had changed.

Since the new board had become hard on the McGintys, Ed had read and analyzed the contract conditions closely, and found benefits through construing contractual obligations loosely, and rights tightly, leaving it to the board to make of it what they could, knowing the OSMs could always respond to a complaint, even one in the form of a violation notice, for such invariably and compulsorily mentioned not only the alleged violation, but also the harm of it, and how it might be remedied, and the time allowed for doing so, failing which a dispute resolution conference was mandated, and if that were to fail, the board could hold the OSMs in default of the contract, and claim its termination. As the whole procedure, found in both the contract and the governing documents, was new for him, and pleasantly drawn out, it took him some time to understand its leniency for OSMs whose object was to earn maximum profit from the Gran Capitan contract, without losing it. To make sure he was getting it right, he took Angel into his confidence, and through him found what the directors could do in respect of alleged violations, and that the same steps were to be followed for each case, and multiple violations could not readily be lumped together. The contract required similar procedure upon an allegation of violation. Besides, the board was hampered in acting on violations, through the need for observance of due process through prior directors' and even owner meetings, and engaging its attorney to prepare notices and provide advice, whereas the OSMs only had themselves, and sometimes Angel, to consult, so could make decisions faster, and in greater secrecy. Once the OSMs knew they could legally live away, they also found they could work outside the condominium, which led to Ed obtaining concurrent appointment as OSM to another, new, district condominium, again a BBC development. Because of the loose wording of the contract, the owners were stuck with the changes.

15

The new directors get lucky in the basement - the struggle takes a new course - suspicions turn into evidence of a conspiracy - what to do about it? - President Manuel disappoints Barney

When Prince lost office at the annual meeting in late 1990, it handed over the records of the association to its successor, Condo Administration Inc. (CA), which held them for a few months then, in need of storage space, found it by returning older records for the board to keep, for which there was space in a condo basement. Some months later, a director searched there for something she didn't find, but was astonished to find instead something much more important.

Another woman, Grace Gambell, had been a founding member of Prince Inc. in 1960, and had become prominent in the unit industry in southern California, along with the firm. Her drive and expertise and vigorous rivalry aimed at keeping others in their place, and Prince on top, had been a significant factor in Prince success. Her drive dropped off with affluence and the lure of leisure, though it remained important to her that Gran Capitan remain a client, because of her longstanding closeness to BBC, and the size and prestige of the condo. So after Prince's service had attracted criticism from successive boards, and even requests not to apply for renewal of its contract, Grace employed her considerable persuasive skills, and knowledge and experience in fixing association elections, and to the wonder of its many critics, at the annual general meeting in late 1987, obtained for Prince a three-year extension of term, 1988-1990. The 1988 board, McGinty-nominated, had been elected at the same meeting. This, now the Bernard Brooks board, claimed a foul, but lacking both experience and evidence, it could only declare no confidence in Prince, and request its resignation. But such thrusts were easily parried by Grace, as she knew the new Prince contract was in order. So when she resigned from her firm a year later, she was pleased it had kept the Gran Capitan business. By then, much of the fire and contention associated with the third option had abated, and Gran Capitan had become just one of many clients of Prince with whom Grace had worked. When she began to spend more time on retirement plans her concerns about past clients had dropped sharply, and when she finally called it a day she had made no special arrangements to safeguard the firm against past problems. Maybe she looked and saw none. More likely there were so many she could not find a starting point that would not lead into the sort of heavy detail she had thrived on once, but which was now boring. But certainly, when Prince lost the Gran Capitan contract at the annual meeting in December 1990, to end its three-year term, there was little concern at base where they kept an eye on the statistics, and were content so long as client numbers kept up. By then

Grace was so deep into retirement Gran Capitan belonged to a dimming past.

Ed's first thought on news of Grace's retirement had been for the records, of which he had but little personal knowledge, but knew they were important. He had supposed that she, being well used to concealing evidence, and skilled in manipulating circumstances to suit the needs of her main client of the moment, Grace would have taken care of everything. So he felt sure all incriminating evidence from the activity in 1988 would have been hidden or destroyed, including that of conspiracy, which he knew Barney alleged to be the basis of the successful play for grant of the third option. Ed had not spoken with Grace on this subject, having total confidence in her attention to such important detail, and her awareness of the danger inherent in Barney's activities, but as time passed, and within the condo resentment of the third option grew, he worried. He also became concerned that the directors who had been his co-conspirators might not have had enough interest in the whole matter to perceive threat, or if they had done so, gone further than destroying personal files, and for the rest assumed that Grace, the one skilled in dirty tricks, and whose firm was document custodian, would have done whatever was needed for mutual security. He did not know that when in office the former directors had not been empowered to order destruction of recent records, because of several sets of restrictions implied in the governing documents of the condo, and set out in taxation and securities laws. Out of office, those directors had no access to them. And even though Prince remained in office for a year after the new-broom board came in, it had lost all capacity for any sort of cover-up, such as fiddling the books, as it would have been pointless to seek approval from the new, hostile, board, and dangerous to act without it. So, after Grace retired, and a new board reigned, the records were firmly in the wrong hands for the McGintys. Ed then suspected a time-bomb somewhere, and he could only hope it would never go off.

He knew the records were double-locked away below, but he had no key, and no right of entry. The new directors assumed the records had been neutered by the conspirators, who had amply shown their devious capabilities. But those new chums had not learned about the barriers against destruction, nor taken into account the ebbing of interest by the former directors and Grace, as they grew away, over time, from the conspiracy, and from control of the condo. The McGintys had the most at stake and Ed, its main director, had dropped his guard, thinking Grace had matters in hand, and it became too late.

Assumptions that the archives in the basement were barren proved very wrong. In fact, even though every document of the fateful period was not there, those at hand were enough. It was a find of the very highest significance for anybody who had sensed a conspiracy that some saw as the Gran Capitan equivalent of the Great Train Robbery; and like it, would take time to clean up. There was much speculation about how this unexpected appearance of secret records had come about, but no answers, other than the obvious one of mistake, and whose it was did not matter to the new directors. As the director at the forefront of the discovery, Libby Ryan, said to Manuel:

"I thought the first lesson all crooks learned was to destroy the evidence", to which he replied:

"And it is; but as in everything, it must be someone's job, or else it could be left to the other guy, which could mean nobody in particular. And I guess the Bernard Brooks gang being out of office for a year before Prince got the axe, and Grace having already retired, the crooks dropped their guard, so it became nobody's work."

Said Libby: "So there was our lucky break. Who could have dreamed it? Yippeeee! Thanks and salutations to the bitch. I'll make sure her pals know she did it; or rather, didn't."

Manuel added: "Go for it, but do it informally. The sooner they start worrying the better. It's becoming our turn now. We must tell the board what we've found, and get their permission for investigating this new evidence for the conspiracy we've suspected all along, besides any other breaches of duty that might appear."

Libby said: "There's a lot of stuff, and it's not organized, so we must get a plan for sifting and culling and noting it up, otherwise we'll get lost."

"I agree. Right. Why don't we allow a few days weekly for a while and see how far we get?"

"That'll do. This sort of work is not for everybody, and some of our directors have no real understanding of the fraud, which they can catch up on as we go, but we don't want to waste time teaching them right now." She paused, then added, "Okay, do we keep all this under wraps, and not tell the owners?"

"You mean not until we've done our homework? Asked Manuel. Maybe we should put it this way. There's a pile of material about the 1988 activity at hand, and we're working on it to see what's in it for the condo owners. That way, no secrets. But we had better see what the board thinks first. How's that??"

"Yep. Right on."

Yet Manuel was so thrilled by the discovery he was almost ready to broadcast news of the find right there and then, and pictured in his mind a lead-in line, like "Let's nail the rats," followed by an account of how the records had been revealed, and appeared to contain evidence needed to prosecute conspiracy, and for other violations of duty by multiple parties, including the former directors. But discretion took over, and he let it rest, as agreed with Libby.

The records gave a valuable insight into the workings of the old board, including incriminating activities, and absence of due process, by directors, Prince, the McGintys, and Angel Tejero. Ed emerged as the OSMs front man and driving force. The researchers quickly saw material apparently damming of the cheats, and working it into the timeframe of the events before and after the special meeting of August 1988 became their challenge, and it soon appeared it could be done.

The find was a great and pleasant surprise to all current directors, along with many condo owners. A case floundering for want of evidence was to be turned around though carelessness, and whose did not matter, for the records were owners' property, and had come into the directors' hands legitimately. They provided a prima facie conclusion that several parties, very prominent among them some 1988 directors of the Bernard Brooks board, had conspired together to advance the interests of the OSMs, without regard for the interests of the owners, which for directors had been their primary duty under the Declaration.

President Manuel became the driving force behind the board's building up its case. The task was made harder by the poor quality of the records of meetings kept by the Prince folk, due partly to their incompetence, and probably partly with intent to obscure deceitful activities. As the work was tedious for all but the very dedicated, and the detail almost overwhelming, most board members lost passion quickly, after initial amazement and resentment at many parties coming together to deceive and deprive the condo owners of their rights. Manuel and Libby stayed the course, but more help was needed, and they turned to non-directors. First Barney, whose interest had been well displayed, and through him, Charles Olly. Together, they compiled a statement of mixed fact and law they called Notes, with attachments, aiming to provide the board's attorney with a good basis for advising. Their consensual view was that several parties, having functions and duties in and about the condo, had conspired to produce a result for the McGintys that could not have been obtained had they not been, as Charles Olly put it, negligent, and deceitful, and in breach of fiduciary duty to the owners. And they noted Angel's letters advising the OSMs at several points, and Ed's adoption of their content in his dealings with the board and Prince, so they became his own contributions.

Manuel was a forceful leader, and enthusiastic in seeking justice for the owners. At times his zeal, and considerable self-confidence, led him down the wrong paths, which would not matter but for them sometimes passing through attorney's doors, by which expensive means he obtained much advice about the legal complexities of condo disputes, but not all of it to do with the central issues. His dominance of the board, which he once had justified with the words 'it's my show', and his fervent belief in his legal theories of the moment, were such that the others had little to say in that area. Of course, as the whole affair was exceedingly unusual, it was beyond anybody's prior experience. It really deserved the expertise of a DA's investigation team, one that specialized in condo malfeasance, and if such a team existed, it was not available for hire by a private community like Gran Capitan. So the investigation had to proceed through the enthusiastic but inexpert efforts of a few board members, who had to get legal advice at times, and even choosing the questions to ask of lawyers was a problem, and so mistakes were made there, and the attorney's fees were the same notwithstanding; and even they found much that was hard going, for it was a unique case. At length, chastened by poor results from his substantially solo sleuthing, but remaining resolute in a desire for justice for the condo owners, Manuel sought further discussion with Barney and Charles Olly. Moreover, although it was but little known so far, he was concerned, as were some owners, about a budget blowout for legal expense, which could turn around with good results in some ongoing lawsuits in other areas of the condo's affairs, but for the time being it was a sore spot, and so he wished to keep away from fee-charging attorneys as much as possible.

Manuel told Charles and Barney that his board was looking at activities classifiable as contract violations, and would soon serve notice of them on the OSMs, as the first step in a procedure to be followed before termination of the contract could be declared. The chance of an end to the management contract that way was enticing. Charles supposed that, with so much at stake, Ed would contest each one, and also look into appeal prospects if things went bad for him. Violation/termination procedure seemed to Charles to aim most firmly at the confirmed violator, and that inherent in it was a bias toward protecting an OSM who was no more than an occasional or minor violator, so that managerial imperfections might not always be transformable into grounds for termination of contract. Charles saw past the simple words about violation notices and termination, and was not sure that courts would deal with all such matters literally, and in any case the prospect of prolonged litigation was there. He saw the alleged violations as only OSM matters, and quite separate from the conspiracy of several parties that had led to the grant of the third option. He took it that if the board was able to terminate the contract for violations, the whole contract, and not only the third option, would be finished, and the three men agreed that would be enough, and nothing more need thereafter be sought from the conspirators, regardless of the extent or nature of their wrong-doing.

As to the conspiracy question, a fairly strong and clear case was present. The third option could not otherwise have been obtained. Naturally there were leaders and followers among the perpetrators, and it was in this area that conflicts of views among the reviewing group first emerged. Manuel was keen to protect the lesser lights, and while Charles agreed with the sentiment, boards acted as a single unit, so that unless a director had distanced himself clearly from a particular decision, he or she was complicit, and could be held liable along with the others. But it also seemed possible to Charles to prosecute only the leaders, as long as everybody knew those might join other directors as co-defendants, and that would be beyond the control of the prosecutor.

While assisting the board during investigations, Barney had spoken with Ronald Smart, who had been a director in 1988 under Bernard Brooks, and was currently serving again under Manuel. Barney took him to have been only a supporter of the front runners in the conspiracy, which of course was bad enough, considering that the Declaration imposed a positive duty on directors to support only the interests of the condo owners. Barney knew he favored contract management, and supposed that accounted for Ed luring Ronald to the Bernard Brooks board. His presence on both boards reflected both his quiet competence, and unassertive personality, while neither explaining nor excusing his continuance on the Manuel Martin board following the basement find. He remained as if the activities of the 1988 board had no connection to him, which was delusive, as he had been a compliant voting director right through. But Barney badly needed moles, to explain some basement records, and some points of board activity, so he planned on grooming Ronald as a helper, while neutering him as a current board member. However, at the point that Ronald was considering Barney's plan, Manuel had stepped in, and told Barney that Ronald was needed to help in the compilation of the forthcoming budget, that for the year 1992, and also in examining possible overcharging by Prince for past services. Barney knew that all that work could be carried out as well by CA, or alternatively by an accountant. But as Manuel would have known that, there was no point in protesting his decision, so he concluded the discussion with the observation that his and Manuel's ideas of good corporate governance differed. In reply Manuel explained that the way he was organizing it Ronald would be excluded by a Chinese wall from relevant committee activity concerning the investigation, so there would be no problems there. Barney, well experienced in the supposed protections of such walls, did not share that confident view for a small and somewhat inexperienced board, but as there were other things to worry about, he accepted the situation, putting Manuel's attitude down to something unstated, but which could surface later. That was the start of a few differences between the two men. Barney remained perplexed that the directors had not seen the futility of an investigation in which one of their own was a prospective, if minor, target. It was like a police investigation team having a suspect on board, and could only be explained by widespread disinterest, and commercial ignorance, among the directors. He did not understand how Manuel could protect him, knowing the risk of hampering the completeness of the investigation, and the bringing to account of offenders. The explanation would come later. Part of it was that Manuel had started to lose interest in conspiracy as a remedy for the condo owners. It was not announced, and it took Barney a while to see it was the fact.

After the find in the basement, the president had openly compared it to a gold strike, and stressed its potential in aid of a lawsuit against alleged conspirators. At the annual meeting of owners later that year a motion authorizing legal investigation had been put and passed, and he had stated to the members present it was the board's intention, if the investigation and legal advice justified it, thereafter to start lawsuits. Another time he had said, in discussing the involvement of a particular director, "they were all in it".

From such and similar comment Barney supposed the case to be conspiracy with multiple defendants, and not being privy to board activities, and for want of better knowledge, he took it that was the way the board was proceeding. From time to time, as matters apparently worthy of the board's consideration in its legal work on the case occurred to him, he sent them on, and that they brought no reply did not disturb him, as he knew that in voluntary bodies, such as condo boards, clerical output was not always of a high standard. But in due course, after allowing ample time, it seemed strange he had heard nothing from either the board or its attorney, as the long Notes should have prompted questions. He allayed his concerns by assuming that the attorney had referred tough points to trial counsel, and that a written opinion on significant aspects of the case was, or soon would be, held by the board. He supposed that it was easier to picture a civil conspiracy and talk about it, than to prove it in court, and few attorneys would have that particular tort at their finger-tips. Eventually, he wrote to the board asking for a copy of the legal advice, and was immediately struck by the offhand nature of the response, and found, after prodding, there was none. That to Barney meant that contrary to his expectations, the board had gone cold on the idea of suing for conspiracy, and instead was concentrating on OSM contract violations, at the end of successful prosecution of which the contract hopefully could be terminated for default. He had not been told. That was astonishing treachery. It was his due to be told.

Delivery of the Notes to the attorney, with a verbal introduction from Manuel, and a discussion about what the directors expected, and what it might cost, had been a small ceremony. The exhibits were managed by Libby, whose clerical help was to be available to the attorney, Tom Apponi, an expert in the law of condos and other community title schemes, whose office was readily accessible from Gran Capitan. He saw that the Notes would take quite a lot of reading time, before he turned to consideration of the possible causes of action, whether or not mentioned in the Notes. It was an interesting and challenging brief, and he wondered from the start if he was up to it, but decided to find out. He supposed from Manuel's words that he would be able, indeed expected to, refer the tough points to a trial lawyer.

On their attendance on him with the Notes the directors had noticed Tom's files overflowing from shelves and pigeon-holes, seemingly into any free space, including the floor, and his desk, so that he had little more than his blotting pad free before him. At one end of the desk the files were high enough to cause Libby, seated in a low chair, and being a short person, to sit up high to be on approximately eye level with Tom, who also was short, and seemed to slump down, rather than sit up, so that Libby wondered if he might submerge there one day, into a legal files equivalent of quicksand. The conference was interrupted several times by inwards telephone calls, of which a few were urgent enough for Tom to excuse himself to deal with briefly, and the visitors could only guess at the frustration of callers, who through ruses had broken past the receptionist, even though Tom was in conference. Not that he was ever ruffled, and after every interruption returned his attention cleanly to the point of departure. Manuel and Libby wondered where their case would rank in his priorities, for which there was obvious competition, and Manuel decided to find out through the making of another appointment for a week later, in order to discuss progress. Tom prevaricated about that, but Manuel insisted, while half expecting a message later postponing it. Disturbed as the clients were, they could not help noticing that Tom had his wits about him, and a strong awareness of the items that made up each pile of files, and pads of notes, like the one he was using in their conference, and had not the slightest tendency to panic, or even to break his even rhythm. He was composed come what may, and Manuel decided that maybe he was just different, and that could not justify their walking out to look for another attorney. Certainly Tom's questions of the visitors were perceptive. And it was no surprise when he explained that the complications and the range of wrongfulness was so vast it would be easy for him to err, and so he wanted permission to obtain an opinion on several preliminary points from specialist counsel. This immediately doubled the attorney's fees in Manuel's mind, just to shape up the case, and apart from expert advice later from a trial attorney on selected topics. Manuel's dilemma now was that he had spent considerable sums on advice and other legal activity on several issues, not only the 1988 scam, with little to show for any of it, which did not sit well with the image of efficiency for himself he had promoted and enjoyed around the condo, and which his detractors did not share. Now Tom was advising that the task ahead could be gargantuan in both time and money. Manuel had been involved in lawsuits in business over the years and was aware that fees could blow out painfully, but he had no prior experience of the law in a condo environment, and had much to learn there. He had known from the outset that the Notes portrayed a multitude of possible defendants and actionable events, and that it was unlikely that one lawyer practicing alone, especially if he were not a commercial litigation specialist, could know enough, or invest the necessary time in research, to come up with telling advice. Yet it had seemed right that the attorney at first instance should have an overall view of the case, via the Notes, before turning to specifics.

Manuel requested Tom to sort the facts and prospective defendants and possible actions into a priority list for their joint discussion. He surprised Manuel by producing it within the week, so that in their next conference they had something manageable to work on.

What Tom did not know at first was Manuel's concern about the legal expenses actually incurred, and in prospect, for several matters at Gran Capitan, and so had lately adopted a minimalist approach to litigation. Ed had sensed the problem about legal expenses and taunted Manuel about having to consider a special levy on owners, which was denied by Manuel, without the denial being thoroughly convincing. But denial made it more important for Manuel to avoid it, in the interests of his image as a competent leader. The truth is hard to find in such a situation. It's easy to crash budgets through the unpredictability of litigation expense, and to keep up appearances many a board faced with a blow-out has deferred expenditure somewhere else, short-sighted policy though it may be. But fear of criticism can produce awkward results. At the time, at Gran Capitan, the existing suits involving other contractors for maintenance works allegedly faulty, and the OSMs in respect of gardening and other disputes, meant that legal expenses were indeed a problem already. If all the cases resulted favorably for the board, in short time all would be well, but otherwise distorted budgets would be the order of the day for a while, absent a special levy. Tom soon got the picture, and modified his own views about the case to meet those of the client.

The legal expense blow-out issue had made Manuel think that Ronald Smart would be the right assistant in framing the budget, he being the most experienced director in that line. And as he had been on the 1988 board as well, he would come grateful for Manuel's protection. And he would work for nothing, as a current director. He was certainly a timely and congenial appointment for Manuel. The budget when produced showed high legal expense, without details and that was, at least for the time being, acceptable to uncritical owners. Later, as owners tired of ongoing the internal conflicts, the legals and their underlying detail would attract more intensive interest from them, and questions; though it was well known that questions from owners on quasi-technical matters often lacked penetration, and so were readily answered by a competent propagandist, such as Manuel, using board facilities in the ordinary way, and the facility of which was unavailable to the inquirer, whose tenacity might in consequence be dented right away. It was clear to Barney that the condo system, with its ingredients of many uninformed or uninterested owners, a high level of administrative and legal complexity, and control by a few authority figures of the avenues for communication and propaganda, favored the power and influence of vigorous leaders.

Barney sustained his discontent with Ronald Smart, and in a circular to owners suggested they not appoint any member of the 1988 board to office ever again, unless he or she first answered on oath a series of pointed questions, which were listed, and the veracity of which he had sworn to in an affidavit filed with CA. All those directors were named. He knew his action was bold, and could seem arrogant to some owners, yet to him it was necessary. And it was also a form of insurance against future strife, as he knew the questions he put up could not be answered truthfully without self-incrimination. Its immediate effect was that Ronald stepped down.

So Manuel arguably had reason to avoid a complex lawsuit based on conspiracy, even though it was the main cause of much pain and inconvenience and millions of dollars over-spent in management expense, to be borne by the condo owners. That is to say, had not the conspiracy yielded the third option, conflict between Ed, on the one hand, and on the other, the new board, and Manuel alone, could not have grown as it had, to amount to mutual and open derision. And there was no end in sight. But for the third option, Ed and Binny would have finished their contract in a few short years, without the problems of their effort to prolong it, and of Manuel's boards to deny it; all engendering much friction and expense for all parties. That was apart from the financial aspects of a conspiracy lawsuit. Its cost was a danger. What the violation-termination path might cost in money and effort was also unknown. No foreknowledge was available. Still, violations were easier to understand and process than a conspiracy prosecution, and much of the procedural work about them could be managed in-house, and so confine legal expense. Many uncertainties remained. And it was not as though termination proceedings, like conspiracy prosecutions, were run-of-the-mill affairs, even for experienced attorneys. There was no machinery for weighing the two in advance, so the board proceeded in the hope of success in its chosen course, the one apparently simpler, and spurned conspiracy, even to the point of declining to take advice from counsel, as will be seen. The directors passed over the possibility of having two barrels for their gun, and settled for one.

Other prospective actions related to single parties, and made a long list. All were sound enough for their abuses and recoverable damages, and if prosecuted might well be profitable for the condo. As Charles had said to Barney and Zina:

"The scene is riddled with fraud, and all activities have to be considered, the very many of them, for how they were wrongful, and in each case its seriousness, and the evidence for proof. There may be too many to be manageable, or for the directors and owners to digest, but those things are for later." Warming to the subject, he had continued, "That the directors were representing the owners in 1988 was no more than an illusion. The board had duties, such as explaining to the owners why it was in the interests of the owners that they consider in special meeting an issue so remote in both interest and in time, the management contract having eight years to run. By calling the meeting the board impliedly stamped its approval on it. It did not inform the meeting that the McGintys were to pay for it, and as that was itself a unique event, disclosure was appropriate. The Declaration provides amply for explanatory statements to accompany notices of meeting, with special latitude for a board, so it had opportunity, to say nothing of inducement or duty, to explain clearly why 1988 was chosen, when much time lay ahead in which to act. And also to say how, on behalf of the owners, the proposal had been weighed up, and what the directors saw as pros or cons. They had figuratively thumbed their collective nose at those opportunities.

"Every director failed, because all were parties to those steps, which were board activities and decisions. Each had ample opportunity to put up a protest flag along the way, but none did so.

"Some owners vote for something brought forward by a board on the assumption that even though they did not understand it fully, the board would not support and promote it unless it were worthy. In a community of 400 units, and with many owners having at best a hazy understanding of the workings of their condominium, it was unsafe and irresponsible not to explain fully a resolution that would affect all owners for years ahead, and in a place like Gran Capitan, in the odd situation of a residential complex being under contract management, nothing could be of greater significance. It was true that the granting of the previous, or 1990 option to the previous OSMs, had been a low-key event, and readily approved, though I think the Hollidays were lucky, 'cos Barney would have been involved a few months later.

"But I think the value to the condo of multiple small actions for offences shown up through the Notes, may be little, whether measured in penalties recovered, or reward for directors' efforts. Little, that is, as compared with the main game of divesting the McGintys of the third option, through a conspiracy prosecution, or termination of the whole contract."

Although Charles was not to know, for there was no contact between the two men, Tom would be very much of the same mind, with the addition that not all current directors or owners would want to sue all former directors, especially those who had presumably come into office with good intentions, and having gained nothing personally out of their wrongful activity, would be hit hard if action succeeded and they were denied indemnity or insurance protection, which was possible as they had seemingly acted negligently and without good faith throughout. For Tom, like Charles, a threshold question was how to distinguish between the leaders and the followers. All directors were willing parties to various abuses of power, but there were too many to include in a lawsuit to be run by Gran Capitan, with its limited resources. Yet the leaders stood out. Tom also advised Manuel - as Charles had earlier - that any director sued could join one who was not, so the ploy of selecting leaders only might not protect the followers, the second-stringers. All in all, it was not hard for Manuel, nor for other current directors, to put aside the prospect of actions against the former directors for specific misdemeanors, and that quickly covered Prince also, because sued alone it could readily claim it acted within the boundaries of its instructions at all times. And so, from one or another cause, the board's, and Manuel's, initial picture of possible remedies and defendants contracted.

There was no getting away from the bogy of costs ballooning vastly. Ed knew of, and made much of cases where a condominium had lost a lawsuit, and large bills had added to the pain. Ed seized on the sensational aspects of cases to warn owners off legal action, and while most knew what he was up to, it would likely be seen as fair comment by some. Barney and Charles agreed that one of the factors driving the cautious approach of the current board to legal redress post-1988, was the risk, faint and unstated, that something would go off the rails and they would finish up personally liable, or at least be shamed.

Once the new board had dumped conspiracy, and were cool to the idea of prosecuting former directors, and that attitude flowed over to the benefit of Prince, which was a small fish alone, the McGintys remained the sole target. The board decided to concentrate on events that could be argued to be serious violations of contract. Such a trend grated against the Jones' and Charle's ideas of both lawsuit management and justice, and even after following the board's reasoning, they were puzzled and discontent.

Barney, more passionate than Charles in this matter, was set right back on his heels by the way the case was wasting. Two things continued to trouble him. The first, if the board failed to terminate the contract that way the case was over, because by then the statute of limitations would have kicked in against conspiracy, and secondly, in the absence of conspiracy charges, the OSMs might be given space in which to divert blame from themselves for alleged violations. An example of the latter was that the former board had paid an invoice from Angel, which turned out to have been addressed to the OSMs, and when taxed about it Ed had indignantly claimed he had only been the board's agent in hiring Angel for the service, so the payment was in order, even though there was no minute of the directors to confirm this version. But messaging during the same period tended to confirm Ed's claim, or at least, not to disprove it. So, Barney thought, if a former director were to support Ed's version in this, or any violation proceeding, in court, maybe he would succeed.

And Barney also felt that, to avoid missing the conspiracy boat entirely, the board should at least commence the proceedings so as to beat the statute of limitations, for time was running out, and after its issue, let the writ sit, or progress slowly, until the violation-termination scene became clearer. He supposed the defendants in conspiracy would be less willing to lie for their friends while they themselves had their own day in court hanging over their heads. But this tactic was more than most directors could comprehend, so the case blundered along, to Barney's continuing despair.

The tripartite discussions had revealed to Barney the extent of the revised thinking by Manuel's board. Without letting on the depth of his disappointment in the change, and in the casual way he had been told of it, he and Charles continued their discussion with Manuel, who seemed oblivious to Barney's concerns, and to have forgotten his former vengeful attitude. But the common ground they had shared earlier no longer existed. At home, waiting for Charles to join them for lunch, Zina noticed Barney was unusually quiet, and took it there was a connection to the meeting, and to break the ice she asked:

"Is there any news from the fighting front, even a little propaganda? Anything will do."

Barney saw he had to tell her, and said: "OK, you win. I'll tell, but it may be slow because to tell you everything going through my mind would be a terrible bore for you."

"Oh, we couldn't have that, could we?" Zina cried, "So start off with small sentences, and expect me to glare at you if they're too small."

"Well", continued Barney, "in essence the board has stood me up. They've given up on conspiracy without a word to me. Something's happened that I can't put my finger on exactly, and I'm still guessing. They're going after the McGintys only, confined to contract violations, and those have nothing to do with the conspiracy. Manuel wasn't giving much away, and as it was all so obvious, there was no point in my banging on. Shameless it was; as though nobody had ever said that the old board deceived the condo owners, which Manuel and his people have been crying out from the start."

"Did you argue with him? Did you complain about being left out in the cold?"

"Nope. Call me chicken-heart if you like, but I concentrated on digesting everything instead, and Charles did too. We can talk it over, and plan, another time."

"Plan, what plan?" asked Zina. "If you can't sue them all for conspiracy you might be up the creek without a paddle. Oh, to think of all the work you put into making up those Notes for the board to give the attorney, and then not to be told his opinion, or even if he went right through them, sounds fishy. Tell me you'll contact Manuel right away and check that out! It sounds contemptuous by both Manuel and the board, unless I'm missing something. But can't you guess at what's driven this change."

"My short list so far is the quixotic wish to protect Ronald Sharp, and maybe others. And a concern about legal expense, which may well be larger than has been disclosed to the owners so far. Maybe there is also a concern that suing past directors would create a precedent for suing current or future directors. That's all I can think of. Y'see I don't really know. But no, you've got it right." He paused, thinking before continuing, "It's not a case of not doing what you said, but more of when. Y'see, I'm hoping Charles will wise me up better about conspiracy, after he's checked it out for himself, and then I have a proposition to bounce off him, and then I'm ready for Manuel."

"Good. Can I hear?"

"Yes, even though it's half-baked. In essence it's to look at conspiracy by a reduced number of players, by omitting the directors other than the three leaders. I'll say that anybody with eyes must see them as serious wrongdoers, who should be brought to account. The other directors can go jump, though of course they were all complicit, and didn't lift a hand or say a word against the fraud on the owners. But the records are not as convincing against them as the others, so the chances of suing them to a useful result are low."

"That sounds neat, and sensible. I take it this narrowing of targets has only come up since Manuel's brush-off this morning?"

"That's so. Until then I was aiming for all directors plus the others, and in my innocence thought the board was thinking along much the same lines. Yet that was a lot of people and that would make a big case. In the meantime he's done me a favor. By wiping out conspiracy in the way it actually happened,

135

he's sent me to this other line of thinking, mini-conspiracy in a way, narrower in scope, but also more manageable, and hopefully acceptable to the board."

"I see. It also gets around the hurdle of the condo owners being disinclined to tackle innocents among the 1988 directors. Besides, while you never get into the minds of individual directors, but we know they and their wives interact with the condo community, so some owners wouldn't favor suit against folks they count as friends, even if in 1988 the same friends were traitors to Gran Capitan. I have to say I was a bit rocked by your news at first, and I'm very disappointed in both Manuel and his directors. That you never heard from any of them suggests he is surely the spokesman, which sounds a bit like the old board and Spinks the policeman. Will it be hard for you to look them in the eye."

"I hope not. But it should be harder for them, or at least the few I know, especially after they realize they let me down, and that I know it."

"Y'know, when the archives were opened all those people were baying for the blood of those they saw as deceivers, but today, it's almost as if they were friends. Like as if Manuel Martin's Marines had morphed into Bernard Brooks' Buddies."

"Indeed. Who would have thought it possible?"

16

The friends review the issues and legal remedies - they conclude it was and remained conspiracy - in spite of being at odds with the directors on the point, they will try to revive board interest in a conspiracy prosecution

Charles came in, and while waiting for lunch he explained to Barney what he had picked up: "I really don't know much, but will do my best. The edges of criminal conspiracy are more sharply defined than the civil tort. Conspiracies in commerce are given special treatment in securities legislation, including definitions, and are statutory offences, which give them boundaries that are relatively clear. Although we talk about conspiracy quite freely, and the media does too, it's not a tidy civil lawsuit, being based on the common law, and on decided cases, with little help from statutory definitions. So proceed carefully, in case some old rule of construction is turned up against you by the defendant's counsel. I can't really add much at the moment, for there's more to come. I sense you've had your thinking cap on since we last spoke, so let's hear about that."

Barney replied: "Thanks for that. My news is simple enough. Drop conspiracy against the directors other than the three top men, and keep the McGintys, and Prince. Don't DA's prosecutions sometimes only go against the most obvious?" Charles nodded assent. Barney continued: "Each of my first-class defendants was in a dominant and active position from the start, and used it to manipulate events to get the McGintys the third option. Of course, I'll write those things down for you to think about. I'd be looking carefully at failures of duty along the way, mainly as corroborative of conspiracy. Until we've had a good look at it all I wouldn't be for going public. Then I'd have to decide between putting it to the board, and going direct to the owners, though helping the board has lost its sparkle for me. I mean, how could Manuel explain not telling us earlier they weren't going on with conspiracy? I'm tiring of one-way traffic. How could anybody miss conspiracy and those three executive directors right in the middle of it? I mean, who else could have been responsible? Still a lot of defendants though, isn't it? But if I don't include Prince, the others can blame its staff."

Charles had been listening carefully, and said, "I see what you want, and I'll look at it. So far it seems OK. But we - or rather the board - would need an opinion from a trial attorney before commencing proceedings, conspiracy being a rare beast. That was to be Tom's job, I had thought."

"We need the advice anyway," Barney replied. "If the board won't get it voluntarily, I could put up a motion for the owners to insist on it. I'd rather not, but the owners deserve the final say, but only after hearing the whole story. Even if it seems, at the end, they don't care about being done out of a couple of million dollars, that's their right, but at least they would have got to understand how they were swindled." He thought a moment, then added, "It's a pity we can't get that advice early. It would be great to have it. If bad, end of case. If good, we'll have something for the owners. Funny to be talking this way now, long after the advice should have been gotten by the board."

"Y'know, what you say maybe overlooks the reality of the board's attitude, and its influence over owner thinking. I wouldn't like you to waste your time on a hopeless mission. I mean, I wouldn't like to see you fight the board and lose. So please consider this, as an alternative. Maybe we could turn enemies into friends. Put the revised conspiracy case to the directors, and suggest they get counsel's advice, the brief for which we would prepare, free. Tell them you don't want to go alone, or without counsel advice, as that could reflect some disagreement among the goodies. If they knocked you back, you'd be going to the owners without board support, and frankly, you should avoid that as the directors pack too many punches, or I should say, too many captive owner votes. A word here and there from them would sink your ship, especially with this emerging concern about lawsuit expense."

He continued, "The first thing is to put a neat conspiracy argument to the board. It would benefit from all the our chewing the cud since the Notes were prepared, and being more succinct, would give the directors a chance of understanding the case, and more important, getting interested. If they agree to get advice, the brief for it could also be kept short, much like your argument to the board, and enough for counsel to say either forget it, or else ask for more detail. So while you digest that, I've a few different slants to offer, if I could have the floor a bit longer, please." They others waved him onward, and he continued:

"Another problem here is that the records of board proceedings are in bad shape. The usual thing of writing them up and later, at the next meeting, correcting them if necessary, seems nowhere to have been followed. It must be assumed that all directors received a copy of the record of the preceding meeting, and that any dissent or abstention made but not shown there would have been rectified right away.

"Applying that to the Brooks reign, it didn't seem that any member either abstained or dissented ever, and so it's hard to see how every director was not in favor of each step. That does not mean that all understood everything, or even that they agreed in every detail, or that meetings were not run in a dictatorial manner by Bernard Brooks or Josh Spinks, or that proxies acted completely in accordance with instructions; but complaints intended to change the record should be made in good time, otherwise the business of a board could remain incomplete indefinitely.

"Because of that collective principle, and the absence of recorded dissents, Manuel has a hang-up about proceeding against directors among whose members he sees innocents besides culprits. So, regardless of the culpability of the board as a whole, or differences among members, he would apply justice by not prosecuting any. As he speaks for the current board, and does so confidently, and the other directors are silent, we can take it his voice is that of the board, and that he simply states its notion of justice. Accepting that is not easy for me, and I would much prefer the matter being aired before the owners, as it should be their decision, Gran Capitan being their property, and their assessments paying for the earlier board having indulged the OSMs so liberally. So if I understand Manuel correctly, conspiracy is off the table, and he has no legal opinion to show us, we have only his word, and his interpretation of any oral advice given by the attorney." Turning toward Zina, he added: "We'd understand if you think it's partly our own fault because we declined to stay on the case after the Notes were compiled. But who knows if our position now would be different anyway?"

Zina didn't answer directly, merely saying: "I think it's a pity that you folks, and Manuel, all having the best of intentions, don't see eye-to-eye in all this. Of course I understand, and support, Barney's attitude, and always your advice, Charles, but I doubt that Manuel would act as he does without board support, even if it were to come after the event. He may sound like a one-man band, but he isn't really, and can only appear so through his co-directors compliance. It's right that the board calls the shots, and just as right that owners who disagree make their objections heard. I don't know that you can truly assess anybody's performance until after their act is over, and while we can, and have, assessed that of the 1988 board, we should hang on a bit longer about Manuel and his directors. So though I'm alarmed, I would give them more rope just now ..." At that point Barney interjected with, " No need to give it dear, they've taken it!"

"I can't deny that," Zina said, before continuing. "But we do get mixed dishes, don't we? Take the position since the McGintys aren't here as they used to be. Sure, their employees do a reasonable job, but without going that extra yard that can make a big difference. The directors see the gaps and put their own efforts in, so they have become hands-on folks more than before. This, to me, reflects loyalty to Manuel, which is good, and nothing like that happened when Bernard Brooks was the leader: directors were more inclined to drop out than to pitch in. There's a down side though. Some directors don't know their place, and so perhaps interfere with the staff at work, and this might produce untimely turn-overs. How else do we account for the new worker-faces we see so often? And if you don't see it for yourself, you won't know. It doesn't suit the board to tell the owners about tensions that could possibly be sheeted home to directors. Maybe the conflict between Manuel and Ed tends to infect the workers in the field. Still, I believe this is the most vigorous and able and cohesive board we've seen here, or Barney and I ever saw at Marquise. Josh Spinks was a big bossy boots, and Manuel is like him in that way, but only that, as he works for the owners, and Josh worked for the McGintys. Oh, but I'm rambling. Forgive me."

Charles responded: "Well said, Zina. Observant stuff. Actually, you've opened my eyes to a few things, for which I thank you." Turning to Barney he said: "I noticed you didn't ask any questions about the attorney's handling of the Notes. Was that because you felt Manuel's answers would be skewed?"

"Yes, especially as there was nothing in writing. And such a discussion could lead to a clash, which might be unavoidable, but there's no need to bring it on until I'm ready."

Charles continued, "They've half shut the door against conspiracy, but as it seems to fit, I'd better keep on looking at it."

Barney had kept as quiet as he could, not wanting to go into detail that might be tiresome for the older man, who really did not fully share his passion for the affair, and had been very much a retiree when Barney had first came to him for a word of advice. He said: "Oddly, for once I've nothing to say, other than that I'll think, and lick my wounds. But I'm not dead yet."

Charles chuckled: "I never thought you would be. Treat it as the first round, and we'll talk about the next in a little while. Violation proceedings are either in progress, or are not. If they are, we can take it they are in good hands. If they are not, we can take it the board feels it has good reason for the delay; not that I see it from here. I mean, if you and I are the parties to a contract, and violation by me is alleged, I believe you have a duty to tell me fairly promptly, and also give me a chance to repair the damage. If you don't, you may lose any right of termination for that violation, because the law may take you to have excused me from it, or to have acquiesced in it, so that it has become no violation at all. Put another way, I doubt the board can store up violations, and trot them out only when it suits its tactics in a lawsuit about something else, such as when the McGintys set out to exercise the third option.

"But Ed, no stranger to legal advice, would already know all this, and more. I don't see anything in the McGinty conduct indicating insecurity about their hold on the contract, and as part of it, the right to the third option. Another thing, we could ask why the board doesn't try to set aside that option, as something quite apart from the other remedies we've talked about. Maybe it has considered doing so, after the find in the basement. The broad picture is that it was the Brooks board, and Prince, who took the main steps that led to that option. The McGintys didn't call the special meeting or propose any motion to it. The board did those things. On the face of things, the McGintys shouldn't be penalized for being the beneficiaries. But if we dig deeper, we find they invented the show, and wrote the script, and acted a role just like the others, with the sole purpose of personal benefit. They weren't innocents receiving a gift from the condo. For us, it's not like needing a smoking gun, but rather adding together bits from here and there, which is good enough, considering we don't have to prove everything beyond reasonable doubt, as in a criminal case, but only that it would be inequitable and unconscionable for the McGintys to hang on to their prize.

"So there are a few puzzles here, and I'm only scratching at their edges. Let's turn a corner, and look at the McGintys wanting to sell the contract. In the meantime they have the benefit of its high compensation. They and our board are at each other's throats, in particular Ed and Manuel, and that's not a good prospect for future peace, or for compromising in order to end the whole affair.

"I hope the McGintys are scared of getting into a fight in court where they are attacked on the way the third option got up. I would be. Conspiracy is the obvious battle field for that. If time runs out for a suit there, expect the McGintys to become bolder. No doubt Ed and his attorney are assessing their prospects all the time, and must find it a riddle. As we do.

"The game can't go on forever. At the latest it will come to an end when it's time to exercise the third option, which It's only a year and a few months ahead. They must exercise it or let it pass. To exercise it they would have to jump the hurdle of contract violation-termination, and we don't know how big that is, and I don't think anybody does, because it would have to be decided in court, where the result is always uncertain, and much could depend on attorney tactics. Mark this though: as surely as we could lose in court, so could the McGintys. I'll say it another way. First, assume a conspiracy prosecution is off the agenda. The third option must be exercised or else be lost. If the contract has been lawfully terminated through violation the right to the third option is also terminated; automatically. The result of the conflict must therefore hinge on the termination proceedings. That would be the battle field.

"Neither side would like to lose. It would be a big win for one and a big loss for the other. That is the point where compromise starts to make more sense. Maybe the pressures for that will become so great that a way around the mutual animosity of Ed and Manuel will be found. Now look. You've been very patient here, and I'm sorry to be holding the floor, especially when I'm not recommending anything much. Yet just to have stated the complications, may help us a bit."

Barney stood up, and stretched: "The part I understand best is that if there's no contract default from violations, there's no termination. If there are none now, there may never be any, given that the OSMs are doing a pretty fair job, and have lots of incentive to keep it up. I know I could ask the board for details of violation notices, but they would be suspicious of me, and hold up a reply, or mess it up, so I'll hang back for the moment. Y'know, if conspiracy is done, we'll never get rid of the McGintys except through the violation/default/termination route, the expense of which could be pretty huge, and if it fails we would be stuck with contract management for ever so long; losers all along the line." He paused a few moments, thinking, before continuing: Maybe we could look for a peaceful solution, even though it's not all our way."

Charles said: "The alternatives to that being only giant lawsuits and expense, why not? And even though Ed hasn't shown much talent for seeing the other guy's point of view, our leaders should be trying everything. But of course, if they, or Ed for that matter, are obsessed with winning, they would only go through the motions of compromise, without bona fide intention.

That happens. But we shouldn't delay a start. I mean, if our case is uncertain, and Ed's is also, both sides would have something to gain from a compromise. If it fails, nobody's worse off than they are now." Almost as an afterthought he added: "Normally I'd suggest you talk all this over with Manuel, but I guess the same old problem, of him dominating the board, and being confident of his strategies, is a bit of a put-off. I'm in the same boat: Grinning, he added: "What about you instead, Zina?" "Ha ha," she laughed in reply. He concluded: "Well, as I'm getting nowhere, I'll go home."

Barney said, as they showed him out: "I'll draft something and show it to you. Maybe we can get a quick reaction from the board."

"Thank you. Good night." Charles walked away.

17

The Jones and Charles Olly continue their probing of the 1988 events - they continue to see conspiracy as the main issue

The chances of the 1988 wrongdoers escaping justice was strong before the basement find, and that event provided the evidence needed for prosecutions by the board, and the owners promptly authorized the board to proceed. But it had not done so. The directors' legal strategy had changed enormously. No longer were their targets to be all those who had betrayed duty and plundered trashed the owners' rights, but instead, only the OSMs, and then simply for such contract violations as could be pinned on them. Those had nothing to do with the conspiracy. Barney felt the owners were being seriously let down. Only through a conspiracy suit could court verdicts denying validity to the third option, and delivering justice for individual wrongdoing, be obtained in one hit. It should proceed, along with the proceedings for termination for contract violations that Manuel had come to favor as the single course to pursue. Benefit for owners from running individual cases against transgressors was uncertain, because of doubtful or limited financial return, while the diversion of directors' energies away from other aspects of condo management was assured. Not enough benefit to interest Barney nor, it seemed to him, the board either. Manuel had not spelled it out like this, but if action could be taken against the dominant directors without impact on the lesser ones, by which he meant Ronald Smart at least, maybe the board would recommend conspiracy proceedings to the owners, aiming to knock over both the third option and the senior cheats in the process. Maybe, thought Barney; but the directors would soon see that once a conspiracy suit started, even one in which the targeted directors were limited to the top three, along with Prince and the McGintys, nobody could guarantee the others would not be sucked in.

The only people who could add useful detail to the Notes were, naturally, silent. Prince was out of the scene. The two sets of directors, past and present, were at arms' length from each other, and the antipathy between individual members on both sides was sometimes quite intense; an example of which was a threat from a former director, made directly to Manuel, to engage The Bandidos to work on him to change his style. Coming out of the blue, with violence from experts in prospect, Manuel freaked out, and temporarily retired with his wife to their principal home in Texas. There he reported the matter to the police, and from them to the Santa Marta PD, who interviewed the culprit, who claimed he had been joking, and had no such contacts, and so there was nothing in it that an apology would not cover. Manuel took him at his word, and accepted his apology, and the police gave the offender a warning to keep away. Ed, too, about the same time, implied a threat of physical harm to Manuel, which he took to the police, who rated it too minor for action by them, and he concluded he would have to be bashed first. And he supposed that men prepared to offer violence in the course of business would not shirk conspiracy.

Upon completion of the Notes the two friends had informed the board they would have no part in briefing the lawyers, as they would not want to appear to be looking over their shoulders. Manuel queried their attitude, protesting that the instructions could be incomplete without them. To that Barney and Charles responded they had put so much concentrated effort into their research and compilation, and hopefully made it self-explanatory, they saw no need for continuing involvement, but if the attorney wanted to discuss any point they would be available to him. There was a little more to it, actually, but tactfully was overlooked. The truth was that early in the peace it had seemed to both, and to Charles in particular, that they should be appointed to an ad hoc investigation team, along with Manuel. They did not say so, but that status could get them away from receiving news and views through his filter excessively, which they did not fully respect in view of his limited legal knowledge, and notable self-confidence. But he ignored the suggestion, and they never mentioned it again. Nor did they hear from the attorney Tom Apponi, who was to be given the Notes, which puzzled them faintly, without causing any concern, for it was not their wish to be involved once the Notes had been handed to the board. They had given as much time as they could to the project and were glad to think they were right out of it. But that turned out to be wishful thinking.

It was not possible to know what owners might think about anything, except that keeping assessments in check was important for all, and very important for some. Still, the deception had been of such a scale, and its consequences so very costly and long-lasting, it seemed reasonable to expect an interest in justice among them, and with it a fatalistic attitude to accompanying legal expense. Taking extreme views of the two boards, the first, created by the McGintys, had actively sponsored their cause; and the second, honestly elected, was now indirectly sustaining them through a misguided approach to a conspiracy prosecution. Moreover, prolonged lethargy and delay by Manuel's board may also have eroded owner resentment against the whole swindle, so that to bring a conspiracy case to them for approval now might be favored less than earlier. Certainly, as time passed, fewer owners put their hands in their pockets to help pay for Barney's occasional circulars, which he took to be the normal condition of condo owners, and a reflex of reducing interest in the 1988 conspiracy. Whatever had been the level of their volunteering in community affairs in their former lives, many owners brought little of it along as they entered into the comfortable and undemanding routine of their condo complex, as though paying assessments there meant they were also paying their way through life. The only other potential source of funds for circulars was the board, and Barney felt unable to go there. He and Charles understood that by not going ahead with conspiracy legal expense would be curtailed, and that was an argument to sway some directors, and owners. But it needed to be noted also that the recovery of damages and lawsuit expense from the culprits was also on the cards, apart from the likelihood of a court reversing the grant of the third option.

As belatedly appeared, a conspiracy action had been dropped by the board, without a proper legal opinion, and yet it still seemed to the two friends that was the logical remedy for the condo, so they made their own analysis. It was overdue legal work, but necessary if the board might be persuaded to get back on the conspiracy trail, and that Barney could propose it now was only possible because Charles would help.

18

Discussion about remedies continues among the friends - an insight into Manuel's position - Barney prepares a concise conspiracy argument - rescission emerges as a talking point

In one of many talks with Barney about the strange situation they were in, Zina summed up her feelings this way: "Condo owners here have the dual distinction of being the victims of very great abuse of owners' rights by directors, and being led by a new set of directors to whom it doesn't seem to matter much."

A worry for the Jones and Charles was that significant violation of contractual obligations came along only occasionally, because OSMs normally guarded their territory pretty well. At Gran Capitan talk of violations was recent, either through laxity by former boards, or by there having being none. Whatever the explanation, once the violation axe was sharpened, it would follow that the OSMs would take care not to be whacked by it. From those thoughts came the idea that the supply of violations was not as regular as water from a spring, so that, like as not, those in hand were most, perhaps all, there were. Tom Apponi had told Manuel that the board should not see termination for contract violation as a pushover, as it would be a severe penalty, with a definite risk of failure, and then attorney fees would add to the pain. But he thought cases worth proceeding with were there, with a caution that a doubt could be created if a witness, such as a former director, or Prince staff member, turned up with a tale in support of Ed.

If the McGintys intended to exercise the third option they could do so only by formal notice shortly before 31 August 1990, which was the expiry date of the then current phase. They must also not be in default under the management contract. Clearly, default was a critical issue. Charles Olly saw it, for present purposes, as failure in the performance of an obligation. Here, it was non-performance of contractual obligations. The starting point was to see if the contract defined default, and it did, liberally for the OSMs. It also seemed to Charles that if the directors intended to say to the OSMs, when they gave notice of exercise of the third option, "You are in default and we don't accept your notice of exercise of option", they should seize the initiative and warn the OSMs now. He saw four sensitive areas if that were not done. The board might be held to have acquiesced in, or forgiven, an alleged violation. The OSMs might claim insincerity by the board in not pursuing remediation of contract violations, thereby reducing opportunities for the OSMs to make good. They might also allege victimization by the board, in that unlawful activity by other parties had been openly identified by the directors, but the malefactors not brought to account. And a question of good faith by the board, which was a contractual requirement of both parties, could be raised against it, because it held grounds for contract termination, but failed to take remedial action when it was timely to do so. Those and other opinions of the dissidents were passed on to the board from time to time, and never acknowledged, which they put down to clerical inefficiency, without being disturbed. However, they were gratified occasionally to find the board taking up their suggestions, although without attribution of their source.

After the appearance of the special meeting agenda, and after Barney had sent a flyer suggesting owners vote against the board motion for the third option, Ed had presented to Prince a letter from Angel for use in arguing to the owners against Barney's representations. Prince having no independent status in the condominium, it received it as agent for the board. Prince and Bernard Brooks board accepted the letter in its entirety, and it was signed by the president on behalf of the board, and sent to owners. Barney was not asked about the truth or otherwise of its content. Its purpose was to undermine his position in owner's eyes. The content was actually scurrilous, and skated on the thin ice of defamation, without falling in. Barney had rejected its contents in a circular to owners, classifying all as either simple lies or close, using scornful language throughout. But the McGinty-linked board took no notice, even though identified as liars. Their failure to sue suggested to Charles and Barney a tacit admission of guilt, and of arrogance supported by power. And so the matter ended, with the crooks escaping again.   .

From fragments of information gathered from individual directors and their family members, and from reading between the lines of official communications to owners, Barney and Charles came to see that Manuel's board was not at all of a mind to deliver justice across the board, but instead had chosen a narrower approach, one that would involve minimal legal expense, and protect the former directors, including Ronald Smart. That, to the dissidents, was not justice for a serious wrong, not the way to make good the financial harm suffered by the owners, gave insufficient weight to the risk of failure in a termination lawsuit, and could result in the diversion of a few million dollars of owners' money in excessive compensation to the OSMs via an extended contract tenure. Moreover, it appeared that the board had not sought further advice from a specialist adviser after attorney Apponi had conducted a preliminary survey, and his was the only legal advice at hand, and it was oral only, and only comprehensible to Manuel, to whom it was primarily directed. And he and the board kept the nature of it to themselves. Their minimalist strategy was thereby confirmed.

Troubled by, and dissatisfied with the board's case management as dominated by Manuel, the two dissidents approached him, and pointedly observed that as Ronald Smart was no longer a director, any embarrassment felt by the current board in acting against him would have disappeared. They were alarmed by Manuel's response that proceeding against all former directors could be unfair to the innocent members. He seemed to be saying that as, in his board's view, one or two former directors were probably innocent, no action should be taken against any. The board had not sought legal advice on all the remedies available to it on the face of the Notes, so were prepared to make a decision based on their own inexpert opinion, and which was possibly mainly Manuel's, which did not seem to Barney and Charles at all sensible.

As the board had started out, post-basement, with the apparent intention of bringing the main wrongdoers to account, it was a shock to Barney and Charles to find that a year on, the intention had dissolved. The board had done nothing, not one thing, toward nailing the directors responsible for the disaster, either as conspirators, or for separate wrongdoings. Though not without merit, directors' views were not a fair substitute for proper legal advice on conspiracy from an expert counselor, and after it a decision by the condo owners, should the advice be favorable.

Charles said to Barney, "Y'know, our side might not see clearly enough the risk of the McGintys making out a convincing case of victimization. Ed and Manuel are quite open about their mutual dislike, evidence of which we see in circulars and records of directors meetings, and Ed's circulars. One of these, the other day, you will have seen, included a recitation of some of the difficulties the OSMs worked under, and announced they could not work with Manuel and director Libby Ryan, whom we know acts as Manuel's personal assistant, and does it so well he can be president even though his principal home is in Texas. It was extremely disappointing to read that, and also Manuel's reaction: disdain of, and fault-finding against the OSMs, which did nothing to close the gap. I would think Ed's attorney will flog the line of the OSMs being victims of discrimination by the board, just as he will grab at anything that comes along. Maybe the board should moderate its language to reduce its exposure. That apart, an obvious victim must be the sensible conduct of litigation between the board and the OSMs. If, in the management of lawsuits, one party behaves intransigently, it follows, by the laws of human nature, the other might too. The maxim about things not being capable of getting worse is not always true. There's a considerable pile of litigation both afoot and ahead, and cool heads are desirable on both sides for intelligent results."

Barney replied, "And it would be so easy for the true interests of the owners to be lost in a clash of personalities in court. So what can be done about it? Sideline Manuel from managing litigation? I like that. He would then say that was playing into Ed's hands, and he might be right. The other directors seem pretty timid. Compromise with Ed? Now that's unknown territory, but it should be looked at. Surely a director or two has considered doing so. Maybe secret negotiations are going on. Or we could talk about the owners buying out his contract, and I could work out a plan for that, so that it would be a good investment, but it would mean giving Ed the dollar equivalent of the unexpired OSM contract, which would be okay, plus something for the third option, even if not a hundred per cent, and that might not be okay. So it's an idea in need of a long gestation period. Change in personal styles? I think not. Those two guys are naturally combative haters. Of course, if litigation proved highly expensive, and interminable, a point will come when owners will say it must end, and directors will start defying Manuel, but that seems a ways off. Early signs may be there, though. Those occasional belly-aches about legal expense and budget blow-out we hear might be mainly the perpetual whingers at work, but also might reflect truth, and that could influence some directors."

Charles added, "A couple of years back I presumed to say to Manuel that I thought Ed was a formidable opponent, partly because he was litigious, and engaged smart attorneys, and was decisive. We needed to recognize that so as to guard against being out-lawyered. I couldn't do any more, as I hadn't been asked my opinion, and as it has turned out, I may as well have kept my mouth closed."

"Well, our president is certainly hard to help in litigation, and given his apparent dominance of the directors' thinking, events will have to turn even sourer before those guys get minds of their own. Zina thinks they have them, and that Manual is only the spokesman, but I'm not fully convinced. And in the meantime the owners will continue as losers all along the line, starting with the OSM contract from BBC years ago."

Faced with letting conspiracy be, or pressing on, Barney chose the latter. He thought: 'Say I do nothing, like the board. That approach cuts out the owners. The issue then is - should the owners be asked their opinion, or should the board be taken to have been elected to decide for them? The board had no mandate for inactivity. To the contrary, when they were asked, the owners authorized the directors to go ahead, find the culprits, pin-point their unlawful activity, and take legal advice on prosecuting. The owners were then to decide upon the legal action to follow. There was no announcement to the owners of change in direction, and no authority from them. To me, the directors took an undemocratic and arrogant path. I would be a jerk and a jelly-back if, believing that, I don't work against it, hard as it would be. So, tiresome as the whole business is becoming, I'll take Charles' advice.' That is to say, he produced a letter containing a draft case for the board to look more intently at conspiracy. In preparing it Barney had in mind the possibility that the board would go ahead and get counsel opinion, and that his letter would pretty well supply the background. The new and critical part was his analysis of the direct and corroborative acts and events that showed conspiracy against the interests of the condo owners, identification of the main participants, the reasons for selecting them, and what could be expected from a lawsuit. He concentrated on two areas of unlawful activity as proving the conspiracy, being the flawed agenda, and the misleading meeting papers, and fleshed out his arguments with supporting detail. Above all, he argued that specialized counsel advice should be obtained by the board, for which purpose he and Charles Olly would willingly prepare the brief without charge. If the advice was encouraging, the board would, naturally, look to the owners for approval of the next step. Whatever the outcome, by following the course he suggested the directors could show they had met their obligations to the owners.

Zina thought well of the letter as being from the best democratic mold, but added: "So, if I see the picture right, if the board declines to act after seeing your case, they will put up reasons of course, and as this board is very influential, you could win a vote from the owners only after a brawl, and I fear you would lose, and all the being right under the sun wouldn't compensate for the strain and waste of effort. Call me chicken, but I don't want to see you done over like that."

Barney shrugged. "You got it. The only thing left then might be a resolution from the condo owners recording that the grant of the third option was a mistake, and condemning the failure of the 1988 board to act in their interests, as required by the Declaration. Not much is it? No teeth."

Zina said: "No, it's not. But such a reprimand would still be a sort of closure. That the conspiracy is only now being considered is really discouraging, and its chances of acceptance by the owners, after gloomy forecasts of legal expense are slotted in, may not be high, even if the board didn't oppose it, and so you face being wiped out. That would be a great shame for the condo, and for you and your many supporters besides. In the long run a reprimand in the way you just said may be the best thing on offer. It would cost owners nothing. Would they vote it in? We can't tell, but it may appeal to some as a clean and cheap way of concluding a nasty case. That they would then be left only with contract violations for redress, and might be throwing away other good opportunities, would be their concern, but the whole ball of wax is theirs anyway. But tell me this please: do you or Charles know if the board has looked into upsetting the resolution for the third option because of the skullduggery behind it? Didn't that come up the other day, or did I hear wrongly?"

Barney paused before answering, slowly: "No, Charles mentioned it. Oddly enough, we don't know if the board has looked into it, nor the effect of the former board and the OSMs having signed a deed to give effect to the resolution. Remember it specified execution of a deed. I've heard that Manuel is suspicious about the way it was signed, in that certain procedures are mandated, and I believe he went into that stuff, but what the wash-up was I don't know. Maybe nothing, because we've heard no more. So we can't rely on the deed not having been signed the right way. Suspicion's not enough. The Brooks crowd will guard their territory."

"But if the resolution was flawed, through fraud, how could a deed made under it change anything? I mean, surely the deed came from the resolution, and if that was unlawfully obtained, as it now seems, the deed might be worth zilch, nada."

Barney slowly scratched his head, then stared at Zina, before replying: "You know something? You're a pretty good musician, and you'll likely become a hotshot attorney if you keep this up."

Zina smiled, saying, "Oh, what a flatterer! I'm only acting out what you've taught me. I mean, I can't do all that listening to you and Charles, without learning a bit. And no, I'm sticking to music, thank you."

"But keep on here a little longer, please, because you've brought on a brain-wave. Try this. We aim for a conspiracy action through the letter to the board, and if the board denies us we let it be, rather than flog a dead horse in front of the owners. Then we look at what we've got left. I think Charles would think like that. And you?"

With a laugh, Zina cried,: "Yes. And I just know that you'll look hard at how the third option was created."

19

The directors deny Barney's plea for resurrection of conspiracy - the reasons for denial are unconvincing to the dissidents, who turn to other means of justice for the owners - they will try to rescind the motion that created the third option

Several weeks after Barney's letter pleading for review of conspiracy, Manuel replied on behalf of the board. Summarized, the board was most grateful for the continuing interest shown by Barney and Charles in assisting the owners find a way to remedy the serious wrongs of 1988; it was invaluable. The current directors were entirely satisfied a conspiracy was behind it. They had very carefully considered the letter with its arguments, and were in substantial agreement with Barney's views. Their concern was that such a case would be quite big, and Ed had already shown he was a determined scrapper, and legal proceedings with him had already cost the owners heavily, which owners had noticed, and recently criticized. Being a prospectively big case, it could cost a lot and take years to finalize. The letter then added words intended to cast doubt on the prospects of proving the case, which amused Charles when he saw them, and he said:

"They've tripped over in their eagerness to turn you down. They have gone past informing you of an executive decision, and added their legal opinion, that the case would be hard to prove, which may be so, but that was the question you wanted them to refer to counsel. Instead, they answer it themselves. If counsel advised the board not to proceed, that would be the end of the matter. If he gave the case a tick, the board could then put the issue to the owners, who could make an informed judgment about prosecuting, for they already know the stakes. It's very arrogant of Manuel to talk down to an owner in that manner, apart from being muddled thinking. It was his letter, whatever the forces behind it. He can't control the urge to be a pretend lawyer, and so has gone off half-cocked again. The board had a duty to obtain proper advice, and willfully failed to do so, and in its absence it, or Manuel, has acted as its own lawyer, and advised itself, wrongly in my view. In doing so it has ruined an otherwise reasonable response to your letter, and confirmed my suspicions that they are blind to their duty to the owners. The owners gave them the authority to proceed, but this was ignored. You come at the conspiracy another way, and get a straight denial, based on hot air. No action of any kind against anybody for the wrongs of the Brooks board. No director, not Prince. Amazing! But it doesn't matter, as no is no, and the board would surely convince the owners if push came to shove. Many find it simpler to follow the leader. Getting into their heads that their leaders here are out of their depth in managing litigation, and are fooling them, almost like the Bernard Brooks board in 1988, is impossible for us, who are running out of gas anyway. Someday someone may come forward to demonstrate to the owners they have been duped again, but that doesn't help us right now. So that seems to be that, and I accept the board's decision, while condemning the directors. We mustn't resent the time and effort we put into the Notes, or the submission, as it was our free choice."

Barney cried, "Okay. Conspiracy's over. This nonsense in the letter is so pathetic as to be almost unbelievable. Right, I see Zina putting the brakes on me. My last word is that we deserved better from the board. And the owners did too."

Still, the Jones and Charles chatted a little more about what the letter said and didn't say, and tried to forget conspiracy. And the way was now clear to look at other possibilities.

A few days after they had digested the board's letter, the Jones were sitting quietly in the evening when Barney started up: "Can we go back to what to do if the board knocked conspiracy? We talked about reprimand, and you put us on to repudiation, and that's what we can look at now. It could be our hit tune. In the Declaration it's called rescission, and is allowed. I've typed out something for you to look at."

Zina jumped up, and came to get it, and read it at once, and after that, as she put it down, Barney asked, "Well, what do you think?"

"Does it mean this motion would go before the owners? It sounds almost cheeky, sort of taking the case out of the directors' hands. What would they think?"

"Who knows? They would be on the spot. I guess somebody could feel upstaged. But surely the correct view is that owners have rights to initiate motions and ideas. The board has had - still has - the chance to do its own thing about rescission, and if they did I'd be ready to stand aside. I can't ask their approval of what I'm about now, as they might bog it down in talk, like with conspiracy."

"You'll show it to them prior to filing?"

"I expect so, but only out of courtesy."

"Still, it sounds bold, like in ya face. Won't Ed have fits? Could somebody sue you?"

"Good question. Let's walk through it. The wording is careful. Nothing reckless. All darn true, all fact. Subject to what Charles might say, I can't see it producing many defamation lawsuits against me. It's a communication with my co-owners regarding our common business, expressing my opinions, based on research. That should be safe. So instead of hitting me, Ed goes to court to stop the motion from being dealt with by the meeting. There are plenty of attorneys and plenty of courts, so getting up an arguable case to block it shouldn't be too hard. You would expect that to bring me into court to explain my words, and show their truth. Bring it on! But if Ed didn't try to convince the owners that the material in the explanation - that's the attachment you've just read - was false and misleading, it could possibly be

154

used against him in court. Of course, if the owners voted down rescission, say for fear of legal expense in a fight with Ed, or whatever, end of story. But then they would have impliedly approved what the Brooks mob did to them in 1988, and I can't see them swallowing that one. Anyway, I promise not to hire an attorney, unless the board pays, as in reality it's the owners' case."

"Of course it is, and always has been." Zina reflected before continuing, "Is this how it is? You worked up a case for conspiracy, were denied, but then found the same material could be used for rescission?"

"Pretty well. It's nice to think the work need not be wasted after all. And there's a little more spin-off. The motion, and any proceedings from it, will be followed intently by the owners, and that would remind them of the message we've been banging on about for so long."

"Well, after all that, who's a clever cookie? I can't wait to see what Charles thinks of it. Now say rescission is voted in - what then?"

"It becomes owners' business. The directors would have to find a way of dealing with it. You, my dear, can stand with me on the sidelines and urge them on. Remember, at that stage it's been approved by the owners, who will understand what it's about, so the directors chances of blocking its progress will be limited, and we will keep it so."

"Wooo …. hoo! What a thrill! At least we'll all know what the case is about, unlike the violations. Am I right in guessing that all our dirty washing could be hung out this way, much the same as would happen in a conspiracy case, and more than from the reprimand motion we discussed?"

Barney replied, "It could be so, but Gran Capitan is headed for a wash-day sooner or later, and the sooner the better, because as the years go by they take memories with them, and fires from bellies. Another thing. Have you noticed the gradual change in faces around here? There's a steady turnover, which means more and more owners weren't here in 1988, so those could may not be as interested as old hands."

"No, I hadn't, though the steady flow of 'For sale' notices should have alerted me. So there's another reason for hurry up. But this is all so exciting. Can we get Charles in on it? Invite him in for a drink or a meal, whatever?"

"Sure. You'd like to do that while it's hot?"

"I think so, don't you? Just as soon as he's available. I'll slip a note under his door."

Charles came, and Barney showed him the proposed motion and its explanation, and asked him to criticize anything he liked, as Ed would be keen to find fault with it. The motion for rescission, simple in form, was accompanied by an explanatory statement from Barney for the benefit of voters, as allowed under the bylaws, and that statement read as follows:

EXPLANATION from Barney Jones, co-owner, apartment 257, proposer of above motion.

The resolution to be rescinded granted an option to extend the management contract by five years, 1995-2000.

Rescission has become feasible, fair, and reasonable following the discovery and examination of Gran Capitan's 1988 records, which process has confirmed to me a deep suspicion, long held by many owners, and myself, that deceit and misinformation and misrepresentation and abuse of power and breach of statutory duty and bad faith, underlay normal procedures relating to both the meeting and the resolution.

I allege that the wrongful conduct covered a span of several months around August, 1988, and shows nothing happened by chance, but instead was planned to produce benefits for the McGintys. Though too long to specify here, the details are now well recorded. In my assessment, activity by them was significant in the passing of the motion for grant of the 1995-2000 option, as were activities of the leaders of the then board, and some staff members of Prince. All played a part, and all were wrongful parts, and all were complicit in the plan. To me, justice requires that owners be entitled to rescind that resolution, with the intent of nullifying anything dependent upon it.

From the start I protested the circumstances of the election of the 1988 board, but nonetheless it was the legal board, and by law had the primary purpose of serving the interests of the association. In practice, the interests of the McGintys were the primary concern of the leaders of that board.

We are entitled to recall that under the management system here, extension options, which are quite valuable, are not purchased, but are freebies. Also that in a very close vote in 1988, the McGintys' two votes got it over the line.

Handing the sheet back, Charles commented, "That reads well. May I have my own copy to read at home? How long before you want to file it?"

Barney replied, "Take that copy. I have another. I'll file it as soon as the wording seems right. There's no special meeting coming that I know of, so it sounds as though it's headed for the annual meeting, in November. It must be filed by the end of the financial year, 31 August, so we have spare time."

With a happy face Charles said, "Y'know, it will be ironic if this turns out to be as big a contest as the conspiracy might have been, and to think the work we did for that is the basis of this. That's a nice turn-around."

Zina broke in: "I wonder if the McGintys ever thought this rescission idea might jump up to frighten them."

Charles replied, "It will be a shock, if not. I expect Ed to claim it isn't available to the owners, but of course he'll have to show why not. I think this. If a body, including a condo, can decide on something through a resolution, it can also change its mind, like people do, and rescind or unmake it through another resolution, subject to conditions which I can't rattle off. Ed's attorney will find them, and if it's strong stuff we could be in trouble, or would be in an ordinary case. This one is unique, of course. Just reading the explanatory statement tells us that. Then there's the deed, and how that will pan out goodness only knows."

He continued, "But could anyone put up a peace proposal while getting Ed all worked up through a rescission play? Surely peace dies the day you file."

Barney was not sure, saying, "Or maybe it only takes a back seat. If rescission is voted, Ed will be playing in a different ball game afterwards, and might, just might, change his style. That is to say, he might add compromise to his shopping list. So who knows?"

Zina added, "I never had high expectations of compromise at any time, but it sure seemed right to talk about it. Maybe a better day will come."

Looking at Zina, Charles spoke, "Right. We'll return to it sometime, as it's a legitimate option, in the right climate."

Barney said, "A change in subject, if you please. It's another thing I wouldn't need to refer to the board, but it would mean cranking up our circular engine again. Do you recall the Dreyfus affair in France, and the heading J'Accuse used by Emile Zola for an article in his newspaper, in which he criticized the Dreyfus persecution, and defended him? Think a bit."

Zina thought, and exclaimed, "Oh! How right on! Wasn't Dreyfus a soldier, an officer, and a Jew, and the victim of a conspiracy? The anti-semites set him up. Was that it?"

"Sure was. Now if nothing else ever happens, I want the condo owners to know just how the directors failed them in 1988, and I thought a circular, headed I Accuse, might be the way to do it."

"Well, that's a good one. Charles, what do you think? Could he could do this without them suing for libel?"

Barney said, "Don't answer that Charles, until you see what I might say. I'd be careful, as we don't want Zina to have to go back to work. Or me either. I'd say the truth only, and make it out to be fair comment to interested parties. But it's early days."

Charles nodded agreement. "Interesting. It might make you feel better, but as everyone already knows we're dealing with a bunch of crooks, some folks might ask about the point of saying it again. Sure though, I'll look at it when the time comes."

Zina said, "Still, it would shame them, again, for what that's worth. Not much you say, Charles. But hang on! Isn't that what the circular warning them off becoming directors did? The one that led to Ronald Smart resigning?"

Barney thought that over. "That's so, close enough anyway. Methinks y'all are suggesting we've done enough shaming. I get it. Okay."

"But just thinking of Dreyfus, reminds me of the harm conspiracies can cause, and the warped minds that can link up to hurt other people," Charles said, adding, "Some of our own conspirators would have fitted well into the Dreyfus scene."

Zina inquired: "As stuffed shirt French officers you mean? It would be fun to dress them up in those elaborate uniforms and sporting long curly moustaches. Make them wear them for a year, as a minimum penalty for conspirators. Dream on, woman. But you mean to run the rescission motion

157

at the next general meeting?"

"Yes," answered Barney. "It's different. It's fundamental. It hits the jugular. Shaming was only a second best. And until we work through rescission everything else can go on the shelf. Charles, do you think the board will take over the rescission?"

"My guess is that someone has thought of it already, like us, post-basement, but they didn't have your analysis to help, so it went nowhere. Will it be different now? I tend to think that differences are developing among the directors, which is natural when they haven't had much success in litigation so far, and yet have racked up some big legal expense. If I were you I wouldn't wait around. Maybe give them an opportunity to change a word or two, but little more. If they did that, there's de facto support. They would become part of it. But go on at your own pace. Wait for nobody."

Barney said, "Good. Actually, I'm happy to go solo, unless they insist on taking it over, so everything's clear."

Cried Zina, "Wow! Ed will have Angel working overtime when he sees it. Do you have to stay while the case is battled out?"

Reflectively, Barney asked, "What's stay mean? It's like suggesting I'll be kept here, which is fine, as I'm not going anywhere. Not that I know of."

"Just poor expression." Addressing Charles, Zina added, "Won't he have to be a witness if there's a trial?"

"You'd think so, but it would depend on the sort of case it turned out to be."

"And I guess that's as much for Ed to decide as Barney. Exciting, isn't it? I'm really proud of you taking this on. It's going to be a pretty fair substitute for conspiracy in my book."

20

A rescission motion is filed - the board will neither support nor oppose it - Manuel and the secretary, as private owners, openly commend it - Barney is more certain the board is split - a director-driven push for compromise of disputation with Ed appears - an owner files a compromise motion which Ed sees as a threat to rescission - he finds a counter - on receipt of the meeting agenda Ed reads the rescission motion and hot-foots it to Angel for advice

Barney's rescission motion was well supported by Manuel and another director, but not by the board. His invitation for limited input to its wording was acted on by the two directors, who were concerned to have it phrased for the highest level of understanding and interest from owners. When the motion appeared on the agenda the same two directors sent a circular to the owners supporting it, and stating that although it wasn't appropriate for the board to support an owner's motion, individual directors could, as owners. Barney, who was glad to have any support, saw that line as and only sophistry, a pitch to disguise a split on the issue among the directors, as there was nothing he knew of to prevent a board having and expressing views on an owner motion, and indeed at times would have a duty to do so. The inaccuracy reminded him of the specious reasoning in the board's rejection of his argument for attorney advice on conspiracy. He sensed the inevitable had come, and that some timid directors were leaning toward a compromise with Ed, influenced by owners' complaints about legal expense, and community disharmony through ongoing contests between the board and the OSMs. Some directors, led by Manuel, remained convinced that the conspiracy should not be rewarded, which would happen if appeasement of Ed was a significant factor in a compromise solution. But they shied away from pursuing the conspirators, and so were more huff and puff than law enforcers. Barney could not see any good resulting from that ambiguous attitude. It might lead to an unduly expensive compromise, with contract management still in place, and have the side effect of knocking the ideal of self-management on the head. He was tiring of the struggle. Zina told him that after nine years of activism, and his sandy hair becoming greyer all the time, and as was getting on for 70, it was time he changed his lifestyle. But he could not walk away yet. It was a crucial period. The emergence of directors wanting to appease Ed was a bad omen, carrying an implication that the McGintys could be credited with some part of the third option period. They would need this to make an attractive sale package, for unexpired years of tenure meant a lot in selling a contract. So Barney, long opposed to the third option, was totally against compromise if it meant rewarding the McGintys for their swindle in 1988. He was not alone.

He was right about a split. And there was a peace move. The exact details were not exposed, but it was there. Evidence came to him in a message from a director to the effect that the resistance game was over, and it was time to parley with Ed, and it would be sensible for Barney to withdraw his rescission motion. Astonished and angry and enlivened, Barney disagreed, and made it known he would be on the look-out for mischief, and was prepared to take legal proceedings to protect his rights. And he added that passing the rescission motion should be their aim, as well as his because, at the least, it could restrain Ed in compromise negotiations.

When the meeting papers came out his motion, number 11, plus its explanation, were in place, alongside another motion, number 12, from another owner. The thrust of the latter was to negotiate a settlement of disputes, for which a plan was laid out, in which the McGinty interests were to be looked upon favorably, and the owners would face several more years of contract management, such as they had endured already, but with compensation and contract conditions amended. Clearly, several years tenure would be needed to make it worthwhile for both buyer and seller of the contract, which to Barney was a concession to the conspirators, not to be tolerated. He wondered how owners might adjust to two significant motions about management appearing side by side, each having features certain to attract some support, and yet likely to confuse some voters unless explained. He felt some guidance should be offered owners in a circular, and who should author it was the next question, and he suggested to the directors they should, although he sensed their finding agreement on the wording might be too hard, given a rift within. But he was very concerned about owner confusion with the two motions side by side, which might, by chance, produce a result adverse to the rescission motion. As the board was silent despite matters of the very highest importance for the condo being in issue, Barney decided he must tackle that task personally, in case the owners shot themselves in the foot again, as in 1988.

He took his concerns to bed, and awoke during the night, still tossing the problem around, and he suddenly saw some light. Did not the bylaws stipulate that owner motions for the purchase of goods or services be accompanied by two quotes for the cost? Was not the appeasement motion, requiring as it did the hiring of a mediator, the purchasing of a service? And so, without the quotes would not the motion be invalid? He guessed the answers to all would be "yes", and rose and looked them up in his study, and confirmed his guess. He would look into it further in the morning, and returned to bed with a smile on his face, which grew bigger as he thought of another point, namely, there was nothing in motion 12 to show Ed had, or would agree, to mediation, and as the board could not compel him, the motion was unenforceable. In the morning he went through the enemy motion again, more carefully, and found an additional weakness, so he then had three points of order available to submit to the chair of the meeting. As time was running out, and the board showed no sign of presenting an explanation of the competing motions, he then prepared a circular to the owners stating his understanding of the motions, and while being fair to the compromise concept, he argued that motion 12 was irreversibly flawed, in consequence of the points of order he had devised, and which were included in the circular, so all owners would know what was driving him. He prevailed on Charles to run his eye over it quickly, then the Jones box-dropped it open-sheet form, which carried no guarantee of reaching absentee owners, but there was no time to spare. Then he filed notice of his points of order right away, this being more of a tactical move than a legal obligation. Later, Zina inquired, "If you knock out that mediation motion, and yours is the only one for the owners to consider, how many votes do you need?"

Barney replied: "Each motion can be decided by simple majority. If number 12 is removed, all we need for 11 is one more vote for us than against us, and the overall numbers of voters doesn't matter. I would have expected a fairly good vote for rescission until the compromise push surfaced, and that may eat into the numbers I had hoped for. Of course we don't know what opposition will come at the meeting, so predictions are unsafe, but I've prepared my case and looked at our meeting procedures, and will give it my best shot. I suppose you're disappointed by the thought of rescission conflicting with compromise, but remember that motion 12 would give the OSMs some credit for the five years of the third option. Ed would claim 100%, and finish up with something not much less, because he's the toughest nut in the bunch. As a negotiator, think of him as like Hitler to Chamberlain and Daladier at Munich, which is history's best example of how and when not to compromise. Now that rescission is in the game, get it passed, I say, then if peace is still an aim, the owners have more chance of achieving it on just terms."

Zina thought about that. She still hankered after an end to the strife, but found Barney's argument persuasive. She said, "OK, so maybe peace's place will pop up another time. It's hard to take it all in. The future is so uncertain any way you look at it. But yep, I get the Munich message. And of course our management system is simply theft from condo owners, and the sooner it's buried the better, no matter that Queensland folks might see it as a good thing. It seems to me that the longer we're locked into it, the more distant self-management becomes. Is that how you see it?"

"I do. And if we don't keep that target clear we might succumb as some others do, peace being a natural and worthy aim. But some who feel that way are short-sighted, and forget the devilish scheming which has robbed them of money and rights for so long. They may not see that we're in the condo equivalent of the Dark Ages here, and if that appeasement motion were voted in, our stay there may be a long one."

Zina nodded her agreement, adding, "What happens if the owners vote yes to both motions? They're not being put forward as alternatives, as I've sometimes seen on agendas?"

"They're not alternatives. In theory both could stand up. However, the chair would have no right to allow 12 to go to vote because of the points of order I've made.   And I believe that if owners vote for 11, they'll see that 12 contradicts it, and so would vote it down should it get past the chair. That's why we sent the circular explaining the two motions."

Ed became very concerned on reading the rescission motion, and immediately left a copy for Angel, and made an appointment to see him the following day. In the meantime he made up a list of discussion points. He didn't expect complete answers to everything right away, but it would be a start.

He asked: "Do the governing documents allow an owners' resolution to be rescinded. Especially one passed years ago?"

Angel replied: "Let's be frank from the start. I've never seen anything like this, so I've got some research ahead. There's time, as the meeting is a few weeks away. Any answers I give today must be provisional, until I've looked closer into everything, but I know you want the best I can do right now. So today's answer is that I don't see why not. That means I don't know of any statute of limitations that applies to rescission of a resolution, but in any case a time bar wouldn't have kicked in yet, because it's usually six years. As to what Gran Capitan regulations say, I must look them up, but I expect that if the owners can make a resolution, they can also rescind it. Time apart, have you or has anybody changed their situation on the faith of the resolution? That's a reason for denial; somebody acting on the strength of its legitimacy, especially a third party …."

Ed interrupted with: "What's third party mean?"

Angel replied: "Here, Barney Jones, the publisher, is the first, the second is the person being talked about (you), the third is anyone who may have acted on the strength of the 1988 resolution, or even read the explanation attached to the rescission motion, and took it as defaming you. For the moment concentrate on people changing their status on the faith of the resolution. Start by applying it to yourself and Binny, and finding a clue in your own affairs. I mean apart from signing the deed. If it's a big thing, like mortgaging the contract - which of course includes the option - that would be a start. It brings in the financier as a third party. Don't overlook others. I expect you will find plenty of folks who took the explanation of the rescission motion as defaming you and Binny, and that's important, but it's not the same thing as them changing position on the security of the 1988 resolution, which is our best shot. Tell me anything that comes to mind, and we'll dig into it."

Ed asked, "This is new stuff for me, but I thought that once a meeting made a decision that was it; terminado. I'd never heard of rescission until now. How come it's allowed?"

Angel shrugged, saying, "I guess the principle is that organizations are in control of their own affairs, and if they can make a decision, they can also unmake, amend, or rescind it. But maybe not if someone, especially a third party, has taken the original resolution in good faith, and changed his or her affairs on the strength of its validity."

Ed said: "That's fucking lovely, I don't think. Y'know what? I'm feeling I'm being shoved into shit here. I hope we're going to do better, else I'm fucked. After all that effort getting the option up, it can fizzle out because of that fucking Grace Gambell. You know how important the option is for me."

Angel, calm as always, replied, "I do, I do indeed. But we haven't covered the field yet. I must check the condo's Declaration, and also look for cases on these matters. And you can lobby the owners to vote against it. And I can look into obtaining an injunction to block the meeting from dealing with it. And more possibilities will come up; just give both of us a day or two."

Ed said, "I know you're avoiding talk about it to save my feelings, but that freaking motion makes me out to be a crook, and I want to know how Jones can get away with that. Isn't there a law of libel or defamation against that sort of thing?"

Angel replied, "Of course there's a law, and of course there's also a right of free speech. Jones says he's been through the records and claims they show all sorts of nasties. You can read the motion, and particularly the explanatory statement, as well as I can, and you'll see he's not hanging back. It's very deliberate wording, and we'll look for a loophole in it, but it may not be easy. If he's gone too far we'll get him. If not, the job's harder."

Ed cried, "Why don't we run through the words now. Don't worry about my feelings. We have to face it sometime. Binny will have fits when she sees what Jones has said. Oh, Jesus, this is so fucking awful!"

Angel would have been content to postpone the careful reading of the papers, because he didn't want to see his friend disintegrate, yet it had to be done. They both read, silently, and each asked an occasional question as they went, but it was gloomy work, and at the end Ed was clearly shaken, and he seemed to Angel to have suddenly shrunk in size. There was so little to say. The words used were known to both men to represent events they both had personal knowledge of, and although he was not mentioned, Angel felt a chill in the background, so that if the matter got into court his own activities might come under scrutiny. At the end Ed said, "Y'know, if that fucking eagle-head Grace had done her job, all the records would have disappeared. She should be facing the music, not me."

They parted company, expecting to meet again after Angel had done some research, and Ed now had to work out how to tell Binny the dismal news. He couldn't avoid that painful task, which he must do quickly, before she heard about it from others. Their relationship had already been battered by her criticisms of how he handled their OSM affairs, added to by suspicions of something unusual in his relationship with Georgia Land. She had been pleased about the large retirement payment, but disappointed and puzzled that after

163

so many years of them being part of the warm Georgia Land corporate family, they were now not just outside, which came with retirement, but somehow, intangibly, they were out in the cold. Ed had said he didn't feel that way, so perhaps she was imagining something that didn't exist.

Angel looked at Barney's motion and explanatory statement again, and again, and his own law books, and got ready to discuss the case again with Ed, who was clearly restless and apprehensive of a bad result. When they met again, Angel said, "It's hard for me to do this, but I can't let you nurse useless hopes. I'm not at all hopeful we can kill that motion. Jones has been very careful. He may have a bag-full of evidence. Okay, some of it could be bluff, but we don't get to know that until the case is way down the line, so we go in blind. But I'll say what I think, and don't expect you to be happy with it.

"To start, we don't have any right to interfere with the business of the owners, so we can't stop the meeting just by asking. We can apply to a judge for an injunction to wipe it out, and at best would get a brief stay, and we would have to move fast with a convincing case of injustice in a further hearing, otherwise it would expire. I'm talking about our number one shot, pal. Okay, I can write a strong letter to Jones, to frighten him into withdrawing the motion and the statement, and apologize. Ditto to the directors to remove it from the agenda. And also state our view that the motion is unenforceable, because of the execution of the deed it authorized, so it should be disallowed by the chair of the meeting. In each case I can tell them of our intention to seek an injunction and punitive damages if they persist. Naturally, we'll deny everything. The hard part comes when we have to back up the denial, and prove that the allegations in the explanatory statement are all horseshit. Tell me how to do that please, and I'll strip for action. My gut feeling is that Jones has compiled this motion and statement with that retired attorney he hangs out with. We contest it, as in seeking an interim injunction, and then a nullity declaration. We make them prove what they say, and we must prove them all wrong. If we fall down here Ed, we may be fucked."

Ed broke in, with, "Them's not the fightin' words I've come to expect from you. I come for you to get me in the clear, and you don't seem to see that happening."

Angel raised his arm to take over, saying, "Hang on. You sound like you don't understand what Jones is saying. We went through it, bit by bit, and I thought he had chosen his words carefully, and had done so anticipating our reaction, and wanting us to have as little room to move as possible. If you didn't get that message, we can go through it again, no sweat, but Ed, this is serious stuff. We not only need to deny, but be ready to prove them wrong when they bring out their evidence. So tell me, instruct me that Jones has listed a lot of lies, and we'll talk turkey. And we'll sue for defamation. Those would be big lies and worth plenty. Now so far we've been talking about the motion. Say the worst happens, and it goes to a vote, and gets up. But that's not a sure thing. Then we still have the deed, and you'll find that's worth plenty.

"Another thing, Binny being a partner, she's as much in the firing line as you Ed, and as you folks aren't as close as you were once, which I truly regret, I have to tell you I must hear from her personally how she wants this to be handled. She could hire her own attorney, and you can guess how complicated the works could be then."

Ed was pretty quiet by now, an unusual condition for one who was used to doing at least half the taking in any discussion. He didn't say, but Angel sensed trouble ahead, because Binny was unlikely to deny allegations she thought carried some truth. She would get to the bottom of it through Ed, himself, and any attorney she hired. And until she was through, Ed was in no position to give him instructions on behalf of both.

Angel was inwardly comforted by Binny's presence as a Jones target along with Ed. He knew that Ed, alone, would pressure him into statements that would prove difficult, even impossible, to support with evidence. That was not how attorneys were supposed to present their cases to a court, and that, potentially, gave him a personal interest in Binny's participation. He was starting to feel he had a personal interest anyway, because in being an activist for the McGintys' cause he had gone overboard a bit, and if Jones had found this he would be sure to hammer Angel with it in the course of a lawsuit, and maybe get him reported to the California State Bar. As Ed had said, fuck eagle-head Grace.

Ed asked, "Can we stop the motion from being heard by the meeting? I don't mean call off the meeting. I don't suppose there's any chance of that. But get an order that it be kept off the agenda."

Angel replied, "Ed, old pal, you haven't been listening. Yes, we can try for anything you like. That's the temporary injunction thing we discussed. Now what I'm going to say this doesn't mean I'm not rooting for you, or that we won't apply. But it may not be easy. It's their meeting, and we're talking about one item of business, the motion that hurts us. We'll be asking a court to re-arrange the agenda. I can tell you now, there's at least an equal chance it won't, and I can't even think of, let alone describe to you, all the sorts of reasons that could operate on a judge's mind here."

"You mean you don't fucking know, don't you?" Ed snapped out.

Angel sat and thought a little bit before replying. "Y'know somethin'?," he asked. "That's pretty well it. I don't know how we can convince a judge that those allegations in the motion are not only wrong, but deliberately and malevolently wrong, and so they shouldn't go to the meeting. Maybe part wrong ain't enough, as interfering with a private meeting is not something courts do just for the asking. Also, they would know that many motions in meetings like this contain errors, even lies, and that owner meetings work around that. If something's defamatory, the victim has a remedy without interfering with a meeting. And a court may feel the issue should have a run at a meeting anyway, to find out what the owners thought of it all."

Ed pondered, lit a cigarette, inhaled and blew out long and slowly, before saying, "I'm getting the feeling I'm asking for the moon here. No, I don't feel you're not interested, only that it's a hard road. Maybe the owners will vote down rescission, and vote for that compromise motion, which would be just fine for me."

"Maybe," the attorney said. "Let's hope so. I can't guess the votes, or even if the chair will allow both to go to a vote, and I don't see any value in us speculating about the possibilities, except that a vote against Jones motion 11, and a vote for motion 12, would be the best possible result for my friend Ed McGinty. But we can't waste time there just now." He did not say, but upon quickly reading Barney's three points of order against motion 12, he knew he had blocked as many holes as possible. So Ed should try the same tactic against Barney's motion 11, though Angel sensed it had been the more expertly prepared of the two, and offered less scope for persuasive points of order.

Ed asked, "All the condo owners will have got the agenda by now, so they all know the Jones' lies. I can send out a circular denying them, and say I'm taking action against Jones, because if I don't the condo owners might think it's all true."

"Great. So, we got a plan. Part of it is to show that someone has acted on the faith of the resolution passed years ago. You must think hard on that one, pal. I know I haven't covered the fact of the deed having been signed after the 1988 resolution, but it will be important, and there's a lot of law to be looked at right there. And I'll look for a point of order against Jones' motion 11. The deed might help us there. I have a copy of it here. All that's to come. For the moment, bring me your draft circular and we'll go over it at once. Right?" Ed again nodded agreement, and Angel continued, "This is fine between you and me so far, but we still have to know what Binny thinks of it all, and I need to know if I'm acting for both of you, or if she is getting separate counsel. That affects everything, y'know. So you have some urgent jobs before we meet again. The circular, and stretching your memory about the impact of the deed on third parties, and updating Binny. She might want me to explain how I see the case before she commits herself, and whether I see her alone, or with you, is up to you folks."

In the evening of the day the meeting papers came out, and the Jones read motion 11, and realized all other condo owners would soon be reading it too, they discussed it over dinner. Barney said:

"I guess the McGintys are busy cursing me and wondering what to do next. They'll do something, but what?"

"Oh, to be a fly on the wall while they talk it over. Y'know, with Binny having taken off, maybe agreement won't come easily."

"All I can say is that Charles and I made it as hard as we could for them without exposing ourselves too much. Actually, we found it impossible to make the complaint strong without also being provocative. We also tried to exclude Binny, but couldn't."

"I see", said Zina thoughtfully. "I feel for her. Like many wives she's caught up in her man's ambition. I guess when she woke up the damage had been done."

"I guess, but then she knew what Ed was doing from the start, bringing his odd ideas here. She had her eyes open when she was active, and they both sort of said 'screw the owners.' Sure she was a victim, in that it all went too far, and I bet he never consulted her about his later moves."

"That sounds likely. Still, it takes a woman a while to understand her man completely. And then to decide what to do. I sympathize with her, because to come out of this clean will likely be hard for her, but not impossible, as it may be for Ed."

21

The Jones and Charles Olly are curious about the absence of response from the McGintys to the rescission motion - a telephone call on the eve of the general meeting brings dramatic news

On the eve of the meeting, the rebels were puzzled by there being no word from Ed concerning the rescission motion, so significant for the McGinty interests. Nor from other persons who might be interested in one or other of the two motions. As to those others, it seemed to show than many owners were out of their depth in respect of formal meeting procedure, which Barney and Charles both knew could be obtained only by experience and study, and even then it was possible to trip up. As to Ed, they had expected his attorney to make noises against the motion, in good time prior to the voting on it. Though he regretted that the prospect of a debate on the issues had become less likely, Barney was content.

The Jones never knew this, but the reason for Ed not taking part in the business of the meeting was Binny's attitude. Unknown to Ed, she had become well informed about the special meeting in August 1988 when the third option was granted, and made this clear when she conferred with him and Angel about a response to Barney's rescission motion 11, the contesting of which was of high importance for Ed. She flatly refused to sanction anything that would amount to a false denial of the facts, so that Angel had no useful instructions, and both he and Ed risked future trouble with Binny should Ed proceed alone, and in doing so imply that either man was also acting for her. That being so, Ed's hands were tied, at least for the time being.

But Binny's were not. Seeing the rescission motion, starkly accusatory of her equally with Ed, alleging in words whose import was clear even if the language used was legalistic, that both she and he were crooks and swindlers, tore her apart. She went into seclusion and shame until she realized she had to find a path forward. With a broken heart, and deep remorse, she turned to her father, and poured out her terror to him. He, Hans Knobel, knew nothing about condos, and a lot about morality, and sensed danger ahead, and to confine it the help of his attorney was needed. He took Binny there, and sat, embarrassed, while she told her story, and she did it pretty well, in spite of occasional bursts of sobbing. It was a long session, at the end of which Hans was convinced, without the slightest doubt, that Binny must scramble out of the case as best she could, regardless of winners and losers. This was to meet the higher needs of the Knobel family, which did not accommodate lawsuits about a member being a cheat and a conspirator, or a case over the third option and the effect of the rescission motion being decided in court, and likely to be reported in the Santa Marta Bee, of whose editions Hans was painfully aware the family newsagencies sold many copies. The attorney, Jack

Roberts, was instructed to inform Ed of the sea-change in strategy, for Binny's part, regarding both rescission and the third option, and he did so by letter forthwith to Angel, who was not entirely surprised, though inwardly relieved. He could face lawyer-negotiations better than a possible State Bar tribunal inquiry into the ethics of his deals with Ed. From the attorney's letter soon at hand, Ed quickly realized that negotiation and not litigation was the name of the only path ahead. And that from then on the effective adviser for all the McGinty interests would be the Knobel family attorney.

The Jones were at home on the evening prior to the meeting when a call came from their friend, Leland Baigent. Barney answered, and listened intently for a good minute before exclaiming, "Well, that surely is hot news!", and excitedly left, telling Zina he would continue the call from the telephone in the study, without other explanation. Intrigued, she picked up the hand-set to replace it, and on hearing the excitement in the men's voices, listened in, until Leland starting swearing, as was his habit, and Barney said, "Hold the language pal, as Zina could be there", whereupon she placed the hand-set on its cradle, and the click was heard was heard by the men, who both laughed heartily, without a word.

On Barney's return after the call he wanted to tell Zina, and she wanted to know, and she said: "I heard something about a palace revolution, and firing Manuel, but little more, yet I suppose there's more, and I'm all ears."

"Yes, Leland gets hold of scuttlebutt that we don't, and he's figured that resentment against Manuel has been building up among a few directors for quite a while. It became active a couple of weeks back, when the court decision in that long-running lawsuit about security was given, and which the board kept to themselves while they sorted themselves out. They were all blown to bits by it. It's been of no interest to me, but of course I've seen references to it, especially in circulars from Manuel, which often spin facts, and ditto Ed, and I've felt their egos might be keeping the case alive, and I guessed that if we lost, Manuel would be shattered."

Zina said: "I don't get it. I never understood what the case was about, and as we had more important things at hand,   we never talked about it."

"Yes, that's how it's been. I could tell you more, but I know you would start laughing as I went, because it would all sound so silly, so I'll cut it short. It was about who should control security. It's been the OSMs. They talked with the board - or rather Manuel talked with Ed - about the financial compensation in changing control from OSM to board. Not surprisingly, the two gladiators had trouble even agreeing on that, and one thing led to another, and into arbitration then court, where it ended with us being knocked out. The word's out it will cost us plenty. As Manuel's forecasts were always rosy, I suppose that's how the board saw it too. Maybe it was to be a big put-down of Ed. It's helped fire that blowout for legals shown in the budget papers. For some of Manuel's enemies that's been a sore point, and they have been bitching about all litigation, and the war between Manuel and Ed, and have got into the minds of some directors, so Manuel's grip on the board has weakened. Then the bombshell of the decision comes along to make it all worse."

Zina asked, "Do you think that by living mostly in Texas - or anywhere distant - Manuel could miss some of the local vibrations that some leaders feel a need for?"

"I'm sure of it. He's the only director who doesn't live here. He misses out on casual encounters and chat that keep people up to date. He can't sniff things out as a resident president can. It mightn't matter often, or in some condominiums, but he's vulnerable when it's a hothouse like Gran Capitan. He relies on Libby Ryan, as his personal assistant, and nobody could do it better, but it seems it's not enough, especially when you lose big cases, and some owners are already doubting you."

"Because of that he might not have sensed his power base was being eroded."

"Agreed. That plus a ton of natural self-confidence. Anyway, the other directors, or at least a majority of them, have shaken off their normal timidity, and taken Manuel in hand, and made him pull his horns in, and closed down some of the litigation with Ed. Leland thinks he's hanging on by one director vote, but there's guess-work in that, as most directors are keeping their mouths shut. Leland has read the judgment, and our copy must be on its way, but things aren't made any better by the judge criticizing the way the Gran Capitan case was handled. That brings us back to what Charles and I have said all along, that Manuel's inexperience in lawsuit management shows up all the time, but his ego prevents him from seeing that he's out of his depth.

"The board has been very busy, as we'll see from its report, which Leland has already seen. He doesn't know if Manuel will resign, or if he will keep a majority among the directors, but we should hear tomorrow."

"And they kept it to themselves! No wonder you couldn't get sense from them about guiding the owners about those two motions. Oh my! Poor Manuel. After all his trying for the owners."

"Yes. Pity. Maybe he shouldn't have fooled himself that condo lawsuits can be run well enough by switched-on business-men, and that moral right is bound to win in court."

"Well, we all have to learn, but usually it's not as publicly as this. The directors seem to have let him think for them, and make their decisions too. That's another lesson. Can they fire him? I hope not. Do they want to? I hope not."

"I don't know, and Leland didn't either. You would need someone to replace him, and I would imagine there's a director or two who would like the top job, but aren't sure enough of their numbers to have a go, or else aren't sure they could handle this troubled condo. And there must be owners out there with the right background, who might show up sometime."

"Do you think Manuel's enemies, the owners who are always rousing on him, will attack him at the meeting? That wouldn't be nice to see."

"I suppose they will. It's a rare chance for them. Remember he's put a few people down along the way."

"Oh! my God! Does Charles know? Can't, if we didn't."

"He's away. I think he's doing it hard on his own with his heart playing up."

"Of course. You think he might go to a daughter? Maybe Rose, in San Diego?"

"I think that's where he is right now, so could be so."

22

In which the motions go well for the rebels - Manuel under fire from owners - Charles speculates on Ed's future plays - celebration of the rescission

To the surprise of many, including the Jones and Charles, the excitement at the meeting didn't come from the two motions, as there was no debate on them at all, confirming that points of order and the rules of meeting procedure are daunting for inexperienced owners. Here the advantage lay clearly with Barney, who knew the field well, and had prepared for battle. The boss of the current administration manager, CA, was there to advise and assist the president on technical points, and as a cordial working relationship between them was in place, and Manuel was for motion 11 and against motion 12, the adviser had no interest in helping those who had reverse priorities. As Charles had expected, enemy owners would have needed to prepare carefully to match Barney's preliminary work. He had promoted his rescission motion, demolished the other with forceful argument, and left his rivals little space in which to move. Without hiring an attorney for guidance, they were lost. But that did not account for Ed's silence. Hiring attorneys had never previously been a problem for him. Barney's motion 11 struck at both his reputation, and his treasured third option obtained, as has been shown, by planning, great effort, and cheating.

Many votes on the two motions had been filed beforehand, and had been counted, and alone were enough to assure the result Barney had sought, without reference to the votes filed at the meeting and still to be counted. So there was not even an element of suspense there. Instead, attention was riveted on Manuel's reaction to the turning against him of some directors, and the consequences in any direction of the loss of the security lawsuit. The board made it clear in a statement issued on the eve of the meeting that a new approach to litigation had just been adopted, so that in effect, Manuel had been rolled. The directors knew legal expense had ballooned, and that much of it was through Manuel's case management, and that owners were talking, and were lying in wait at the meeting to have their say. As he was the front man, and the chief decision maker for the board, he was also the focus of sharp criticism from several owners, some of whom had studied the financial papers and were able to pin-point bad areas. The other directors, who were equally to blame, through inactivity as against his ill-aimed activity, went unscathed, and generally failed to stand up for Manuel when he came under serious and persistent attack, from which he didn't flinch, even when accusations were both bitter and personal. And as the meeting went along, and voting for the new board was announced, it was clear that he had kept a majority of directors on side, and this was important to the Jones and Charles Olly, because the owners would not now be easily convinced to make peace with Ed at any price, which appeared to be in the minds of some of those, including directors, whom Barney classified as the Munich Men.

The Jones were so pleased that the rescission motion had got up, and content also with the denial of motion 12, they held a small celebration with a handful of like-minded owners the same evening. Everything concerning Gran Capitan's current affairs was fully discussed, and deep satisfaction expressed.

Charles came home in time for the celebration, and was the object of much explaining by his friends of the events of the day. Like most of them, he had been unaware of the court decision, and the directors' revolt, and decision to settle outstanding lawsuits, and was astonished, and the more so because of the timing, coincident with the meeting. His views were much in demand, and he said:

"I can't tell any better than you what may happen from now on, but here goes. For me, the rescission is a great success. It's a good start to righting a serious wrong. The voting in favor was good enough, considering owner disinterest though time passing, and the distraction of the appeasement motion. So you could say the owners aren't ready for a quick fix just to get peace with Ed, and the appeasers should take notice.

"Besides, even though Manuel is hurt, he is still president. While I think a couple of his fellow directors fancy themselves to take his place, he is too powerful for them at present, so they'll wait and see. They all bring energy and sense to their specialties, and so together make a very good board, if you close your eyes to mishandling of lawsuits and justice for owners. No natural leaders there though, for guys like him and Josh Spinks come along rarely. Generally the other directors lack the cojones for a fight, so won't act until Manuel falls over, as he very nearly did this time. One change in allegiance from a board member and the numbers could be against him. The danger then would be the Munich Men. So long as Manuel is on deck, and has the right support, and gets better legal advice than has been his habit, we can rely on resistance. By that I don't mean we should be chasing complete victory over Ed. I don't think our directors are either clever or aggressive enough for that. I think it's important that owners like ourselves, who see the option of self-management as important, keep our voice heard, be it through Barney's circulars, or your own. If ordinary owners don't keep the self-management flag flying it could fall one day.

"A problem about the same authorship of circulars is reader boredom, of which Manuel's many circulars, which are often loaded with spin, are an example. Where spin is gross it should be shown up, and that's where owner circulars have a place, but not all from the one source please.

"Consider this. Why should a loss in court and legal expense be a reason for our collapse. We lost, we'll learn from that. Agree that Manuel led us astray. Money has been wasted. But why dwell on those things, done and irreversible? Sure, be more careful next time, but don't lose a battle and take that as meaning all is lost, because the war is about the bigger issues of a few million dollars, and making and keeping our condo management user-friendly and economic.

"I think you want my ideas about what Ed might do. I ignore Binny here, because frankly I don't know where she fits in at the moment. We know enough about Ed though. We can wonder why he didn't do something about the rescission motion. Astounding! Not even a point of order. Remember he usually has an attorney barking for him. Yet here was a clear allegation against him of deceit and conspiracy, and he didn't crack a boo. In passing, recall those accusations have been flying around here for a long time and none of the accused has denied their truth. So you might wonder why our directors haven't chased them down the conspiracy road, but don't get me going on that, as it's too late, unless it crops up in a future battle with Ed about the rescission. It just might. Now I'll mention something new. I've been a little concerned about time running out on us for a conspiracy prosecution. Now that rescission is the new flavor, that problem is over. Please don't ask me to explain further; not tonight anyway.

"Going on, we should expect Ed to make much of the deed. He must claim it was separate from the resolution of the meeting, and was validly signed. That would be a good argument from him, but if Manuel has his way, it will be contested. I once heard it said by Grace Gambell of Prince that even if the signing was flawed, Ed had a right to call for it to be signed correctly, because of the words in the 1988 resolution 'that a deed be entered into'. However, since then the old records have produced incriminating evidence of malfeasance surrounding the resolution and hence the deed, so she may be wrong there. The weighting could be different now. Ed needs to breathe life into that deed, or a substitute for it, to make his case for the third option, which is worth maybe three million dollars of our money to him. Expect to hear from him. There may be nothing for the board to do until then, but that's not our concern. I'd think the rescission stands until or unless Ed brings along some heavy artillery, and whatever it is, we must hope the board will meet fire with fire. I know the legal costs would worry some folks, and this is an area where multi-owner authorship of circulars could be important, different voices singing the same tune. We shouldn't underestimate the strength of the owners' case post-basement. That was gold from heaven, and owners should not squander it by allowing weaklings, or Munich Men, make bad decisions.

"As Zina once asked, 'If the meeting and the motion were based on wrongdoing, and conspiracy, how could a consequential deed change or purify that?' We may get the answer from a court one day. Our side would have to get the wrongdoing into evidence in court, so as to put the judge in the picture. In effect, it would be stating the elements of the conspiracy. It would be quite a large legal task, just as proving the conspiracy in another sort of suit was always going to be, so that's not new.

"My speculation done with, don't you feel that Ed's bargaining position has lost some punch by the simple fact of rescission?"

The gathering murmured assent.

Leland had been listening to the old man intently, like the others. Looking at Zina he asked: "May I propose a toast?" She nodded and waved him on, and when she and Barney had topped up their guest's glasses, he led a toast: "The rescission. May its strength grow and grow."

23

Charles is moving on and some of his past is revealed - analysis of the failed lawsuit - the hoodwinking of owners at Gran Capitan reviewed - ingredients for improvement discussed - Zina makes a shock announcement concerning the Jones' future

Charles decided to go to live with his daughter. After disposing of his household effects, including the gift of his fishing gear to the Jones, and shipping prized furniture to his new home, he spent the final two nights at Gran Capitan as their guest. He was ready to leave town after closure of the condo sale, and on the night before Barney and Zina held a small dinner party, to which they also invited Rose - standing by to help her father - along with Leland and Peggy Baigent, and another couple who were supportive condo owners, and also fishing enthusiasts like him. All were jubilant at the recent turn of events.

Charles naturally gaunt face seemed thinner, and his friends supposed it was due to a mixture of age, the stress and activity of recent events, and his heart trouble. Besides, he was in the middle of a major change in life style, so the hosts planned an early night.

Barney and Zina were occasional fishers, but not as enthusiastic or regular as Charles, who frequently fished the lake and its tributary streams from his small boat, or the banks, or when the seas in the Santa Barbara Channel were calm enough, from a charter fishing boat that catered for groups there, and for cleaning guests' catches to take home. He kept his catch in a home freezer, and gave out fillets to friends from time to time, which the recipients prized, and reciprocated with hospitality, when he was well regarded also for his wit, and self-deprecatory manner, and no fault on his part led his friends to take him to have been a more prominent and successful attorney than had been the case, with which position all parties were content.

The gathering was jocularly speculating on how Charles would keep up his gifts of fish from San Diego, when Peggy Baigent became more serious. "You may not know," said she, "That it's not only us and other locals whom Charles has fed fish to …." At which point Charles half-raised his arm to silence her, but she gently pushed it down. "No," she continued, "there's more to it than is generally known, as I found out by chance recently. Y'see, he needed a ride downtown, and I took him. His destination was the Salvos Homeless Shelter on West Sutter, almost opposite the Santa Marta Music Club where Zina and I go, she to play her piano, and me my flute, which we can't do at home because of the house rules." Rose interrupted with "Pardon, but why so?" Peggy replied, "It's all about noise control. To some people all music is noise, and to all of us some is nothing else. Distinguishing is too hard for the directors, so a complete ban is the rule. Pity for us, but such is a musician's life in a condo." Rose nodded her understanding, and Peggy continued. "So, being interested in our friend, and having seen him once before going in with a parcel, I went there one day and got to chat with the supervisor, and learned that he was a regular donor of fillets, which she knew he had even bought from the market when he had run out of his own catch. So that's another side to our Charles – philanthropic fisher!" She smiled at him, with, "Please forgive me for outing you." He shrugged, and said, "Just a hobby. It's not as available where Rose lives, though her home has other splendid attractions."

Zina asked, "As you must leave us, to our great sorrow, this might be the moment to tell us how you came here."

"It was like this," he replied: "We - Mary and I - had sold our home and were ready for a condo, but it had to be accessible for our family, and fishing and of course, a decent climate. Both of us were into retirement, and we hit upon Gran Capitan, and bought in off-the-plan, then fitted it out in our minds, and had planned all the details, when Mary became ill, and died far too quickly. You may as well know, she had long-standing emphysema, which of itself was not a big problem, but sadly it cloaked the development of lung cancer, so that when that was diagnosed it was too late. Ironically, she had been a nurse at a cancer clinic, which had caused her to quit smoking, but again, too late. I'll spare you other details, but the girls and I agreed it would keep me closer to Mary's spirit if I lived here, and that was a good decision."

The meal over, the party moved to the easy chairs, where they chatted while Barney and Zina offered coffee and brandy. When they settled down, there was a silent understanding that Charles should have right of way this night. He broke the silence:

"So, I've been here 12 years. I must say that had I any idea that things might turn out as they have, I would not have come, but sold the unit instead. But I wanted to live with Mary's memory, as we had together planned this as our home."

Excepting Rose, that had been news to all the others present, who sat silent for a bit, then he continued: "For the first few years the dream was what I wanted, and near enough to what I had expected. I had even made allowance for the probability of occasional difficulties within a community of several hundreds.

"Half way along I realized that serious conflict lay ahead, and so I had then the chance to move on, but chose not to, maybe because I was comfortable, and was interested in what was going on. The dream had taken a hit, but on the other hand the local events were a reality, with some legal aspects that I found stimulating. I was not familiar with the law of condominiums until turmoil started, and then I became absorbed in catching up, and I know that you, as concerned owners, have gone down the same path. We know very well our lessons have been costly in terms of both our money and our contentment in our common home, and as I go on my way I hope for better things ahead for you and the other owners, and that the condo can become

"Gran" in fact, as well as in name." He paused, contemplatively. The others kept quiet, until Peggy asked:

"You mentioned a change in your understanding half way along. Would you care to tell us how. We're all interested in knowing just what brought us all the bad luck we know about."

Charles remained silent a little longer, and the others knew his precise manner well enough to be patient while he got his answer right. He then continued, "Peggy, so often a happening has more than one cause, though it's simpler, and matches our impatience, to be content with one only, and to look for no more. That happens here too, and I'd like to take your time to take the notion further. For me, the disturbing current started with the McGintys putting to the board in 1987 a prepared 25 year contract. The prospect of success must have seemed real enough to make that effort worth-while. Such a hope was unlikely to be dropped in a hurry. We all know it was denied, and that the directors were not of a single mind there. We know also that a few months later, the McGintys manipulated the elections so as to have directors amenable to their wishes. Not that it was said like that. Rather, the new board was to be welcomed for its concern for owners' needs, and the prospect of harmony between it on the one hand, and the OSMs and the administration manager on the other, which also carried the implication of furthering the owners' interests. The whole thing stank: the effort, the propaganda, and the result. For me, Gran Capitan had changed, could not be the same again." He paused again, and the others knew he was running other matters through his mind. In the meantime Barney quietly looked to his guests' cups and glasses, until Charles continued:

"The supremely important factor about the contract is that at the time of its signing at the commencement of this condominium, it was loaded for the OSMs and against the owners. That contract, and its bias, controls us still. The key elements were leniency in respect of violations of contract duties, which naturally also meant contract termination was made so much harder, and the high compensation, which we now know has increased our assessments by hundreds of dollar annually, and by thousands all up, and by millions for all of us together. It was value transferred from the owners to the OSMs. As long as those elements stayed intact, the incumbent OSM was on a very good thing, just as BBC had been when selling the contract in 1980. That outfit knew those things from the start, and we did not, until Barney alerted us. He showed how it was set up to deprive us, and how, later, the 1988 conspirators also stole our money, in the style you know well, and which would be the envy of any number of other crooks. Other contract provisions were, and are, a disgrace, as we've seen in very recent years, and I'll leave them aside, for enough's enough. In my opinion the owners could have, and should have, sued BBC early on, for breach of fiduciary duty about the contract, but nobody thought of it, at least until after Barney did his bit, and by then it was too late. Why? Because a right to sue, or claim any sort of legal redress, can be lost through inactivity by the aggrieved party, or by its accepting what happened. Recall that after the developer ceded control of this operation to the board, we the condo owners, voted that contract, and so it became our contract, and that was always going to be an obstacle for suit; not that that question came up. I suspect that voting that contract was facilitated by the presence of owners and directors who, unknown to buyers, were BBC stooges. So we had owners approving a contract that was to cost them and their successors millions above a fair thing, to say nothing of the consequent stress for decent directors and owners. To that approval, of doubtful quality, the time-lapse factor was grafted on, and gave BBC effective immunity from suit. So while the change for me came with the conspiracy to extend contract tenure through a third option, it was attributable in part to the earlier event of BBC setting up the contract as it did."

"For the condo owners it's been a killer contract from the start", Leland interjected. "And it's just too bad we missed out on suing BBC. And it seems to me we've missed the boat again by not running down the 2008 committee and Ed and Prince for the conspiracy about the third option, which we mightn't even have known about but for Barney and you."

Charles continued: "Quite so. The bad contract was a lure for OSMs to cement their hold on management here. They knew, better than us, the good thing they were on, so along came the McGinty pitch for extension. An outsider could only know by going into the numbers, which Barney did, and then Manuel, and that told us enough to make it most unlikely that extension would be approved by the owners prior to management modeling, but the swindlers pulled another fast one by leaving his modeling motion off the agenda, so there was no contest. It's hard to win when the other side cheats."

Zina asked: "Isn't it a funny thing that it took us so long to wake up? Look at this way. Add to the 400 original owners the second wave, being buyers from the pioneers. Guess that makes 450. Few of them, on their own, could be tricked out of ten dollars, let alone the thousands for each of us, or millions for the total, as has happened; in truth a work still in progress. I'm ashamed we could be so gullible."

"I agree about us being suckers," added Leland, "but remember we had no watch-dog to warn us. I think that if you're a first-time condo owner, it's a little like going into hospital. You're in their hands. You're only one of many sick folks. You'd be out of order telling them how to run the place, or arguing about their fees. Above all, you trust the institution, and everything about it. Not that I want to push the comparison too far, but I feel we all came here feeling the place and its systems, including management in all its aspects, were not for querying or changing by us as individuals. Our interests would be well enough served by the contracted managers and our elected directors; like doctors and nurses. And I think that attitude has worked well enough in very many condos, and our experience here isn't typical."

Peggy said: "That's sounds right. For this train-wreck of ours to happen

180

you needed men who became directors who were both crooked, and dumb enough not to see they were victims as much as any other owner. That's a funny combination, I guess."

Leland had a slightly different slant to offer. "I see the only victims as us, who had the wool pulled over our eyes at every point. The insiders who set out to rob the owners weren't victims in my book, because they were not innocents, but chose their path. They had a clear choice. We didn't. They knew everything important, and we knew but the half of it."

Charles held up his hand for a chance to speak: "I don't disagree with any of that, but there's another factor that takes Gran Capitan into the rare category. It was what the OSMs did with the directors they sponsored, and who became the 1988 board. The current that disturbed me was, as I said, the push for long tenure without review of contract conditions, including OSM compensation. The conspiracy was quite another current: actually a wave, even a tsunami, when we saw it clearly, almost three years later, after a new board had uncovered the past records. But it didn't stop there. That is to say, the day for remediation and retribution, or justice if you like, was passed over by the new board, and that to me was as much anti-owner as the OSMs creating their own board of directors. Now we're in the position where the owners are sick to the back teeth of board-manager squabbling and litigation, especially when we seem to lose more than we win, and the attorney fees and court expenses mount up and increase our assessments that are already too high because of the compensation under the contract. There was no more important single suit than conspiracy, yet our board didn't see it, but chose instead to run minor matters which arguably were kept on the boil as much through personal antagonism between Manuel and Ed, as for the true interests of the condo owners.

"I said the push for the third option long tenure was a disturbing factor for me, and it turned out to be only one of several issues. Go back to the formation of the contract. Go forward to the making of the conspiracy. Farther forward, to the failure of the new board to prosecute conspiracy. Far, farther back to the strangeness of the management rights system, as it's called in Queensland, and wonder how indifferent its government can be to the rights of owners of condos there, to allow management rights to displace owner rights. For it was there that the McGintys got the notions that they linked to the weaknesses of our Californian set-up. Where do we stop counting?"

Barney spoke up: "The way you put it, a condo development is also a minefield, and if the condo owners are lucky they won't get blown up as they go through, but the risk is always there. The danger is magnified by crooked developers and crooked OSMs and even by crooked directors. You can get through safely with luck and by watching your steps, but fraud can't be prevented, and afterward the victims are left with a right to sue, which they can take or leave, and we know what we - or rather our directors - decided there."

Charles ended the chat with: "Right. Well, as I leave I'll be glad to know y'all will continue alert, which will help the owners navigate the difficulties ahead, whatever they may be."

Barney broke the ensuing silence. "It's an ill wind et cetera," he said. "But for you coming here we couldn't have put up the fight as we have, so I'd like to propose a toast, when you're ready." To which Leland added, "And I'll second it." So prepared, the toast was to Mary and Charles, which touched the old man considerably.

After final farewells had been exchanged next morning, the Jones sat silently for a time, until Zina said, "If you have a minute I have some more news for us. We must work harder at giving us smoking. We should be able to get on top of it now the pressure's off you here, and after hearing about poor Mary. The other matter will take longer, so please be patient, and here me out. I've been thinking with my left brain, you'll see. Now I'm going to suggest we move from here. Oh, look surprised, of course!" She paused while he did.

24

Zina's plan for moving to the Towers is discussed - Barney agrees - keeping both condos debated

"I've checked out Towers of Gold," Zina told Barney. You know it well enough, inside and out. Now ask yourself for how long our lives here can be fun. When I go to the Towers for bridge or tennis or anything, I compare it with Gran Capitan, and it seems much better. But if it wasn't the Towers it should be somewhere else, as I don't think that you being in the epicenter of every storm about this place is a sensible way of living. Y'see, the way it's structured, there's no getting away from our tension and storms. There's no rainbow on the horizon. Even if Ed is subdued - and that's a big if - there's no guarantee that our directors will be smarter in handling legal issues than any we've had so far, nor that our owners will take a real interest in what goes on, but instead will leave everything to the board which, as we know, can mean in reality leaving it to the most dominant director, someone like Josh Spinks or Manuel Martin. Now that would be in order if such men were blessed with great wisdom besides their powerful personalities, but that's such a rare combination it would be unsafe to rely on it. It may seem too extreme to even mention this, but to my mind our past events and poor leadership in management issues, suggest the possibility that new directors will one day lead our condo owners into another bad management arrangement. So even if we finish with Ed as OSM in a year or so, we might fall into a new deal that's just as bad. Why? Because our system doesn't encourage new blood for the board of directors. I mean quality blood. Why would any half-decent new chum feel that being a director here would be a worthwhile use of time and effort? Most owners don't care enough, so the ambitious guys get a smooth ride in. Or Manuel engineers compliant souls into vacant seats. Test what I'm saying by a look at the set-up at the Towers.

"The chances of us going backwards like that are less with you and someone like Charles paying attention, but with him gone now, it's all you, or if not, then too much you. The only way you'll ever get out is by leaving. Oh, one day you will have won all the fights, and then you might say there's no need to leave, 'cos we've won, and everything is in good shape. But that will be too late for retirees, who should have more pleasant things to do with their time and energy. You may not know this, but your beautiful habit of smiling whenever possible is seen a little less lately, and that will never do.

"We've discussed some of this before, but I must remind you of some singular differences between here and there. As it's self-managed, we don't hear of board-OSM conflicts. The directors are pre-selected through an introductory system to show owners exactly who and what the candidates are. They revolve, as some directors can't stay in office longer than two consecutive years, so there's new blood every year, alongside the more experienced hands. A non-resident director cannot be an office-bearer, and more than two aren't permitted on any board. The candidates for election are listed randomly, which gets around the donkey vote effect that sometimes comes with the alphabetic listing we have here, and which allowed Joan Abernethy to get on the 1989 board to prop up the Brooks-Spinks power bloc. She knew nothing about administration, and had no experience of any sort to commend her. It was not known that she was a close friend of Brooks wife, and came in only to support Bernard, and get his team a majority. It worked. They then had four votes and held the reins for another year, and you know better than me the harm that caused.

"I guess you know the owners there have a few committees reporting to the board, and their memberships are turned over occasionally to give more owners a say. It's also a way of introducing future directors. One committee runs an occasional newsletter, funded by the condominium, which carries owner opinions, besides messages from the board, and provides a forum where decisions can be trashed, or praised, as readers wish. When you compare our system, you see that our owners are so often in the dark. Our board's loaded circulars, always signed by Manuel, may be heavy with spin, but how do you know, how do you find out? We owners have no place in which to make statements or ask questions. Well, maybe at a general meeting, but only if you attend, and most owners don't. And then you need to be at ease in public speaking, and desirably know more about the governing documents than suits most owners. So the other side of an issue has to be put by circular at an owner's expense, as we well know. It's the only way to get coverage. CA's style of reporting board meetings is loaded in favor of the board on the big issues, which is only to be expected from an administration manager dependent upon it for re-engagement. A newsletter might and should balance the official propaganda which we get here. We need open owner appraisal of what's happening. Being presented with a motion to vote, out of the blue, without time for owners to reflect and digest, isn't the only way to do it.

"Few owners have the know-how and concern to do and send circulars as we have done, and the expense is always a put-off, and any points made that way can be instantly dismissed by a few words from the board, which might be misleading or wrong, yet the owner will not have the resources to keep it up, and send out follow-up circulars, which the board can. Every other government - taking a condo board as its government - in the country has an opposition and a media to help keep all the facts in view. If you were to ask me I could give you examples of the board misleading owners, if only by not telling the full story. I'll guarantee that if we had had an owners' newsletter in place, the stupidity of the dispute about security would have been known long before we lost the case. I have great faith in one like they have at the Towers. It would be of little use though if it were only another voice of the board.

"Another thing, the residents mix better than here through a monthly social together, and I believe good numbers come along. I think the tensions here put some folks off coming along to ours, for fear of meeting people they find disagreeable, or being sucked into a political argument. And yet some of our people need to get out and mix, it being too easy to cringe alone in a unit.

"At the Towers renting of units out is very tightly controlled, minimum six months, and the commissions belong to the condominium. The board has to approve each lease, official forms must be used, the tenant must know the rules, and the owner is responsible for everything the tenant does. Above all, there's a limit on how many condos can be rented out at the one time, though I don't know the numbers. At any rate, I get the feeling there are fewer tenants at the Towers than here. Actually, in this as in so many other ways, the early promise of Gran Capitan, the nod and wink stuff from BBC that it was to be very much residential-owner-occupied, has been bent badly. We all know it's terribly important in a proud unit complex that the tone of the place be sustained through the quality and number of tenants. That affects values too, because buyers often check what gives with renting.

"Auto parking at the Towers is controlled better than here. As you know, you need a ticket to park, there's a time limit, violators are fined, or have their autos towed away. Not like here, where all comers can enter, and if they overstay, all the security men do is stick a notice on the vehicle, which means nothing to some cheeky devils. Residents can't bring in commercial vehicles, or recreational equipment like boats, without prior board approval. And though I don't know how it works, the board takes an interest in prospective unit buyers, to keep standards up.

"Altogether the Towers is, I believe, a more civilized place than here, catering more completely for retiree owners like ourselves, and I think the design and amenities and maintenance are almost as good.

"I know, after we finish with Ed and the lawsuits, and you've spent half your retirement on the job, you could turn to making Gran Capitan like the Towers, and it would then be a great place. But I suggest you leave all that to somebody else, because getting there could take more time and health than you've got ahead of you. Another thing, if I may say so, again, is that without Charles the struggle just became so much harder for you.

"It's odd that male dominators have been in charge here for so long. I was glad when Manuel came in like a strong savior to lead the charge against the Bernard Brooks crowd, as we don't know what further mischief they had in store for us. If you can concoct and succeed with one swindle, why not two? Manuel would have none of that, but still, his ego and over-bearing style have produced something nearly as bad. He's wounded now, so coming from Texas for meetings where he faces hostility and very little of the adulation he once drew, may become a lonely business, which he may tire of. But whoever we have at the top, it would take years to get in place systems similar to those at the Towers. Maybe never, because it would mean change, and there's always somebody against that." She paused: "Oh my God, what a bore I am. All that! I suppose I felt I had to get it out while I had the chance."

Barney had been listening, silently. He said: "That's a pretty good pitch, my dear. I like your comparison of the two places, and how you've pin-pointed stuff we could use here. Actually, I've been troubled by some issues without telling you, and now seems to be the time. I've looked at the report on the security case and at some of the stuff in the board circulars and board records of meetings concerning it, and I believe that if owners had been able to see more, the case could have taken a different turn long ago. But then they were in a fog, because there was no critique of anything the board offered, as there would have been if owners had been in on the story through a newsletter.

"The report from president Manuel to the owners, distributed at the meeting, attributed the loss of the security case to deviousness by Ed, and shortcomings in court by our trial attorney. At the same time he expressed astonishment at the result, which was another way of saying the judge had got it wrong. So he would have us believe it wasn't his fault. But if you read on, and not many owners will, you'll find the judge criticizing our case management, meaning Manuel's, implying that the result could have been different but for that. He was not talking about our lawyers at that point, but about us, the client. WOW! Besides, the court made no order as to the expense of the case, so that if the usual rule is applied, we will pay Ed's fees besides our own. I seem to remember Manuel saying once that if we lost the case Ed had to pay our costs, and that we could appeal, but he couldn't if he lost, and I wondered how a hard head like Ed could have agreed to something so unusual.

"But two other points trouble me, from the aspect of due process. The office of administration manager is supposed to be put to tender each year, but instead CA was directly appointed, I guess through Manuel's direction or influence. He explained to the meeting that CA did a good job at a reasonable price, which seems true. However, the Declaration has provisions about the control of spending, and unless the board gets competitive quotes it's not behaving correctly. Another point of concern is that in its report of the meeting CA stated that because its main man was counting votes while the criticism of Manuel was in full roar, he could not take it in, so could not report on it. That was a cop-out. The bylaws require full statements of all meetings. With three representatives of CA present, and a meeting expected to be fiery, CA should have come prepared to cope. As it was, the 370 owners who didn't get to the meeting were left in the dark, and didn't learn how Manuel had come under fire. Those instances show closeness of president and administration manager, which is not at all uncommon in condos, and even necessary, can be abused. Seeing it so blatantly just makes me wonder if there's more out of sight. A newsletter would be the place for it to be shown up to owners, in the interests of them being better informed."

186

Zina interrupted with a gesture, and continued, "That's right. The great sadness of Gran Capitan is that a newsletter wasn't running when the McGintys were on the extension path, then rigging the elections for directors, then engineering the grant of the third option. There was enough suspicion about each for serious and open debate, had there been a newsletter. As it was you were the only to make a noise, and nearly won through your circulars, missing out by only one vote. It can't be proved, but it seems most likely a newsletter would have turned the tide. One vote only, you said. Remember?"

"Remember?" cried Barney. "How could I forget? Every word you said is right on. With either one vote less for them, or one vote more for us, we would have got up. Even though the McGintys are discredited, we all know we're still in a bad hole here, and all because our owners didn't know what they were doing; more than once. Conflict between Ed and some directors is embarrassing for owners, who hope that wise heads will produce a compromise solution, but no deal that keeps the condo under contract management for much longer is worth a squirt in my book. Maybe Manuel should stand aside, as president at least, so as to defuse the bad feelings with Ed. But only maybe. He won't anyway."

"No, please leave him in charge, for he seems the best available", Zina replied. "Just get him to loosen the reins a bit. But saying that is a sad reflection on the interest our owners take in community affairs. I mean, out of 400 owners we see nobody better than a man who has let us down, and doesn't even live here."

"Agreed. That's borne out by the list of candidates for the annual meeting. There's little change, and above all nobody stood against Manuel. But I put to you there could be more change if the owners were better informed, which could only happen through a newsletter. Switched-on owners could get their views across, right or wrong wouldn't matter, for the open sharing of views would be the aim. Gran Capitan would become more of a democracy that at present. More like Towers."

Zina thought about that, and said, "I agree. This could sound funny, but y'know I've never seen a newssheet at the Towers, even though I knew they were there. Yet, come to think of it, the girls I play with do talk as if they know a lot about their local issues, much more so than I've noticed here. I must follow up."

"Well, certainly we could have gotten our ideas across to the owners better that way. I could have discussed the difference between a government that operates though the separation of powers, and here, where the board kids itself that it's okay, and also that the directors are smart enough, to act out the functions of all three powers."

"Is that like a DA being the judge in the same case?"

"Sort of."

"I guess also the basement find could have turned out better with a newssheet here," said Zina. "As it is, owners must wonder how come it all fizzled out."

"Right! Another thing, do you know how the Towers handles legal advice? I mean, in big places like these, where directors are rarely attorneys, maybe one should be on retainer, and attend meetings. Legal issues come up all the time, and getting the directors on the right path up front could save us from going down the wrong streets. I may be wrong, but I feel that if an experienced attorney were to keep abreast of legal issues, and advise promptly, the directors wouldn't be pushed into deciding something alone, or on the unreliable advice that can come from half-trained employees of firms like Prince and CA. We might also get to use the one counsel, instead of jumping around the shop, as we seem to do."

"Zina answered, "No, I don't know about a lawyer at the Towers, but I can try to find out. There's no hurry?"

"Not at all. But back to your idea about moving, it may surprise you, but I take it seriously. As of right now, we've made a contribution here, even if not as successful as we had hoped. There's still a stack of fighting ahead, as Ed will keep fighting, and it's impossible to predict how it will all wash up. If he wins, Gran Capitan might never get to give its owners the chance of voting on self-management. I can't discount the chance of some owners, including directors, becoming so tired of the struggle they'll surrender, with the best of intentions, of course. So there's a reason to keep Manuel on the job, or at least on the board. Whatever his faults, he's the best director to counter the appeasers."

Zina, looking puzzled, asked, "Do you realize what you are saying. That Manuel should stay here and fight, while you talk about leaving the place, and the struggle?"

"I see." He digested the message, then said:, "It sounds selfish of me, I agree. I plead guilty. He had the chance to enlist me and Charles into a warrior committee but he spurned us, and it's too late now. And frankly, I've worked up such a distrust of the guy I'd be a hypocrite to make out I could accept his decisions on legal issues. The only reason I'd like to see him kept in harness is that he has the determination to put Ed in his place, and is not a weak reed like some of his colleagues. Although they don't trust him now as much as before, even if reined in he seems the best scrapper when Ed is the opponent. Will that explanation save me from a prison sentence, your Honor?"

Zina laughed. "Yep, but only because I need you home here helping with our own plans."

Barney said, "You say it's time I stood back a bit. Part of me wants to hang around and be part of the action, while another part tells me to cool it, get up and go, and make you happy."

"And you!" she threw in. "This is not just for me. A lot is for you, who having done his bit, and more, should try to avoid stressful situations."

"Right we are. So my answer is I agree in principle, so we can start talking about how to implement it, remembering I'm still in uniform here."

"Thanks honey. You can't imagine how pleased I am. I'm sure you'll find some way of using your great knowledge to the advantage of the Towers, and also have a more relaxed life. When you're ready I'll tell you how we could finance it, though you'll have better ideas about that than me. The main thing is that, if we wanted, we could keep this place too, and besides renting it out, have it for occasional family vacations for the children. One of my friends at the Towers does that, and we could use her experience."

"Well, having a condo close by for the families would be great. And if we keep it I'll still be entitled to a say here, so I wouldn't be walking out on them in the tough times. So sure, there's an upside. I'm afraid though we'll find the downside heavier. It simply wouldn't sing as an investment. It doesn't matter to us how happy your friend is with her deal, because we all manage our money differently. The thing to face is that so much has to come out of the rent income. Commission at 12%. Taxes, higher because a rental unit is a business, and not a home. Assessments. They're dreadfully high here, though guts and determination and brains can turn that around one day. Maintenance of unit fittings and surfaces. Insurance. Allow something for the inevitable vacancy periods. We'd be lucky to net two per cent on the value of the unit, and you know that's not good investing. For the number of times our families would want to use it, we'd be better off putting them up at some fancy place. And anyway, wouldn't our vacation condo have to compete with vacation attractions all over the world, so we mightn't see as much of them here as we would like. Moreover, it would be a fluke if someone's vacation dates fitted our unit's vacancy. I mean, we could hardly kick a tenant out just to suit a family on vacation. Sorry to be a sourpuss about this. Really am."

Zina replied: "Please don't be. I had no idea about the money side of renting. Some people must have a bad time of it. But not us, because we're using the left brain: that's you! And by using that we'll know to sell this unit in the same market phase as when we buy into the Towers. See, I do pay attention!"

"Of course you do: always. Any more surprises for today?"

"No, that's it. There's nothing like condo living for excitement!"

She got up, and kissed him as she went by.

25

Other friends see more fighters for the cause are needed and step up very effectively

It was only a few days after deciding to move to the Towers that Peggy Baigent ran into Zina on a street within the condominium. As they had a few things to talk about, and the time to spare, Peggy invited Zina to her place for coffee. They hadn't met since the evening with Charles, and had some loose ends to tie up. Leland would probably be home, and if so would be sure to want to carry on from that point. That was alright for Zina, and it would give her an opportunity to tell of the Jones more recent decision to move on. She wished to do this as it would not be nice if Peggy got the news second hand.

Leland was home, and after greeting Zina he asked the women to hang fire with the coffee, as he would like to be in on the discussion. He did not have to say he expected that it would concern the troubles that had engaged their interest for so long. While waiting for him Zina opened up to Peggy with her news about moving on, explaining that it would be better for Barney to detach himself from the constant struggle at Gran Capitan, which seemed endless, like a road with no turning. As Gran Capitan was the Baigents home, she refrained from making comparisons between it and the Towers, though she had delighted in doing so in presenting her case to Barney. Instead, she now stressed the benefits for Barney in shedding his mantle of savior of the owners from the inertia of the directors, and the tenacity of the McGintys, that had consumed his passions for so long. And it was obvious that the move, physically so short, would not hurt their close friendship.

Zina asked, "What am I to do about telling Leland?. He could think it funny not to be told while I'm here."

Peggy replied, "Yes, tell him by all means, but he'll want to tell you something too, and it will be better if he gets it off his chest first before being side-tracked with your news, important as it is." Zina assented with a nod.

Leland came in, and sat with the others at the kitchen table. Unaware of the women's discussion, and being keen to bring Zina up to speed, he went on with his own news at once, and said to her:

"I'm glad you're here, because Peggy and I have some news for the Jones. We've taken in everything that was said at Charles' dinner, and realized it's time we became more active, especially as he's away. We don't want you and Barney to feel alone. That would never do. In our own dumb way we've come to think that a compromise is the best way to go. There's no clean-cut winner in our plan, but it removes the risk of great financial loss through losing the lawsuits ahead. We don't think our people have the nerve for it, especially as it could drag on for two or three years, with appeals. And while it drags on Ed would stay in the OSM seat, and for years and years more if we lost. If we could reduce the problem to money, by getting Ed out, and closing down all the management contract stuff, our owners could finance the purchase of closure easily enough, and recapture most of the cost though reduced assessments ahead.

"It seems to we haven't laid a glove on the McGintys in our lawsuits, and the fearful thing is that by keeping that up into next round, all of us here will be hurt badly, in spirit, and in our pockets too. Putting it bluntly, Ed is better at litigation than our board. Charles told me that once. I believe it. And who among us wants to be on a board led by Manuel, or by one of those Munich Men? Not I, for one.

"So that's something of the background that has put in our minds the notion of a settlement with Ed, out of court. We're travelling part blind, because we don't know everything that's going on, and the directors only tell the owners what they choose. After the disclosures at the annual meeting there's probably not much left to tell, except details of the violations on which the board would pin its case for contract termination. Why that's a big secret is beyond me, but we can't hang about waiting to find out. It will be revealed not later than when Ed gives notice of exercise of the third option.

"In the meantime we have another approach in mind. We would say that both the McGintys and the condo owners have weak points in their cases that could be their undoing. If the McGintys lost, they would forfeit the option, and pay a lot in legal fees. I can't say they would lose the rental brokerage, because I just don't know. If we lost, we pay the fees, and would be stuck with another five years of exorbitant management compensation, and the prospect of a progressive lowering of unit values through our high unit assessments. And we would not have certainly broken the management regime we dislike so much. Upsetting that would still be a task for another day. The work that you and Barney have put into that has been marvelous, and sadly would have to kick-started again.

"We've just come to the point of talking this over with you guys, so it's timely that you came, and can take our notes home, and we can discuss the idea another time. Here, I'll show you."

The women had been listening carefully as Leland held the floor. As he paused for breath Peggy topped up the coffee cups. Zina had been looking for an opportunity to tell Leland what she had told Peggy about moving, and Peggy helped by saying, "Before you go on there's something Zina might want to tell you. She told me just before you came."

"Oh," said Leland, "I've cramped her style by holding the floor. Sorry, Zina. What's the news?"

"It's just that we've decided to move from here to the Towers. It's only a decision, about which we've taken no action yet. It's been my idea, and it's based on my concern that the strain of trying to get justice here might get Barney in the end. It was in my mind earlier, but when Charles started his move out, and I saw how much more of that legal stuff would fall on Barney's shoulders only, it seemed right to bring up the moving idea. I expected a fight about it, but he was more easily convinced than I had hoped for, so we are both firm on the idea now. We're so glad we won't be too far away from your dear selves, so we needn't shed many tears about it. Does that change anything in your ideas?"

Leland had mentally sifted the elements of his and Peggy's draft plan as Zina's news sank in, and felt nothing needed to be changed.

"Right. That's real news. Frankly, I don't know how Barney has lasted the course. He's one tenacious critter. I understood he could want out at some point, and it's come. We have to do what we have to do. So I'll show you these notes of ours, hoping that he and you will criticize them before we go public."

"You mean I'll take them with me?"

"Right. Here's your copy. Maybe you'd like to glance at them in case something needs to be corrected before you go. He handed it to Zina, who read, and the others did also, although they knew them pretty well off by heart. This is what she read:

AN OUTLINE OF A POSSIBLE FIX

The background is that without a settlement we face much litigation and inconvenience, as do the McGintys.

I must explain about the manager. I think we need a full-time resident manager. We don't need, and can't afford, one whose compensation is too high, such as the one we have at present. Big dollars won't be offered to the new guy. He or they will be paid a good salary for a set range of duties to be agreed upon. As he isn't going to be buying anything, and won't have a right of sale of his contract, capital considerations can't concern him. As to the length of the tenure, I'm suggesting three years, but a bit more or less would also do. It has to be long enough for him to settle into the job and show his best style, but not too long for us to see the end of the deal if something goes wrong along the way. He can tender again, and as he'll have his feet under our table he would be favored to be reappointed.

The letting business isn't something that has jacked up owner assessments, which have sprung only from the OSM compensation, so it costs us nothing to leave it with Ed, and doing so could make it easier to crunch a deal. It will become a wasting asset for him, I think, because the new manager must have the right to handle lettings for those owners who want to hire him, and some will switch, and few new ones will choose Ed above the new guy. The McGintys own the office, which should never have been allowed, and that gives them some leverage. Can't be helped, but the owners will want to plan for an end to that sometime. It may come up during negotiations. We aren't without muscle here. We can create another office readily.

A golden hand-shake for the McGintys won't go down well with some owners, and I don't like it one bit, but it would be recovered soon through smaller compensation and so lower assessments.

The main points are set out below.

FROM THE MCGINTY SIDE:
1. Depart at the end of the current tenure phase, ie, 30 September next year.
2. Forego any claim to the third option.
3. Retain the office.
4. Retain the letting brokerage.
5. Be paid $ ... K by the condominium, ie, the owners.
6. Allow the new manager to use part of the office, on commercial terms.
7. Cooperate with the board and its new manager in transferring the office systems and devices attaching to the OSM job, with financial adjustments as per standard business procedure.
8. Permit the new manager to run his own letting agency in the shared office without poaching McGinty clients.
9. Withdraw existing defamation proceedings against any director.

FROM THE OWNERS' SIDE:
1. Find a new OSM by tender, meaning simply the amount he would want as salary.
2. Give him the right to run his own rental brokerage for such owners as may ask, without poaching on the existing rent roll.
3. Allow him the use of the office space to be rented from the McGintys, or else build a new office.
4. Release the OSMs from all contract termination proceedings.
5. Allow the existing rental brokerage to be sustained by the OSMs.
6. Pay them $ ... K.

Those seemed the main things, but of course there will be more, and a lot of discussion. The McGintys will have to talk with the committee, unless both sides turn the proposal down flat. I'll stand by,

Leland Baigent (333)

Zina read the paper without interruption from her hosts. At the end she looked up and said, "Congratulations. That's a good effort, and I hope it rings everybody's bells. I can't think of anything that you haven't covered, though the stuff about the rental brokerage and the office is new territory for me, and I'd guess for a lot of other owners besides. You want me to take this Barney? Is there any message for me to take?"

"Only for him to add or criticize as he likes, and call me when he's ready for a discussion," replied Leland. "He knows that if there's to be no deal we'll be into lawsuits."

Zina nodded her understanding of what she was to do.

Peggy added, as Zina was departing, "Y'know, it seems to me that there's a lot to do, whether it be in implementing a compromise, or preparing for court. There mightn't be enough time for both, so the sooner the owners and Ed know if they have a deal, or must go to war, the better for everybody. There's not much more than a year ahead, and that's not a lot when you think of the procedures that must be followed for getting owner's approval of anything."

Both Leland and Zina murmured that they understood, and agreed, both thinking of their inexperience in such a complicated field.

Back home Barney was pleased with what his friends had done, and had little to add, at least for the moment. Zina had been worried he would drop their plans for moving house, and stay on to help Leland and Peggy, encouraging them as the new flag-bearers. He thought about doing so, but decided not to. He said to Zina: "I'll tell Leland he should send this circular in his name. Adding my name won't make any difference. I'll assure him of my help whether I'm here or at the Towers, so he will only have to ask for it at any time."

Zina could see Barney would be easing himself out of the struggle, and that on selling their Gran Capitan condo his status as an activist there would be drop off sharply, and with those prospects she was content.

That the McGintys would be startled by the rescission was predictable. In fact though, the combination of rescission and an antagonistic partner had left Ed high and dry. So, unaware of the facts in the McGinty corner, the Baigent mission bore more fruit than they could have hoped for, as shortly afterward the board received a letter from the attorney for Binny and her father seeking discussions based on the Baigent paper. With this letter came another from Angel Tejero, for Ed, to the same effect. Patching up had commenced. Self-management and market-based management expense in a year or so, when the McGintys' legitimate tenure ended, had become real prospects.

TIMELINE

1979 Gran Capitan unit sales "off-the plan" commence. Jones go to look. Sign up.

1980 Developer BBC creates 5-year management contract with buyers called Holliday, with an option for a further five years [first option]. Jones close and move into their condo.

1984 Hollidays ask for and get extra option for 5 years from 1990 [second option].

1985 initial term of contract expires. Hollidays exercise first option (1986-1990).

1986 Hollidays sell management contract to the McGintys.

1987 starting in June, the McGintys request a new contract for 25 years, which becomes a contentious issue between some directors and McGintys, who engage their attorney to plan an election campaign for their nominees to become the next directors. They are voted in, and form the 1988 board.

1988 in March, new board sends circular supporting McGinty interests.

1988 in March, McGintys convince board to grant 25 year contract, a plan that falls over in May, upon Jones sending a circular to owners proposing management review.

1988 in April, Jones files motion for management review.

1988 in July, board decides to hold special meeting of owners to consider granting a further, or third option, to the McGintys, five years from 1995.

1988 in July, agenda for upcoming owners special meeting sent, omitting Jones' motion filed in April. He protests.

1988 in August, owners meeting narrowly approves grant of third option. Jones declares dispute, and invokes arbitration.

1988 in November, general meeting approves Jones management modeling motion. Interests supporting the McGintys returned to office with reduced majority.

1989 in April, arbitrator's award, upholding grant of third option, is handed down.

1989 in elections in November, "new broom" directors become the 1990 board, hostile to the McGintys and the third option.

1990 in September, the McGintys exercise the second option.

1990 in November, longstanding administration manager (Prince Inc.) loses office, hands over Gran Capitan records to replacement, Condo Administration Inc. (CA).

1991 in March, CA requests board to take charge of old records because of lack of space. Placed in locked basement.

1991 in May, directors look in basement records and are astonished to find incriminating evidence against the 1988 board, Prince Inc., and the McGintys.

1991 - board commences investigation of records and proposes action for conspiracy and other wrong-doing. Initial board fervor dulls, to the disappointment of the Jones, and their ally, attorney Olly. The board changes course, and backs off the remedial action first proposed, and so disappoints the Jones group, who then look for other avenues for bringing justice to Gran Capitan condo owners.

1993 - remaining dissatisfied with the board's attitude to the conspiracy, Barney hits on the technique of rescission of the resolution by which the third option was deceitfully obtained from the owners. The archives had revealed evidence of the swindle on which the third option was based, and recitation of its detail in his motion ensures a strong vote from the owners for rescission. The effects startle the McGintys, though not in the same way. Binny is shocked by the implication she is a swindler, and becomes a weak link for the McGintys, and even more so after her father, appalled at the possible impacts of major litigation on his family's proud reputation, intervenes to support Binny, and engineer damage control. Ed's influence suddenly drops. The combination of rescission and an antagonistic partner leaves him high and dry. The story continues in chapter 25.